Praise for The Butcher's Sons

"The complexity of love — brotherly, fatherly, romantic — told through the eyes of brothers Dickie, Walt, Adlai, and their father Pat in *The Butcher's Sons* is at once universal and compellingly particular. It's a wallop of a read, packed with beauty and brutality — often in the same sentence — and poetically wrought by Scott Alexander Hess."

—JAMIE BRICKHOUSE, author of
Dangerous When Wet: A Memoir

"A brilliant storyteller, Hess cuts a brutal, vital keyhole into the lives and loves of a lost era with the emotional craft of a master builder, and the gentle caress of a poet. A deeply beautiful book, I fell in love with *The Butcher's Sons*."

—DAVID DRAKE, Obie Award-winning writer of
The Night Larry Kramer Kissed Me

"In his brutal and moving third novel, Scott Hess exhibits exciting new range by tackling the tense, dramatic story of three wholly different brothers living and working together in Hell's Kitchen in the 1930s. The risks for these "Butcher's Sons" are many, and the stakes sky high, as each finds his own definition of what it is to be a man."

—HELEN SCHULMAN, author of
This Beautiful Life

The Butcher's Sons

scott alexander hess

LETHE PRESS
MAPLE SHADE, NEW JERSEY

Published by LETHE PRESS
118 Heritage Ave, Maple Shade, NJ 08052
lethepressbooks.com

ISBN-10: 1-59021-074-3
ISBN-13: 978-1-59021-074-1

Library of Congress Cataloging-in-Publication Data

Hess, Scott Alexander.
The butcher's sons / Scott Alexander Hess.
pages cm
ISBN 978-1-59021-074-1 (pbk. : alk. paper)
1. Irish American families--New York (State)--New York--Fiction.
2. Brothers--Fiction.
3. New York (N.Y.)--Fiction.
I. Title.
PS3608.E844B88 2015
813'.6--dc23

2015006743

Cover and interior design
by MATT CRESSWELL (INKSPIRAL DESIGN)

For the Hess men,
Richard, David and Earl.

prologue

The brothers were dirt of the same road, but a road casting out in so many directions, lost with §so much gunk and otherness, that it was like once good earth now overwhelmed with strangling and poisonous vines. They might have been like blood should be, sharing a sameness, but there was never any heart-tether marrying them. Their same-dirt was like that of a ruined and flood-washed path, stung with nature's hate and strewn with ripped and wretched limbs. From the start, the brothers were flailing, blind and incomplete, like bastard pups thrown off in the river, lost to one another, gulping survival, thinking there was no one near. They had no chance, since they were never brought together by their father. He held no interest in them. They were his burden to love.

Part

One

Dusk settled over New York, and with its lilac light softened the grit of the city's ceaseless urging. It was dim in the narrow butcher shop. The meat case ran the length of the shop and served to display the various cuts and as a counter to take money. It was the only lit thing in the place. Slabs of beef and intestinal swirls of sausages were colored pink and pretty from the bulbs inside the case. With night, its glow brightened against the blackening shop in the way a barely swaying door, opening between a black room and a lit room, gently reveals light—a gradual and enticing change.

Dickie, the oldest of the three brothers, sat on a stool, against the shop's far wall. "Get me a beer, Rat," he said. "Then I'll tell it."

Adlai, the youngest of the three brothers, stared out at 10th Avenue, following the soft, dull rush of taxis. His head popped against the window glass as Dickie smacked him for not moving fast enough.

Walt, the middle brother, flinched as he watched his younger brother stiffen with mild fear. Walt did not move from the long, glass meat counter where he leaned. Since a kid, he liked the feel of cold glass on his arms.

This shift to evening made the case's light seem heaven-like to Adlai, as he turned away from the window, the sun, far off west, was sinking fast. He ran for to the cooler in back for the beer. He hated the cooler; he was afraid the giant metal door would snap shut and trap him. But he did not want to be hit again, so he fetched quickly.

Walt tilted his head to see out the long window fronting the shop. There were strategic spots in the glass giving view to things on the Avenue, past carefully sketched advertisement signs (Adlai's work) telling of pork loins, pig bellies, skirt steak and hog hocks on sale.

"You don't need to tell it today," Walt said.

Adlai crept back in with two beers, waiting.

"Bring it Rat," Dickie said, reaching. "Go back and get one for yourself. Time you get a taste for it and have your first drink. It's a celebration for fuck's sake."

Adlai would soon be sixteen, and he had alcohol a few times already, but he didn't correct his oldest brother. It was full on night, and the light from the meat case had turned into a glorious hot glow, casting a ghostly yellow on Dickie's handsome face: Blond, Irish, blue eyes, built small and tight, like a rooster. One kid once called him pretty. Dickie reacted by biting a chunk out of the boy's arm.

The front door swung, and the customer bell rattled. Mikey, the kid who lived down the street, was out of breath. "Old man's...coming."

"Where?" Dickie said.

Mikey didn't want to stay, did not want to say more. But he knew better than to not answer Dickie. Like everybody in the neighborhood, he'd heard the story about what Dickie did to a guy once with a tire iron.

"Stopped two blocks up on a stoop. Just resting."

"What the fuck?"

"He'll get here," Walt said. "Just tell us if that's what you want. It always makes you feel better."

Dickie had been suffering the same dream for ten years, and it spooked him. He thought by telling it, it might go away.

Adlai was skirting back in with his own beer, back to the long window, looking out again at rushing taxis, their yellowness paler now in night. *They all look empty,* he thought. He sipped the beer.

Dickie sat forward on his stool. To Walt, the glow of the meat cooler brightened his brother's face like a sideshow spotlight, keenly theatrical. Mikey hadn't managed to slip away, just stood at the entrance like an awkward usher, the door half-open, so he could flee any second.

There was a wail of a fire truck far off. Lately, Italian gangs had been causing trouble in Hell's Kitchen, in the Irish neighborhood.

"I get out of the crib, crawl like a monkey."

The siren faded and lights of passing taxis spooked in through the window, swiped across the room and landed spastically on all three brothers.

"I get out and crawl right here in the shop. My knees are full of saw dust, and I can taste it, and it tastes like salt." He reached out, as if he were going to disturb the thin layer of sawdust on the floor at his feet, at all their feet in the shop. But he didn't bend.

"After I taste it, I start throwing up blood," he said.

Walt shifted a little and coughed. He'd heard the dream many times. He knew, though he would never say it aloud, that the dream haunted and frightened his brother more than anything in his life.

Adlai sighed, just a bit too loudly. It was better to stay silent until the end, to let Dickie move things along when he was telling the dream.

"What's that?" Dickie said.

Adlai realized his mistake, and he laughed from nerves. Walt flinched for the second time and pulled his arm off of the cool counter glass where he rested it, because he knew this was bad, but he was too slow, too lumbering, too passive. He was the largest, gentlest of the three brothers.

Dickie flew on Adlai, taking the short spit of a laugh as a slapping affront. He had the runty boy on the floor, in a headlock. He was scraping his fist on the boy's skull, and that made Adlai moan, which made things worse.

"What are you fucking crying now?" Dickie said, giving the kid's head a light whack on the floor.

The knock was harder then he intended, and blood seeped and Adlai, terrified of blood, actually began to cry which irked Dickie further, and Walt realized this had gotten bad fast. He had too often seen his brother lose all control.

"Fucking pussy," Dickie said. He was hollowed out and mad with an escalating unnamed fear, and he pummeled all that rage into his brother to make it disappear. "You shut up, Rat." He popped the boy's head into the sawdust on the floor, and the stuff got stained with blood.

Mikey escaped, and the customer bell rang. Big Ed came in followed by their father, Pat. Big Ed, a meaty boxer and behemoth-sized young thug, flew at Dickie while their father stood at the door, like a fearful passerby watching a burning house in the distance with equal parts awe and indifference.

Big Ed ripped Dickie off the boy and lifted the runtiness of Adlai off of the ground, hoisted him up like a slab, held him above his head, shoulder muscles straining in a dirty white tank top, then carried the boy out onto the sidewalk and away. Dickie rolled in the thin layer of sawdust, on the butcher shop floor, quiet and dumb.

"All right now," Pat said, turning on a light. "Why did you let it get so dark in here?"

The room, which was filled now with a flat fluorescent glow, lost the mystery and madness. Walt drank his beer, and Dickie got up, and Pat moved slowly to get a beer too, to come back, to make a toast to his oldest son.

It was Dickie's eighteenth birthday.

two

It was dark and quiet, and Big Ed looked huge, bear-like near Adlai, who was crumpled on the sidewalk. It was a summer night, and the air was hot, stale. The kid touched his head, over and over, pulling a bloody finger to his lips, like he could paw-clean himself. He seemed ashamed of the wound. Big Ed was hunched down, squatting, his sturdy feet and big calves and muscular thighs making an L shape up into his waist, holding up the bulk of him. He was only 19 but appeared older, due to his size and a dark, wandering look of barely disguised despair in his eyes. He had been large since he was fifteen. He looked across the street at Gem's beauty shop, which was open late. He rocked like he was ready to spring.

The ladies at Gem's were in curlers peering out across the street because Big Ed was a looker. Ed had a heavy cotton cloth wrapped around his head to keep his wild and thick black hair tamed. The ladies at Gem's silently noticed that hair, its dark beauty, and wanted to run their hands through it. He stood, took the rag off his head, then knelt and pressed it onto Adlai's cut head. The rag soaked up the blood.

The boy winced, and Big Ed held the pressure, then wrapped the rag slowly, gently around Adlai's forehead. There was a breeze, and from the open door of Gem's across the street floated women's harmless gossip and laughter.

Ed tied off the rag, and his own hair fell loose into his eyes then swayed back and forth with a sudden sweet and hard night breeze. The air still had a grit to it, a reminder of meanness. There was the smell of meat that always lingered near the butcher shop, but the breeze calmed Adlai, and he smiled. A voice behind him spoke.

"You shouldn't have laughed that's all," Dickie said. "Come in and eat something. You're all right."

Big Ed was still kneeling in front of the boy, shielding him really, though the violence had died off with dusk and the completion of that awful, ceaseless telling Dickie was so obsessed with.

"We're going to the docks tonight," Dickie said, his voice getting softer, like he was walking away, ashamed, maybe more that his runt brother allowed himself to be beaten than for his own action.

Big Ed stood up, because the mention of the docks was business, and the business of the night was on him, the secrecy and consequences and fears. He was no longer able to focus on the kid.

"You keep that rag tight around your head," he said, a parting gesture, making the moment of kindness more real.

He was at the door., Behind him, the soft hush of women's talk at night lilted, and ahead, the fake brightness from inside of the butcher shop and Dickie. But then, something tugged once more. He turned, slumped, and petted Adlai on the head, then he went in.

Adlai was left alone, and he, too, looked across at the women in the shop, but it meant other things to him. He was fifteen, and maybe not full grown, but he was sure he would always be small, thin, frail with an odd face, a face that those women gawked at but didn't want to get close too. He was pretty, they whispered, all them boys were, but they never said it outside of their gab circle. Everyone knew Dickie, his outbursts, and that he once punched a girl in the gut for ridiculing him. The girl, that Mae-Ella Peters was pure trash, always causing trouble, they said, sad case, but still. Adlai imagined getting up and crossing the street and stepping into the beauty shop. He imagined strange things like that, things he never would do.

Dickie wandered out. He was not much taller than Adlai, but the tight muscularity of him spoke to his strength and hardness. He kept his wide, strong back to his brother. His hair was very short, and white blond.

"You gotta toughen up, Rat," he said. "You're going with us tonight. You can't just keep on like you are. Big Ed will keep an eye on you."

Adlai leaned against the glass window of the shop nodding to his brother. He could see one of the signs he'd made for pork sausage for sale. The red *e* in the word *sale* had faded, and he thought of someone named *Sal*, from a book he once read about a man and a poor girl, named Amy, who suffered horrible headaches. He laughed softly, wondering why that had come to him now. Dickie spun on him and stared, but Adlai stayed still and made no move that would anger his brother, so Dickie finally laughed, but more slowly and deeply. Adlai thought: *He's sinister.* The thought made him uneasy.

"Big Ed is gonna show you how to box too. He's gonna get you in the ring this week."

Dickie threw sharp, aimless punches into the reeking, hot night air, then went into the shop, and Adlai soon followed.

three

They were in Dickie's car, having left the butcher shop after the small birthday party. Walt had skulked away to meet his girlfriend, Pat had gone to bed and Dickie had told Adlai he was going along for the ride. It was late, and they were driving under a clear, hot, night sky, over the bridge to the Brooklyn docks.

Sitting in the back seat, Adlai wondered how he could know so little about his oldest brother—he didn't so much know Dickie's habits or likes as feared them. Dickie was mean. He liked nothing better than to scrap and didn't care if his face or hands showed he'd been in a fight as long as the other man was bloodied too. Adlai felt as if they weren't from the same bloodline. *We are nothing to each other, but we are stuck with each other.*

Dickie's close buddies were there. Bug, named for his almond-shaped green eyes and white eyelashes and near albino hair, was up front, drinking, while Dickie drove. Big Ed was canned and contorted next to Adlai in the back of the old Chevy. Adlai was comfortable, his tiny nothingness like an extra canister of gasoline or bottle of beer shucked back. Ed did not complain, because that was not his nature.

"What are we gonna do when we get there?" Bug thrust a pale thin arm behind into the narrow wisp of air in the back seat between Big Ed and Adlai, the bottle he held out teetering there until Adlai grabbed it since Ed couldn't move freely.

Adlai sniffed the liquor, tipped it and drank. He liked the taste of whiskey.

He took a deeper draw, then reached to Big Ed, who still could not move. Big Ed nodded, tilted his head, opened his mouth and winked. Adlai felt silly but dripped the liquor into the man's big fish mouth, slowly so it didn't choke him. Only a few drops dribbled off onto his thick lips. Big Ed was only four years older than Adlai, but his size and strength made them seem worlds apart. The fact fascinated Adlai.

"You worry too much, Bug," Dickie said, swerving off the bridge to the docks.

Dickie slowed. The car sat and idled. Dickie was grinding his teeth, building his strength. No one knew what he planned to do or why they were at the docks. They did not know how he had been planning this night, or something like it, some big move, since he was 15, when he half-forced himself on a stupid girl named Mae-Ella, though she later squealed and asked him to do it all again, and he refused and wanted to hit her but did not. Not that time. The long, wide blacktop dock facing the river was dark and still. He shut off the engine.

"Why are we here?" Bug said.

Ignoring Bug, Dickie held a breath, secretly thrilled that he'd made it this far. It was after that night with Mae-Ella that Dickie had begun to devise his life's plan, and that he admitted fully to himself the truth about his father's weakness, his worthlessness. He knew he had to create his own might and destiny. He started up his little, half-assed Irish gang, The Butchers, with his buddies Bug, Big Ed and the oafish, but brutal, red-headed O'Halleron. They mostly played cards and drank beer in the back of the butcher shop, though lately they'd managed to shake down a few local businesses for protection money, threatening to smash shop windows or beat someone up. And after tonight, Dickie believed in his gut, things would really change.

Dickie started the car and pulled slowly up the drive leading toward the main section of the docks, up a dark, thin corridor of night that blew open into a wide area fronting the long expanse of water. Ships, sleepy and dull, bobbed like small corks. Further down the dock, under the summer moon, they could see a black car was parked. A match lit, and a litter of men were evident. Dickie shut off the car again. They sat quietly. Then he drew a gun from under the seat.

Bug saw the gun Dickie held, and his eyes widened like his namesake. "Where did you get that?"

Dickie hushed him.

Bug thrust his white-bone arm back, like a stick, reaching for the bottle. Adlai handed it up.

"That's the Lucianos out there now. The Coriglianos are coming. We'll wait until they get here before we make a move," Dickie said.

"What move?" Big Ed said, leaning up toward the front, drinking from the bottle. "We have nothing to do with them."

"Exactly," Dickie said. "But we're gonna. I heard about this meeting. They're fighting over something in our neighborhood. Turf war. I heard about it. I've been waiting for a chance for us to make a move. To get noticed. I think we can get involved with them. Things have gotta change for us."

"Why would they want to talk to us?" Bug said. "We don't have anything for them."

"That's why I didn't tell you dumb fucks. You would've tried to talk me out of it. You got no balls," he said. "Sometimes a man has to take a risk to get noticed."

Dickie kept his eyes front, looking straight ahead toward the docks as a shaft of headlamps swam across the scene, signaling the arrival of another car.

"This isn't making any sense Dickie," Bug said.

Dickie opened his car door and got out. Bug reluctantly followed, and the car's back door jawed open, hanging like a tooth, in the gritty, airless night.

"Shoot," Ed said. "This is dumb."

Ed's six feet of bulk was canned too tightly. Adlai got out and went around to help. He did not know whether to reach in and pull the man out. Dickie and Bug were moving toward the dock, not pausing. Ed grunted loudly, then with a thrust was out, standing. He looked at Adlai.

"You wait here," he said.

"Dickie wouldn't like that," Adlai said.

Looking at Ed, and past him to those cars and the ships, bobbing, Adlai thought something was starting for him, some turn in his life that would drag him up and out of the dreariness he had experienced. He was shaking a little, a mixture of fear and thrill, but he didn't want to be left behind.

Big Ed turned and went toward the other two, and Adlai trotted to keep up with the man's wide, hard strides. They all met and stopped far enough away from the cars, in darkness, so they weren't seen.

One of the two cars on the dock turned on its lights, sending broad scoops of fake yellow toward the water's limitless horizon, off to nowhere thought Adlai. A man was walking with conviction toward another man, not hurriedly, but definite. He was wide and dark. Dickie whispered to Bug, and they both moved ahead a few steps, then Bug held up a hand for Ed and Adlai to follow.

In the distance the cars' lights beamed brighter, as if surged with electricity, then they failed and disappeared into the ocean as the scene went bleak and still, and the dock went very dark. Adlai kept his eyes on his brother, who was inching toward the other men, moving in darkness. They didn't notice his approach.

Big Ed was fidgeting with something in his pocket as he and Adlai and Bug crept closer. Adlai's heart was racing, and the whole thing felt increasingly unreal but also arousing in a primal way. The air was incredibly still. Dickie was getting near the cluster of men.

Four Italians, two on each side, were facing one another, as if preparing for a fight. They all wore dark suits and hats. The men on the left were a little smaller in size. One of the men on the right had a bit of red satin circling the center of his hat and looked in control. He used his hands when he spoke. Dickie stepped up to them out of blackness, and they saw him.

"Who the fuck are you," the man with the red on his hat said. "Get the fuck outta here, you stinky Mick. Who is he?"

All of the men had pulled guns, though they held them limply at their sides, and Dickie too had his gun out. They waited.

"We're The Butchers. We're from Hell's Kitchen, and I understand—"

One of the men, Adlai was not sure which, started to laugh, and the man with the red satin on his hat stepped close to Dickie. "Get the fuck out of here you sissy punk, before you hurt yourself," the man said.

Adlai had never seen anyone speak to his brother like that and go away unharmed. He froze, feeling, in an uncanny way, a new and sudden strengthening in that frail line of brotherly knowing that connected him with his brothers. He knew there was more, that Dickie was going to do something. The same way he knew Dickie would hurt him when he laughed earlier that night at the shop during his telling of the dream.

Dickie reached toward the man's back, grabbing him by the shoulder. The man spun on Dickie and with a loud grunt lifted his gun and smashed Dickie in the head with it, and Dickie fell.

"You stupid fuck," the man said. "This Mick is nuts."

Adlai saw the gun hit Dickie's head and saw Bug step back. There was a scant pause. Then came an incredibly loud, brutal, ringing sound that he thought was something from the wide, black sky above, like a distant cannon or a burst from a comet. But then came the fast, vicious sound of Dickie's screaming voice in unison with the other men's voices, and Adlai saw that Dickie, still on the ground, had lifted his gun and shot the man with the red on his hat. The other men were rushing to the man that Dickie shot, who had fallen to the ground. Then came the sound of Dickie's voice, yelling for them to go, and all of their feet running, and all of them racing, and Bug howling like a beast, and Ed lifting a stunned and frozen Adlai up for the second time that night, into the air and swinging him back toward the car, thrusting him into the back seat, thrusting his own bulk in after, cursing loudly.

Dickie was in the front with Bug, and the car was started and moving, and there was shouting and the sound of feet pounding toward their car and then gunshots from the Italian men pursuing them.

Adlai snapped closer to Ed in terror, but the gunshots had not hit the car. They were whirling away, back up over the bridge, and Dickie was talking fast and low to Bud. Ed was still cussing, and Adlai was shaking and more alive then he had ever been, but terrified because he had wet himself, and he could not figure out how he could hide this from Dickie, how he could hide this?

four

Walt sat alone in a booth in the hard glow of the coffee shop. Nothing stirred. The nightshift waitress was in back with the cook, smoking. Walt had on a tie, and his hands were folded. His brother Dickie had taken his goons and gone off on another hair-brained, late night scheme, dragging Adlai along this time for some reason. He sighed, not wanting to think of them now.

The coffee in front of him was cold, black. She promised to come, and he refused to leave. It had been over an hour. Through the window the sleepy street was peaceful, and he was patient. He had always been a patient man.

He was tall, dark, not like his brothers who were smaller, lighter. His shoulders were wide and his hands big and paw-like. At seventeen, he was what some women called gangly. He had a pleasant face, warm, wide, brown eyes. He had been in love for over three months with her, with Adriana, and it had done little to alter his life plan. It fortified him to think he found the love of his life, that that part was done, that she would share the dream with him.

The dream had nothing to do with his brothers, his father, the butcher shop. He would enter University in the fall on a hard-won scholarship and would some day be a doctor, though only he knew that. His father thought he would get a degree then run the business. He hurt, physically when he thought of that man, his father, Pat.

There was something in his father that was too broken to be surviving, too spent too soon, too oblivious to what was happening in their family. Walt couldn't bear to see it. His father's life, the war, his estranged family, the thing with their mother Angie, it shaved off any layer of humanity left in the man.

His brother Dickie had become so blatant, shaking his violence in the old man's face. Yet Pat did not change or react. He ground the meat, set up the shop, swept the floor. He lived in a harsh unchanging light of routine, graying and decaying. Yet, Walt thought sipping his coffee, he was not really that old.

Through the window he watched her approach. She moved steadily but not hurriedly. He was not angry with her for being late. He sighed, relieved she had come. The first time they kissed, he could not stop shivering for an entire day. She was small, but full bodied. Her hair came to her shoulders in thick dark thrusts, and her breasts were large. She was like a dancer. She wore a calico dress, with a single flower, something purple and bulbed, stalking down the front of it.

"She is perfect," he whispered.

Adrianna entered and paused at the door. He loved how she stared at him, saying nothing before smiling. She moved gracefully to the torn, red leather booth, setting a worn canvas bag on the floor.

"I had to work late." She placed her small caramel-colored hand on the table, flat with her palm down. Adriana was a year older than him and already in University.

He placed his large hand over hers immediately, as if a gust of wind might blow through and sweep it away. "It's all right. You want pie?"

"No."

He was not surprised by her answer; she ate very little. She sat across from him and shut her eyes, and a thrill skirted up his back because he could stare more easily in that moment. Her eyelids were lavender, though most would simply say brown. She had the classic face of a beauty queen, but it was her gentility, the near-frail sweep of her, that made him secretly coo.

"You should stop working," he said.

She smiled, , knowing he loved to touch it. She worked cleaning high rise offices because her father thought it built character. They did not need the money. Her father was a wealthy and respected psychiatrist.

Walt wanted to take her away that night, but he could not. They both needed to finish school, which would take a good long time. Her father brought her to America when her mother died of scarlet fever. Adriana's father did not approve of Walt. Walt shivered, though he tried hard to hide it.

The diner was still empty, though the waitress glanced out once from the kitchen, in a shifting, pale cloud of cigarette smoke and radio music.

"How is your brother?"

Walt lifted his cup and sipped the drab, cold coffee. There was no denying Dickie was doomed, he thought. Who knew what he was up to, running off with his thugs, the ridiculous Butchers, as he called them. He would be stalking around with those misfits, moving toward limitless acts of violence, shifting his focus completely from the butcher shop, and in his mind managing some grand, deadly schemes. Then it would all fall apart, because it was all very fragile to begin with, just dressed up in harshness and stupidity.

Walt loved his brother and knew him as if they were twins. He imagined Dickie would not live to see thirty. He worried about Adlai too. He wanted to confide in Adriana about all of it.

"It's his eighteenth birthday?" she said.

Walt smiled. "Let's go," he said.

A siren rang far off, the hot night moving on as Walt and Adriana left.

five

Adlai found the smell of raw meat comforting: a rooty, earthy scent that made him think of things buried, of dirt hardened, of solitude. This was not to be confused with the smell of rotting meat, which he also knew well because grinding machines could hide bits of things, keep them cocooned in there even after cleaning for long periods of time. Rotting meat disgusted him. Raw meat, that smell, he considered gentle.

He sat on the concrete floor in the back area of the butcher shop where deliveries were brought. Adlai crouched like a rabbit trying to disappear; in shadow, he tried to sniff out something to centerhim after the horror on the Brooklyn docks, but he could breathe in no night scent, no wandering lilac from a neighboring yard, nothing pungent, not even the stink of alley trash in the heat. Up near the doorway leading to the front of the shop Dickie hovered.

There were three chairs in a small circle. Bug and Ed sat, Dickie stood and on the third chair lay Dickie's gun, like a museum piece to be studied. It had taken on some of the blood of the man Dickie shot. Dickie drank from a bottle, then he started to laugh softly. Bug twisted his fingers together, snapped his knuckles over and over and sighed loudly.

"I don't know," Bug said. "This is really, really bad."

"What were you thinking?" Ed said.

Dickie drank again and did not look up.

"You got us all involved in this now. Even him," Ed said, indicating Adlai.

Dickie glanced at his youngest brother. "Get off the fucking floor."

Adlai hopped up and went to the circle, hovering over the chair where the gun was lying.

"Give it to me," Dickie said.

Adlai had never held a gun. He figured he never would, though he'd thought of some day holding a rifle. One of the only stories his father had told his sons was of how he hunted with his father when he was young in Ireland. Adlai lifted the gun gingerly, as if it could go off at will. He took it by the long thin end and realized he was touching the blood of the man who had been shot, the blood that splattered onto the gun's tip. He handed it over to his brother.

"It's not a fucking snake. Hold a gun by the handle," Dickie said, grabbing it. "Sit."

Adlai sat, glancing at the other men. Then he looked toward the back garage doorway that opened up into the alley. It was dark, and he realized if someone came from there, quietly, they may not be noticed.

"These families, the Lucianos and the Coriglianos you know how much money they have?" Dickie said, his head still down. "They got houses, cars, broads. They strut around and live like fucking kings, and you know why?"

They were all silent, and Adlai kept his eye on the back, the opening to the alleyway, and despite the heat he felt cold.

"Because they are not afraid to take care of business. To deal with a situation in the way in which it needs to be done," Dickie said. "They don't sit on their asses and wait for things to come to them. They are the makers of things."

"You're not talking sense," Ed said. "We are in big trouble here."

Dickie lifted his head. He still had the gun in his hand, and he stood up. For a moment, Adlai thought his brother may shoot.

"I didn't know he would hit me," Dickie said softly. "Or laugh like that. You know I can't stand that. I won't stand that ever."

"Why were we even there?" Ed said.

"I was going to talk to them. There's no reason we can't talk to them. The son of a bitch shouldn't've laughed at me."

Bug, who had intermittently been sighing and cracking his knuckles, spoke out in a high ragged voice.

"They are going to find us, and they are going to kill us. You shot a Luciano. They don't give a fuck about nothing. They are going to kill us."

Then Bug cut loose with a raw harsh noise close to a wailing, as he lowered his head and continued to crack his knuckles. They all turned to Dickie who still faced away. He was shaking his head and for a moment Adlai thought of his father, of that broken man, and while he feared and hated his brother's violence and insane bravado, he could not bear to think Dickie could ever be broken.

"But they don't know who we are," Adlai said. "They said that. That's an advantage. We are nobody."

Dickie turned, and the men looked at Adlai. There was a long still silence. Ed began to speak, when the entry to the front of the shop opened. It was Pat. He stepped in. A cool light forced its way in with him. Morning had come. They had been up all night. Pat looked around and didn't seem to notice anything out of the ordinary.

"You boys want breakfast?" he said.

He didn't wait for an answer, slipped off as silently as he came, taking the cool, innocent morning light with him. Adlai wished his father had come in and said something to make sense of the horrible mess. But then, that wouldn't be his father.

Dickie took a slug of the bottle, glanced toward his little brother, then handed the bottle to Big Ed.

"Come on let's eat."

The three of them left, but Adlai stayed. He stared out at the back alley entrance, still expecting someone to wander in, someone vile. The night drifted off, gently replaced by a light wash of dawn and a sparrow's voice, which made a slow, consistent chirping, bringing forth the day.

six

Big Ed fitted the soft, rubbery thing to Adlai's head, placing it gingerly over the rag cloth he'd tied across the boy's forehead the night before to blot the still-tender wound Dickie inflicted. The motion disturbed the wound, and new blood seeped through. The helmet tipped dangerously side to side when Adlai moved because he had the skull the size of a child, and the boxing gear was meant for a grown man. Adlai adjusted the helmet, brushing back his unkempt, light blond hair, thinking of how he would soon turn sixteen. The three brothers had birthdays close together, all birthed in heat.

Some nights, in his bunk, the dark stink of his brothers near, their snores filling the room in spits and drones while spills of moonlight crept in then out, as he drifted from sleep to dream, he wondered if he would ever grow to be a real man.

Gleason's gym was huge, cathedral-like, but with no ornamentation and windowless. *Dark and musky*, thought Adlai. The walls were padded, and a boxing ring sat empty, ghostlike and dreary. The place was not crowded, just a negro shadow boxing in a far corner and a skinny Italian slamming mercilessly at a swinging heavy bag. Both men wore stark white shirts, silk shorts, laced-up leather shoes. Adlai was overwhelmed and puny in his brother Dickie's cotton hand-me-down gym trunks and tank. There was a smell, not unlike his room, wafting around, male and untidy. It was a sweaty and exhausted scent, like too much was wanted and too little was happening. Adlai shivered, despite the clawing heat.

After breakfast with Pat that morning, they had gone back down to the butcher shop and Dickie had sent an increasingly hysterical Bug home. He'd told them all to lay low, that he needed time to figure it all out. Ed got Dickie in a corner, towered over him like the heap of a man he was, and leaned hard into him, like he could trap him there. Adlai couldn't hear, but Ed kept glancing his way, and he knew it was about him, his part in it all. That's when they turned to Adlai and announced he was going to learn to box, to defend himself. Ed was going to teach him.

"Well," Big Ed said, "hold out your hands." He scratched at one eye then bent to pick up a pair of tattered boxing gloves.

There was a low animal scream. The skinny Italian had gotten into a fast ramming motion with the heavy bag, and it was pounding back at him, knocking hard until he finally fell into it, hugging it tightly like a lover, swaying with the monstrous thing, cheek on leather, sweating and groaning like a speared boar.

Watching the Italian, Ed shook his head.

"Sunday brings in the dopes," he said. "He's at it too fast."

Adlai shrank back. He knew he was a burden.

"I said hold out your hands kid."

Adlai held his hands straight out, and they shook. Big Ed looked down at him, at the kid's slender pale fretting fingers and frowned, then he took hold of one hand like it was made of glass, and held it aloft. With his other hand he pushed the fat boxing glove over the rail of Adlai's fingers and bony wrist. He shifted his grip, and the glove slid on, outsized and monstrous. They stood not far from the gym's metal door, which squealed as it opened, then slammed shut with a vicious ring. Hot air blew in. The day had warmed quickly. Summer had at last rammed its sweaty fist into the gut of the city, stifling every street corner.

A big man lumbered in, looking at Ed. Adlai recognized him as the young Polack from the neighborhood. That's what Dickie called him. He'd won every amateur fight he'd gotten into, since he started last year. The Polack slunk past, drank something from a tin cup. He paused, threw his head back and drank more of the thick milky gunk in his cup. Then he laughed.

"Beating up girls now, Ed?" he said.

Ed had been a fighter, or wanted to be, once. He'd won a few fights, then he had an accident, broke his wrist and got sloppy; too big, too fat, that's what Dickie said. Big Ed spit, then yanked the glove back off of Adlai's hand.

"Sit down," Ed said, then walked toward the Polack.

He wasn't looking at Adlai when he told him to sit, his eye was trained on the Polack who was also not moving, looking back at them, stray drops of the chalky liquid he drank dropping in globs onto the gym's wood floor.

Adlai sat, the big leather helmet swaying far to one side, blinding him. He let it settle there, following Big Ed's back as he moved away using his one good eye. Ed had on the same greasy white tank from the night before, when they'd gone to the docks, but Adlai noticed a circular rip in the back of the tank that yawned open, then shut, as he moved. His meaty, sloping shoulders swayed and popped in thrusts of movement as that little hole yanked open, then shut, like a phantom mouth, like it might shout at Adlai to "Get out, scram."

Adlai saw the edge of an inked, black -inged tattoo on Big Ed's back itching out from that mouth in the greasy tank's rip. He realized he'd never really looked at Big Ed from behind. It seemed impossible that Ed was only four years his senior. Adlai felt weak because he hadn't eaten much breakfast. The liquor from the night before still sloshed around in his gut. He watched Big Ed approach the Polack. The helmet covered one eye, shrouded his tiny ears and muffled the sound, smothering things. It was like being in a tunnel.

Big Ed leaned into the Polack. Both men threw their heads back, like haughty lions. Big Ed's meaty shoulders raised, and the swamp of his thick, black hair the ladies at Gem's beauty shop gossiped about swayed strangely, almost elegantly, in that hot, raw, boxing gym that knew only ugly fists and harshness.

The Polack rammed his hand into the front of his pants in some vulgar gesture, then he said something and spat and moved away and left Big Ed alone.

Adlai saw the mighty rise and fall in Ed's shoulders. Ed did not go after the Polak, but instead went toward the gym's door, waving at Adlai to wait. Even with the helmet muffling the sound, Adlai heard that angry door smash open and shut as Ed left.

The negro boxer turned and looked to the door, then to Adlai, squinting as if he were not sure whether he was looking across the room at a boy or a tossed off bag of something. He wiped his black brow, then shifted away into a corner where Adlai could not see him. Adlai adjusted the helmet to try to see better, but instead of the negro, he saw the skinny Italian, sweaty and panting, still holding onto the ragged heavy bag. The Italian, who was barefoot, turned his cheek and noticed Adlai. Then he leaned forward, as if to get a better look at the stray boy on the floor.

He slapped his hands together, then whistled and moved quickly toward Adlai, speaking loudly, in a harsh rasping voice. It occurred to Adlai that on the floor, huddled there, the man could run straight at him, then kick him like a ball poised at a goal line. The Italian talked fast, though the voice was muffled through the heavy, leather helmet's padding. Adlai struggled with the thing again, twisting it up, so he could grasp what the man said, all the while watching the Italian's large, hairy, naked feet moving faster toward him.

"Dickie's kid brother ain't it? Ain't it? Dickie, that broke my kid brother's nose."

Adlai got up on one knee, still watching the naked hairy feet coming at him. The gym's door cried open, and another swell of heat blew in, and the sound of other feet on the floor pounded as the Italian reached Adlai and swooped at him, placing his hands securely on the helmet on the boy's head. He hoisted Adlai up by the helmet, holding him aloft, shaking him. Blurred with movement, Adlai could see the man's blood-shot black and raging eyes. He felt limp and lifeless, dizzy. Suddenly there were hands from behind on his shoulders yanking him away from the grip of the Italian. He was wrenched backward, and he felt hot breath on his neck. Big Ed had him, gripping Adlai like a bag of groceries on his hip, moving back quickly.

"You want Dickie; that's who you want. "

"That pansy will do fine for now, an eye for an eye."

Big Ed kept moving back toward the door, and Adlai remained still, the leather helmet slipping around on his head, covering his eye, then his ears again. The black boxer stepped up to the group of them.

"You all right, Big Ed?"

The skinny Italian swung around.

"Get away from here nigger."

With that turn, that angry motion of vileness, Ed made a fast run for the door, carrying Adlai under his arm. They hit the sidewalk. The sticky, waved heat of the day was intense and the clattering rush of noise frightened Adlai. Ed ran, carrying the boy like a sack until they got a few blocks away, then he stopped.

"I went to cool down, so I didn't start a fight. I never thought he'd bother you," Big Ed said, setting Adlai down on the sidewalk. "You're never gonna box. That's just stupid."

A horn blew, and far off something metal roared then quit abruptly.

"Come on," Big Ed said going fast down the sidewalk. "Let's go get a Coca Cola."

Adlai ran to keep up, the burdensome helmet still affixed like a growth, flopping side to side, keeping him only half in the world, as Ed led them swiftly away.

seven

Savage. Adlai wrote in the delicate layer of sawdust that covered the concrete floor. He was awaiting the morning meat delivery in the back of the shop. The carcasses, head in tact, bloody, dripping, or sometimes wrapped in sheath, like a kidnapped child, would come soon. He'd guide them in and imagine, often, that they were still alive, or lowing softly to be set free.

They came first from across the river, where they were clubbed, stunned, bled, gutted (Dickie told all that in bright detail). Then they were shipped downtown to the meat packing district to be stripped out, cleaned up then finally, feebly he thought, carted up to shops in the blazing heat.

Huddled there, waiting, Adlai wanted to write *"the beauty of the savage beast,"* but he wouldn't allow himself to acknowledge that voice so fully, that voice shrouded too deeply in the shame and different-ness and the constant ringing of the customer bell up front, the jangling metal reminder that Dickie was watching.

A bead of sweat dropped from Adlai's pale, angular forehead into the S of the word he'd written, as he crouched, hunter like, close to the concrete sawdust-covered floor. With his finger on the sweat bead, he smeared the S to the A to the V then swiped over it quickly, deleting his secret.

A truck roared up the skinny back alley through the morning's mad and glittering rush of heat. It was the delivery truck and behind it, another car, honking, hollering voices, men. The delivery men stopped fast and were slouching in with the carcasses, slung over shoulders like bags of feed or garment bags, harmless really, if not for the hooves dangling, snouts lagging off lifelessly. Adlai hated taking in the meat delivery, coaching them off to the big refrigerator where the carcasses got hung on silver hooks, left to die, he thought, knowing they were long dead, and he was foolish. He dreaded this chore, but Walt ran the register and Dickie worked the customer counter. That's the way it was.

The delivery men worked silently, barely noticing Adlai, but then turning with the onslaught of a hard voice penetrating from the alley.

"Move that fucking can. It's too fucking hot."

Bug was there, and Big Ed was just behind. Their car was trapped behind the truck, taking in the heated fumes of pork, beef, loins, blood. The plastic flaps separating the small back area from the refrigerator and the shop front swam like their own wave of heat, and Adlai stiffened, ready for any blow. Dickie came out, lighting a cigarette, then stopping.

"Hey Dickie," Bug said, coming in from the alley.

Big Ed also stepped in and lit a cigarette as the delivery men finished with the carcasses, rushing the last into the refrigerator from the trucks out of the searing morning.

"We got some news," Bug said.

Dickie didn't move from the swaying flaps, just raised his hand and swatted, and Adlai thought at first it was a fly, then realized it was him. He was meant to go.

"What are you doing on the ground?" Dickie said.

Adlai stood and moved swiftly toward the flaps to the store up front.

"Watch the counter. I have business," Dickie said.

Big Ed backed up, and the delivery men vanished, leaving hunking scents of animal, their footsteps marring patches of sawdust on the floor like excited boys' paths in a new snow. The three men huddled back by the door, Bug eyeing the alley as if a randy troop of Italians would fly at them, blazing with machine guns any second.

"You shot Sal Luciano," Bug said.

"Yeah?" Dickie said, unable to suppress a slight grin.

Big Ed, towering over the two, still in the greased and sweat-stained white tank, but wearing new blue pants and a high boot, shifted from one foot to the other.

"Like your kid brother said, they didn't know who the hell you are. We're nobodies to them," Bug said.

Dickie's grin vanished, and he sucked on his cigarette. Ed shrugged, also sucking on his smoke.

"Word on the street is it's a Corigliano hit. That they set it all up," Bug said.

The customer bell rang up front, and Dickie turned, then dropped his cigarette butt and squashed it with the end of his work shoe. He wore a white apron hitched over his tank and pants. There was a smear of yellow on the front.

"Yeah?" Dickie said. "Won't the Coriglianos deny it?"

Dickie rubbed a hand over chin stubble, then slowly took off his apron, and dropped it into the sawdust. Before it landed he kicked it viscously, like a dog ready to nip him, and it flew in the air, then fluttered down, white, wide, landing spread out and full.

"Maybe they ought to know it was The Butchers that did the job," Dickie said. "Maybe it's time we get in with the big guys."

Big Ed took a deep breath and stepped forward.

"Don't worry, I'm not gonna do anything that stupid. I'm just talking," Dickie said, smiling, then slapping a hand on Ed's back.

Up front the customer bell clanged again, then once more. Dickie turned. "Adlai," he yelled. "You busy up there?"

"It's okay. I got it. It's okay, Adlai yelled from the front.

"I got an idea," Dickie said.

Big Ed and Bug stood still, waiting. The flaps swayed, the customer bell rang, and in the distance, down the alley out back, a spit-shined black car turned fast and came barreling. Big Ed yanked out a gun and cocked it, and the car came close, then turned the hairpin curve that led back out of the alley. A boy with a mess of freshly cut red hair, a bow tie, and a flask, hung his head out, singing a song about a girl named Mabel. Ed put the gun back, wiped sweat from his forehead, and the three men stood still, quietly, not talking, not looking at one another. The customer bell went still.

eight

The day was busy, long. Dickie had disappeared, leaving Adlai to reach up and take customer orders and wrap meat. Walt watched his little brother, moving gently, elegantly and deliberately like a dancer, he thought. The kid was doing well. Better than Dickie in some ways, though nobody used the band saw and cleaver like Dickie, whacking off pieces in full view for customers to see.

But Adlai took his time, wrapped the meat like he was taping up presents for holiday, handing them over to the men and women with a strange movement that could be mistaken for grace. Walt figured he was nervous, afraid of making mistakes, so he worked as if the cuts were delicate china.

They rang up a lot by closing time. It was a very good day, though Walt had been distracted. Checking the big white clock on the wall over and over, urging it to move faster. He was having dinner at Adriana's house, with her father. He'd only met the man once, and it had not gone well. Tonight was important and, he hoped, a step toward his dream to marry the girl. He'd never been invited to the house. It was not quite five o'clock.

"Lock the door," Walt said.

"But it's early," Adlai said.

Adlai hoped to stay after closing with Walt, to tell his brother about what had happened at the docks. Dickie hadn't said anything to Walt, and that frightened Adlai.

"Go on," Walt said.

Pat had left early, gone upstairs to sleep. He had headaches lately. Walt wanted plenty of time to shower and put on his good suit. He wanted to be early. The dinner was at seven, across town on the East Side. He tossed his apron and got ready to head upstairs, leaving his kid brother to finish up.

Adlai was hunched over, looking at his reflection cast within the dim light of the glass case, his fair hair and lithe frame and paleness matching the light glow within there. He felt, as he always did, invisible, too light, too pale and separate from his brothers, the runt, clearly, but more than that. His view of things was scattered and weak. He often wondered how he'd gotten mixed up in a family like this and how such a mistake was allowed to take place.

He was musing, staring as Walt shut off the lights and knocked on the glass from the customer side. The broadness of his brother now only lit from the case-glow was statuesque and brilliant.. He was a good man and would make something of himself. He was kind too. He was not at all like Dickie.

Adlai turned off the case lighting, as the back door leading up the narrow stair to their home snapped shut, leaving him in that bland, dusky light of a fading summer day that he loved. He sat down on the floor. It was quiet on the Avenue and the sky was clear. He could peek through holes in the signs he'd made and see jagged slices of sky. Also, turning back to the case, he could see the chilly wedges of veal, beef and pork that his brothers had so expertly sliced and placed for sale. He'd never been taught to use the knives or saws. It had never been considered.

Above, he heard the light clatter of feet, like hooves, he thought, like animals, wandering about looking for lost things, planning. He had no plan. His brothers would both be out for the night, and his father would be asleep. He leaned into the glass, the case swathed in grayish light. There were pig's feet resting gently at one edge.

A horn blared, a car rattled past, and he felt a rustling wind, slipping in from outside somehow, and looking away, then back, he thought he saw the pig's hooves move. But that was nonsense.

He had no exact plan, he thought, but he did have one thing he meant to do that summer. He'd found out about it from a strange, shy fellow at the movie house one late Saturday, a nearly empty double feature.Nobody knew he'd snuck out with a nickel for the movie, and nobody noticed when he snuck back in. The shy, pale man whispered to him in the dark theatre then scratched words on a piece of paper and shoved it into his palm. That was what Adlai planned to do.

The shuffling feet above stopped, and all was still. He got up and went upstairs. They would scold him if they found out he'd sat still too long, alone, staring at the case, thinking ridiculous thoughts. He glanced back quickly toward the meat case, just checking the pig's feet, just making sure they were still there.

nine

The building where Adrianna lived was on the city's Upper East Side. It was brick, tall, very large and foreboding, speaking to an elegance Walt found foreign and intimidating. He knew of a competitor's butcher shop on the east side, where they hacked meat slabs in the window like a circus act. He knew of York Avenue's heavy, lolling spots in German town. He'd never, however, seen a building quite like this.

It was white-washed brick, angelic, and it rose high into the sky, slicing in and becoming more and more narrow as it rose, its tiers, like a cake. . There were wide, trellised windows with wood shutters and trails of flower boxes jammed with striped petunias and other exotic drifts of vine and ash colored planters. He craned his neck. Far up, there was a woman leaning out of a window, smoking, her hair long and her dress red. He stood across the block, under a painted sign hawking Mueller's Lunch Counter. There was a light breeze, and a sudden scent of honeysuckle drifted furiously past. The street was quiet, and it was nearly seven. He'd meant to be early but the intimidating building had stopped him, and he'd stood back, afraid.

Nearby, a tower's clock tolled and he crossed quickly, leaving the queer rush of honeysuckle behind. Two glass doors opened from the sidewalk into the building's formal lobby. A dusty old man in a dusty war-like uniform stared at him, not moving, like a wax figure. The bell had tolled seven.

"Yes?" the wax colonel asked. "Name?"

Walt tugged at the collar of his clumsily pressed white shirt. There was a stain on one side, meat blood scrubbed and bleached and faded like the dusting of a rose petal. . His pants were tight, two years old. A middle aged woman with stark white hair, wearing velvet pants and a sheer cream blouse, slipped out of shadow, near the lobby elevator. She was staring at him, like a hungry cat, Walt thought, lasciviously. She laughed harshly.

"Dr. Scola," Walt said. "I'm here to see Dr. Fortunator Scola."

The woman laughed again, though more softly, moving toward him like a panther, like she hungrily scented the blood in his collar, noticed the too snug fit of his pants, tasted his fear. Walt took a deep breath to center himself.

"The Doctor," the woman hissed.

She passed him fluidly, not stopping as she went out into the street.

"He's expecting you. The 12th floor. Go on," the door man said.

Walt moved quickly toward the elevator, late now. The door came open, and a small black man smiled.

"Twelve," Walt said.

The man yanked the door shut, and the machine rolled up, hissing like the strange woman in the lobby. He shut his eyes, took another deep breath.

"Twelve," the operator said.

The doors opened to a long hall, carpeted with strands of honeysuckle sweeping forward. The coincidence made him shudder, and he moved to the apartment. He had to get his balance, to regain his nerve.

"This is the girl I'm going to marry," he said softly, rapping twice on the door.

There was silence. The old elevator sighed back down. He thought again of the madwoman in the lobby and imagined the carpet vines climbing up his legs. The door opened.

She was in a simple, white dress. Lace around the shoulders, arms bare, and a slight shift in coloration from the top of the dress to where it hit above her knees. She wore high-heeled shoes and a strand of pink pearls. In her eyes, Walt found courage. Adriana smiled, and he followed her in.

The hall was long and rather dim. Paintings of dark haired men in flaming and ancient battle scenes lined the walls, which Walt though was a dreary choice for an entry. He kept his eyes on Adriana. He was sweating.

Several clocks chimed. Two began at once, dinging, then a third and a fourth came in, one with the chirp of a cuckoo and another with a long, sad bellow. Adriana led him to a living room off the hall. It was wide, with two large windows cloaked in heavy drapes. The room fed into a dining area where a long, formal mahogany table was set for dinner. A dark, elderly woman in maid's attire stood away from the table. Walt knew Adriana's father did well as a psychiatrist, and he'd never understood why she worked. She wouldn't tell him anything beyond that her father said it built character.

Walt hadn't imagined it all to be quite so grand, so dark and ancient looking. The room was lit with standing lamps. The Doctor was sitting on a velvet sofa with tassels tracing its bottom. Adriana gently took Walt's hand. There were two large ornate side chairs and a gold trimmed mirror with a hairline crack in its center behind the sofa. The room, the entire home, had a sad scent of something old, lost and dying.

"Papa, you remember Walt?" she said.

The man was near fifty, dark-haired, thin with a strand of a mustache, glasses and wearing a tweed suit. He sat very still, and Walt thought of the waxen old man in the lobby. Walt stretched out his hand, and the Doctor stood and shook it.

"Llegaste tarde, que' americano típico."

The Doctor turned and went to the dining room and sat at the head of the table. Adriana led Walt in, and he noticed her hand was shaking and cold. He'd never known her to be anything but bold and fearless. When they made love, she insisted on striding on top of him, maintaining eye contact, telling him dark and fantastical things. He always thought of her as the most powerful woman he'd ever met. She released his hand and sat at the table's other end, leaving the center seat for Walt. The elderly maid had left and now returned with a large, ornate china tureen, filled with a brownish soup.

The table was covered with an ornate, though thread worn, lace tablecloth. There was a full china setting for each of them, yellow dishes with lavish flower blooms on the side. The napkins were cloth, and the tablewear silver. Walt thought of the dinners with his father and brothers. The stink of meat, Dickie's liquor and cigarette smoke. He felt a rush of shame.

The maid spooned soup into his bowl. The Doctor was eating already. Walt glanced at Adriana, and she managed a smile and tilted her head, and he saw the beauty of her, of her entire being, in the glass-like scant reflection of her eyes, which caught the chandelier. He had planned to ask the Doctor about his work, to get comfortable, then broach the subject of courting his daughter, or marriage. He felt hopelessly lost.

"Walt is going to study medicine," Adriana said. "He's very smart."

The Doctor was engaged solely with his soup. He did not look at his daughter or at Walt. When he finished, he set down the silver spoon, and this triggered the maid to go for another dish. Walt knew his collar was wet, stained. He suddenly feared the old blood stain may reopen, may begin to drip new blood on the lace tablecloth. He felt he was losing ground.

"You're line of work must be very rewarding. Being a psychiatrist. Helping people." Walt said.

The maid served the fish, anemic looking sole with a drizzled sauce whiter than the fish itself. The Doctor looked directly at Walt and laughed. Then he glanced at Adriana, then he ate his fish.

A silence was finally broken by the mad rush of clocks, the series of chimes and gongs coming from different rooms in the house. Walt ate slowly. He felt a bone on his tongue, from the fish. The clocks finally exhausted their mad tolling. He wanted to spit out the bone but couldn't without being noticed. So he chewed it.

"¿Por qué haces esto, Adriana?"the Doctor said to Adriana.

The maid was clearing the fish. Walt managed to swallow the bone but it hurt his throat. There was another pause, then Adriana stood up. She put her delicate hands on the table, and Walt shuddered, as he always did when he stared too long at any area of her body.

"Because I love Walt, Papa." She said this with little emotion, more like a declaration, like a line read from the side of a box.

The maid stopped and moved away from the table, though she had not yet cleared the Doctor's fish plate. Walt looked to him, and the man again laughed. One curt, short, full-bodied laugh.

"I'm going to marry your daughter," Walt said.

There was a weak gasp, and in the rush of fear that followed his proclamation, Walt realized he'd made a mistake, done it all wrong, gone too fast. He felt beads of sweat dripping from his chin, onto the tablecloth, and the raw and ragged tear of the fish bone slicing down his throat made him feel like something had crawled in and begun gutting him.

"A friend of mine owns a shoe store on the West Side," the Doctor began.

His voice was mildly accented, soft and steady in tone. The maid again disappeared, and now reappeared with a pudding.

"He is a very good man. He also came from Argentina to begin a new life here in New York.'

The maid dropped round spoons of a pinkish mixture into their dessert plates. The globs covered the elegantly etched flowers.

"He struggled greatly. But he has found his way. His daughter went to school with my Adriana. She is not a pretty girl. She will likely stay with him all her life. He is a widower, like me."

The maid returned with a grand silver urn and, without asking, was pouring coffee. Walt imagined she did not speak English.

"Not long ago, he was approached by three young men. Thugs. Irish thugs who told him he had to pay for protection. When he did not, one night very late, his front window was smashed. So . . ."

He lifted a cup filled with coffee and waved his hand with vague dismissal. The china matched the plates with the blooms dripping down the sides.

"I know of your brother. I know who you are, the type of man you are," the Doctor said. "You will never marry my daughter."

Walt looked toward Adriana, who at some point had begun to cry.

"I'm sorry Walt. Please go," she said softly.

He waited for her eyes to rise, to see him there, to show that glimmer of strength, the woman he knew she was. He wanted to wrench her from the deadening table, the suffocating and dark room's vileness. He wanted to tear her away but when he stood, his legs shook. He was sweating, he was overwhelmed and angry and sad. He moved out of the room and toward the door, thinking only of his brother, both of what Dickie would have done in this situation, that violence, and also of how he, at that moment, wanted his brother to die.

ten

There was a sudden, violent, onslaught of brutal and deadening heat. It was after midnight, and the city was a furnace of unrest, escalating anger, petty arguments broiling into bloody fist fights, smallsquatty fires igniting in dry bristling edges of dark spots near the river. Children were awake, somewhat dazzled by the strangeness of it all. Hydrants, untapped, sprayed ferociously, and mutts dashed through over and over. The heat wave, they said, would only get worse.

The garage door in the back of the butcher shop was open, but no breeze blew. Things were still as if an ancient drought had come to stay. Dickie had set up a card table and chairs but abandoned the game. Too hot to move, he was drinking in short gasps, figuring things out. There was a single oscillating metal fan on the floor, craning up and shooting hot air at the four of them, Dickie, Big Ed, Bug and the heavy, young, red headed O'Halleron. Dickie's four, The Butchers.

A deck of playing cards, smeared with grease, had been shanked aside, and began to scatter from the fan's wind, though the poker chips remained. The beer had lost its foam. They all smoked. In a small, oddly ornate chair, dragged in months ago by a neighbor woman to be fixed but forgotten, Adlai sat sipping warm beer. He'd very recently gotten a real taste for it.

"It's too bloody quiet," O'Halleron said.

He was the only one who'd retained an accent, lilting and Irish, from his parents. He'd been born in Dublin, and brought here when he was six.

"I thought someone was bringing de' Gormley gals," he said, standing and stretching.

His shirt swooped up as he reached higher, a slab of belly rolling out, shafts of reddish hair, matted and sweaty.

"We got business," Dickie said. "Fuck on your own time."

The massive red head loomed near the table, restless. He turned, noticing Adlai in the corner. For reasons unknown to the rest, Dickie didn't react harshly to O'Halleron likely due to the man's brute strength and dumb, child-like nature. It was well known that O'Halleron could not read and that he had once twisted an enemy's head neatly, so the man's eyes were forever looking behind him.

"Who's there?" O'Halleron said, looking toward Adlai, who didn't move, just sipped his beer in shadow.

"I want to hit some stores. Shake them up for protection money," Dickie said. "Then I want to look at Harlem."

Bug stopped dead.

"Harlem?"

"Just to see the racket. They're into all kinds of shit. Making lots of money," Dickie said.

Dickie paused and surveyed the dank and gritty back room, lifting a hand in an uncharacteristic gesture that was at once regal, king-like, gentle.

"This can be a great time for us."

"You killed a man Dickie. Don't you think they're gonna get you?" Big Ed said.

There was a clink of glass, like chimes from a clock or the falling of a delicate china figurine. Adlai had set down his glass in the corner. They all glanced at him, then back to Dickie. At the same time, from down the alley, came footsteps, heavy and deliberate.

"The Coriglianos are taking the rap," Dickie said. "They're saying they did it."

"There's gotta be more to it," said Ed.

Big Ed turned, listening to the approaching steps. They were slow, beast-like, stopping, then beginning again, as if someone were weighted with something heavy and iron, laboring to move forward.

"You worry too much Ed," Dickie began.

The shadowy figure stopped in the doorway, leaning into a wall, as if he may topple. Adlai gasped.

"Walt?"

Walt staggered in, moving with great effort. His shirt was buttoned but there was a rip scraping down one side showing pale skin. He had a cut on his cheek. He moved in slowly, toward the table and the men, lifting his arms upward. He was speaking, but very softly, near gibberish.

Dickie stood up, went around the table, and as he did, Walt took several bold steps forward, like an aerialist desperately trying to make it from the thin high wire to the safety of a platform before plunging. He flung himself at Dickie, and Dickie laughed.

"The golden boy got drunk," Dickie said, catching his brother, gripping him with his steely arms, holding up the much larger bulk of Walt.

Walt pulled back, and Adlai emerged from the corner, moving gingerly toward the table. Walt put his arms on Dickie's shoulders, as if steadying himself, then he gripped him around the neck. Dickie was smiling. With a rush of something buried and awful, Walt began to squeeze the air out of his brother. The movement was swift and brutal, and came too quickly for Dickie to knock him away. Dickie raised his arms, flailing, and Adlai ran to them. He pounded on Walt, hitting at him like a tiny bird on a mythic beast. Realizing what was happening, Big Ed got to the three of them, yanking Walt off. Dickie swayed back, gasping for air. Adlai, crazed and dizzy from the beer was still beating at Walt's side, until Big Ed touched his shoulder and bent down to him.

"Go on, it's okay now kid. Go on."

Walt had fallen to the ground, lying on grease, sawdust and bits of ancient gristle.

"He's just drunk, Dickie," Big Ed said.

Dickie walked to his brother; his breath labored. He kicked him in the gut three times, then, still gasping and red in the face, turned and went back to the table. Adlai had not left; rather, he had hidden himself again in the corner, watching.

"Shit," O'Halleron said. "Should have brought women. Women change things."

"We'll start on my plan tomorrow," Dickie said. "Adlai get your brother upstairs. And bring more beer."

From his corner, Adlai went to Walt, knelt down, touched his cheek. Walt was moaning, and something brown was drizzling out the side of his mouth. Adlai thought he might be crying.

"Go on," Dickie said softly.

Adlai took hold of his brother's arm, and Walt roused, trying to stand. Half way to standing, he fell, trapping Adlai under him.

"Shit. Come on," Big Ed said, moving to the two.

"All I do is pick people up around here," he said, reaching down and hoisting Walt up, carrying him out and upstairs.

Adlai hopped up, unharmed and went in after Big Ed, to get more beer.

eleven

The heat had drawn Adlai out. He'd woken in the middle of the night, his palms sweating, one hand scratching at the surface, scratching for the scrap of paper the shy man had gingerly pressed there, like a coin, like something precious, that night at the movie house last month.

The house was still, both brothers sleeping deeply in the room they all shared. Adlai half woke, digging a nail into his wet palm as if he would cut deep into the soft skin and retrieve that piece of information that had somehow burrowed there. There was a slim cut. He sat up and sucked at the cut, then slipped out of bed and opened the bottom dresser drawer, his drawer (half his, since Dickie kept his gun and girlie magazines down there too, invading his youngest brother's space.) Adlai tipped open the old oak drawer and reached to his underwear where the paper was hidden, though barely, as he knew no one would bother looking into his things. He could likely have left the old scrap in the open.

Walt's railroad pocket watch, which he'd bought second hand and fixed and kept shined, lay on the dresser open. It was after midnight. He had barely been asleep. His brothers had both fallen out, sacked, after the ruckus in the back. Adlai was still dressed, so he just had to slip on his shoes. He went out and stole through the kitchen down the stairs and out through the back, down the alley. He'd snuck out before, sometimes not coming in until morning, and his brothers had presumed he'd just been up early.

The scrap of paper with the name and address of the place was stuck in his palm now, sticky with the trace of fast drying blood from the cut he'd made with his nail and cemented there with the insane heat. It was as if it had become part of his skin, part of him. He hailed a checker cab, holding out his palm with the scrap of paper welded there, stigmata like, and this made him feel like a miraculous journey was finally beginning for him.

He was fully awake, and not sure why he'd chosen this night. He'd had the scrap for a while, and had been thinking of making a move for weeks. Something about Walt, the beastly collapse of him, the meanness of Dickie, the fullness of those two, like biblical heroes throwing themselves at one another, drunk and passionate. He was going to be sixteen, and he was ready for something to begin.

He gave the cabbie the address, reading it from his palm. The driver was of an undetermined age, harsh from behind with a slash of frizzed hair, fur on his neck, and dark patches on his jowly cheek that was lit partially when he turned from the wheel.

"What? That's not where you want to go," he said.

His accent was thick and indiscernible. Eastern European, or Slavic. Heavy like that wild wall of hair. The cab stunk of something rotten. Adlai repeated the address, and the cabbie grunted then went silent. Though there was little traffic, the cab trudged in the heat, light after light halting their progress. The cabbie swung east and slowed.

"You sure?" he said.

Adlai stayed silent. He wasn't sure what he'd do when he got there. He'd done nothing more than listened to the shy man at the movie theatre, held his gaze while he told him about the place, taken the scrap, and known he would go. He wondered if he would see the man there.

The cab yanked over to the curb and stopped near the entry to a slim cobblestone-covered side street, barely wider than an alley. Near the entry to the street, there was a wooden bucket lying on its side like a shot animal, and further down, Adlai spied piles of trash, and against one wall, a wide wooden slat doorway that looked as if it could lead into a barn.

"Well," the cabbie said.

He reached up to pay the fare, but the man wouldn't take the money in his hand and seemed to be formulating an opinion about something. Adlai threw money on the front seat and got out quickly. The side street was deserted, save for a light and voices at the far end. The cab did not go forward, rather sat idling at the entry way, as if creating a mythic doorway back to the real world.

Adlai stood for a bit. He didn't know how late the place would be open. He hadn't thought of that. There was light and sound, so it seemed to be all right. He stepped past the upturned wooden bucket which was wet and dark on the inside. He suddenly thought of pig guts, bled animals, as if the bucket was stained with blood. He looked up into the night sky. Sweat beads on his forehead drizzled back into his blond hair as he hunted for the moon but could not find it. Someone called. A small, funny looking man in a broad rimmed hat was walking his way. He was shouting something, though his thin voice was lost in the night's desperate heat. The man stopped a few feet from Adlai and put a hand to his mouth. Then he belched loudly.

"Sorry," he said, in that same thin voice.

Adlai did not move at first, but then he turned quickly, frantically, searching for the checkered cab which had finally pulled away. Sweat was dripping off of his face. He put his hand to his cheek. The scrap of paper in his palm loosened with the sweat and stuck first to his cheek, then fluttered to the ground.

"Oops," the man said.

Adlai turned and began to walk away.

"Don't go," the man said.

There was a gentle desperation in the voice. He turned back.

"You won't get in over there," the man said, motioning to the bar at the end of the street. "Not that they wouldn't want to let you in. But you look like a child. Are you?"

Suddenly Adlai felt weak, his legs wavering, so he sat down on the cobblestone street and again looked up for a moon, something familiar to bring him back. He wanted to lie back. The man plopped down next to him.

"You can't stay here like this," the man said. "There's a place in Brooklyn. Near the Navy Yard. If that's what you want. Young men go there."

The man leaned in and whispered in Adlai's ear, as if the message could be picked up and thrashed around by someone near, and turned back at them. He told Adlai where to go, where boys like him went, the only sort of place he could go at his age.

"But I wouldn't go there alone," the man said, standing.

His broad hat shadowed his face, and like the cabbie, his age was indiscernible. But his voice was gentle, reedy and soft.

"You take care," the man said, moving back toward the bar, unsteadily.

Adlai rose and went to the mouth of the alley, and turned out of the side street. The checkered cab he'd taken was idling nearby, the wild-haired driver leaning out the window, smoking. The cabbie shook his head with what seemed like legitimate concern, and waved Adlai over. Adlai got in and went home.

twelve

The three brothers were around the large beaten oak table, in mismatched wooden chairs, having breakfast in the kitchen of the apartment over the butcher shop.

Pat stayed at the polished white stove in the window corner, like a day dreaming short order cook, hovering over a cast iron skillet layered with bacon. Light smoke floated through the kitchen, tainted with the fried and fatty strips but also with a sweet gentle molasses and rich hickory scent. Pat was an expert at crisping bacon, known for it, and when the three brothers did sit down together, which was once a week and most often breakfast, he made them a feast of the stuff. They had toast, coffee, and jam with it.

The windows were open wide. The kitchen, which next to the living room was the biggest room in the apartment, sat directly above the space in the shop below that was the refrigerator for the carcasses and meat slabs. Pat said that drew a coolness to the kitchen. The living room was dark, more a wide passageway to the bedrooms with nothing soft or female, nothing of a home in it. Just two chairs and a side table, one lamp. Pat was turning the strips, and humming.

Walt was slumped in his chair. He hadn't put on his shirt, just wore the loose white boxers he'd passed out in. There was a bruising purple stain on the side of his stomach where Dickie had walloped him the night before. He was muscular in the arms and chest, with a thin layer of fat on his belly. A girl once told him he was well-built in a sloppy way.

Dickie was reading a newspaper, folding the pages back into deliberate halves, crisply as he swept through it, hunting for something. He'd already dressed completely in black pants and a gray shirt, though the heat was dreadful. Adlai wore his pajamas, the same pair he'd worn for years, a soft cotton long sleeved top and long billowy pants decorated with small winged things, either moths or butterflies, too faded to tell. The pajamas still fit, though were shorter up the leg and arm. He yawned deeply.

"Up late kid?" Dickie said, snapping a page of the paper in half.

Adlai lifted his head gently, toward Dickie. The newspaper covered his brother's face, so he only saw hands gripping, folding, and the white cropped blond crown of his brother's head. He dared not breathe. Any reaction could solicit anger from Dickie. He knew not to answer, tremors running down his spine, and something thrilling too, like the drab gray moths on his pajamas were feeding off the day's heat and feeding off of him, his skin and bone, and gaining color.

He held still. Something was about to happen. He'd been obsessed with that concept, that this summer something was going to happen to him. He suddenly, fearfully, realized he had no control over when or how this thing would happen, or how it would unfold.

Dickie snapped the final page in half, finishing the paper, creating a narrow half page, and uncovering his face. There was a hard snap and sputtering of flame from the stove.

"Almost ready boys," Pat said.

All three of them turned to Pat at the stove, hungrily, momentarily yearning as if yanked back to some form of fleeting innocence, as if this meal, this talent for crisping their father had, was the only thing left that brought them back to each other and to their father. It was the one remaining thing their father did for them, and it was an action of the past that had remained, while all the rest, the things of childhood, those pale, lacy and powerful little memories, had vanished.

There was a bird cry, an odd singing. It was a loud rattle, a passionate noise.

"That's a wren," Walt said.

"Where'd you go last night?" Dickie said, looking straight at Adlai.

Pat was delivering the first plate, stacked with perfectly crisped and savory pieces of bacon. Walt took it.

Adlai had fallen back, deeper into his chair, deeper into his pajamas, pulling the collar toward his mouth and hoping the moths would swallow him. Dickie could not know, Adlai thought. He'd been gone an entire day once, nobody noticed. Dickie could not know.

"I had the dream last night," Dickie said.

The wren sang again, a lighter cascade of notes, mating sounds, gentler than before, longing. Pat stood watching his sons eat. They all had plates now, with toast, bacon, coffee.

"How much of it?" Walt said.

"It started later this time. I was still on the floor, in the sawdust. It was red and sticky cause I'd already chucked up the blood," Dickie said.

All of them were looking at Dickie. The folklore of his dream, the fact that he had for so long been obsessed with telling it fascinated them. It was the unlikely and vulnerable revealing he expressed when telling it that made them listen. Each time something new came out.

Dickie was chewing bacon and his body shuddered as if with fever.

"The sawdust was like candy, like coming together, like the dust and blood was making it into something sweet. Then in the floor, from below, an eel came out, from the floor and it was steaming," he said.

"Eel?" Pat said, turning away, looking out the window.

"Then I woke up. And Adlai was gone."

The telling was short this time, and they all turned to the youngest. Adlai had pulled his legs up into a knot, into his chin, and he held them close. He hadn't touched his bacon.

"I wake up sometimes. I can't always sleep. I went for a walk," Adlai said quickly.

He held his legs tighter, gripping them so hard that they hurt.

"Angie did that," Pat said, still looking out. "Sometimes it can't be helped."

The wren sang again, joined by another, closer now, in a call and return unison of chords and chortling, almost like delicate laughter. The room was still at the mention of their mother's name. Dickie laid down the paper, and Adlai let his legs fall back to the floor. Walt took five strips of bacon and shoved them into his mouth.

He could always bring them back from the brink of things, from the edge of knowing that they couldn't bear. He could do that. The bacon filled his mouth and puffed his cheeks and he smiled. Dickie took five strips and crammed them into his mouth. They looked to the youngest. Adlai was relieved, momentarily, and gently picked up four strips, folded them in half, and put them in his mouth.

They all chewed, ate, while the wren sang, then another bird joined, some cawing thing, a violent more reckless call, an angry shrillness that filled the room with something mean but bright.

thirteen

They went out in Dickie's car in the morning to sniff around and see what was being said on the street about the murder at the docks. They stopped at Kramer's first. O'Halleron waited in the car, like some sordid and conniving get-away driver, leaving the auto idling in the savage heat. Big Ed and Bug went into the store with Dickie.

Kramer's was a small, family-run grocer, like most, dolling out supplies lately on credit, hoping to collect at month's end from children sent to get flour, sugar or beans. The place was long and narrow, with a few display shelves, two fans running at either end of the store, and a glass chime in the window not moving, as there was no breeze and the fans' weak output did not reach there.

Most things were stacked on shelves behind the long counter, and the grocer, Ed Kramer, would fill orders slowly and deliberately.

The sky had gone fiery white early that day, the morning sun, relentless and scalding in its reach. As the three stepped in, they paused to let their eyes adjust. Kramer was leaning on the counter, speaking softly to a young girl. She turned as they entered, and Dickie waved at her.

"Wait here," Dickie said softly to his two men.

Kramer stood up, handing a bag to the child and stepping back. Dickie moved over to a shelf display, where a few dusty pickle jars sat. He lifted one up. The girl was taking her time getting to the door.

"Go on Mary Alice, your mother's likely waiting," Kramer said, in a tone falsely serene and ragged.

The girl, tiny and barefoot, wearing a dark blue dress with her hair in pigtails, stopped near Dickie and tugged at his pants.

"Buy me a piece of candy?" she said, casting eyes that were oddly bright and violet up at him, almost seductive.

Dickie pulled away quickly, looking at Kramer.

"Rots your teeth. Go home."

The door swung open and shut, and the movement stirred the air enough to give the glass chimes a shake, its melody glittering for a moment. Dickie was at the counter. He set down the pickles.

"Make these yourself?" he said.

Kramer had stepped back further toward the long row of shelves holding dry goods.

"We do," he said. "What are you boys doing around here?"

"We used to come by here. Used to help you out," Dickie said.

Kramer sighed, glanced at a big wooden clock on the wall.

"Things are different. The Coriglianos got this area you know that."

Dickie smirked.

"Yeah I know that. But there's things you don't know," Dickie said.

At the door, both Bug and Big Ed puffed their chests, as if soldiers summoned to battle.

"Get on home Dickie. You don't belong here. You boys go on home."

Dickie leaned slowly into the counter. His face was taking on a light reddish look. His eyes were open very wide.

"You sick or something Dickie, you better get on home," Kramer said.

Dickie slammed his fist down on the counter just as the door swung open, and the chimes made the faintest music. The door did not close. Big Ed and Bug were blocking the way, but the man shoved his way through toward Dickie.

It was not a direct Corigliano, not blood, but a member of their tribe. A gopher to pickup cash likely. He was a fat kid in a tight suit, sweat staining his collar, as well as the thick waist of his cotton pants, the cuffs of his long sleeved shirt and the rim of a straw hat that made him look a bit like a carnival barker. He strode to the counter. Big Ed shut the door.

"I don't think we've met," Dickie said, extending a hand to the fat kid.

"Who the fuck are you?" the fat kid said. "Kramer you got what I need or what? It's too fucking hot."

"We're The Butchers," Dickie said.

The fat kid swiped at his brow, scrunched his forehead.

"Oh yeah, so the fuck what? Get out of here you dirty Mick. We got business."

Dickie flinched. The chimes swayed and as the kid turned to notice the sound, summoned by some stray memory of some stray summer, caught off guard by that delicate phrase of sweetness, as he turned Dickie lifted the heavy jar of pickles and slammed it into the kid's head.

Bug was touching the chimes, making them dance, and he kept that up as the kid squealed and fell to his knees, blood spurting out of the side of his head, one shard of glass from the expertly shattered jar holding firm just above his ear, gushing. Dickie bent to the floor, plucking the shard from the kid's head.

"I'm Dickie, leader of The Butchers. Now we've met," he said, placing the shard in the kid's hand which was flailing toward the gash.

Dickie stood up and turned to a stunned Kramer.

"Sorry for the mess."

The fat kid was struggling to his feet, mumbling in pain. Big Ed still had the door open, and Dickie quickly led them out into the heat, which remained impervious to any human action, still scalding and strangling the city with its ceaseless blaze. They got into the waiting car.

"Where to?" O'Halleron said. "Want to eat something?"

Dickie was in the front seat.

"You really did it now." Bug snorted in hard nervous gusts. "You really did it."

"Go to 125th," Dickie said.

"You still on the Harlem thing?" O'Halleron said.

Dickie leaned into the open car window, a hot wind blowing at his face. Bug put a hand on the seat from the back.

"Just get us out of here fast," Bug said.

Dickie leaned further out the window as they sped along. There was a slender cut on one hand caused by a stray shard of glass from the pickle jar. He held his hand out the side of the car, into the hot wind, letting tiny trembling bits of blood blow out and away as they strayed further uptown.

fourteen

The butcher shop was busy, though many of the women and children that clamored for soup bones and chuck roast wanted credit which Adlai gently, easily gave to them. He hadn't been told not to. His father was off in his dim and quiet room behind a shut door, where only occasional sounds of a woman's voice singing on the radio, or his father's genteel moaning crept through. His sick headaches were back.

Walt was irritable and distant. He'd told his younger brother to work half the counter while he took care of the other half and handled the cash sales. During slow spells, Adlai watched his brother, hunched into the counter, oafish, hung-over and broken, somehow older than he was just the day before. He noticed how large his brother looked, his white butcher apron not tied in back, hanging sloppily, his shirt gray and his hair sweaty and swept to one side.

Adlai had taken his time dressing. There was some shifting movement that had got into him from the night before, some lingering remnant of a glance the strange little man in the hat had given him, some doubtful sneer from the cabbie, that made him feel more alive today.

He wore a navy shirt, buttoned all the way up, and matching dark blue trousers, his church pants. He'd spit shined his black shoes. He'd doubled the large white butcher apron over in back, so it fit snugly around his waist. Several of the women taking their time studying chops and sausages had smiled at him, and one had asked him if he was new. The attention was electrifying.

Folded neatly in his front pant pocket was the vague information the little man had whispered to him the night before. He'd written it on another scrap of paper so he wouldn't forget it, as if it were one important clue in an unraveling mystery that could vanish at any minute.

Mrs. Haas, a round and jolly German woman, was running a fat finger along the glass case, muttering . Adlai was just tall enough to be able to reach over the high meat counter to hand customers wrapped packages. Under five foot tall, Mrs. Haas was too tiny to look up and over, so they smiled at each other through the glass casing. Mrs. Haas as seen through the glass, was like a circular and boldly decorated doll, eyes bright and blue, mouth piqued and red.

"I suppose a chop will do, sweetie," she said.

Adlai reached in to grab the meat, letting his head feel the slight rush of coolness. In there, he saw Mrs. Haas' face looking through the glass.

"Have you been to Brooklyn?" he said, retrieving the chop and pulling it out.

They both stood up, but could no longer see one another clearly. So they leaned down to the glass again.

"I have relatives in Brooklyn. Why do you ask?" she said.

"I was wondering about the ships in the Navy Yard. I'd like to see them some day, but I've never been to Brooklyn," Adlai said.

She stood up, putting her hands on her waist, and Adlai could see a compact but mighty bosom. He stood too and wrapped the meat while she spoke.

"Well I don't know. I don't think that's such a good spot, really, to visit."

Adlai finished up and handed the package over. A chubby hand put the coins down, the soft voice drifting over the counter.

"I have always wanted to take a boat ride down there though," Mrs. Haas said as she left. "I do like the water."

The customer bell rang. Walt was hunched again, this time his head in his hands, as if he might be sick. There was a pretty, dark haired young woman at the door. She stayed away from the counter, as if she'd wandered into the wrong store, as if she'd wanted the movie show a few blocks up or a woman's hat shop and was horrified at the scarred and bloody slabs of beef. Adlai was going to offer his assistance, when Walt straightened up.

The sound Walt made was a sound Adlai had never heard.It was low and guttural, animal like, beginning very dark and deep then tearing out and up in volume between a moan and a scar of weeping. The girl drew back, and pressed herself against the wall, as if there were a hidden passageway, a way out and away from the horrible moan. Walt hurried from behind the counter and went to her, grabbing her by the shoulders, then kissing her straight on the mouth. Adlai froze, nervously fingering the scarp of paper in his front pocket, feeling like he was watching a picture show, not his brother, not this shop. There was a small boy trying to get in, which threw the couple off. Walt stood back, then took the girl's hand roughly and pulled her back behind the counter, then to the back area where they took deliveries. The boy stepped in and looked around.

"Anybody here?"

There was a lull, and Adlai stayed quiet behind the high counter, repressing a sudden urge to giggle.

"Yes, how can I help you?"

"Pound of bacon. The Mulligan's account."

The kid spit out the words fast, as if he expected a fight, as if he were cussing or telling a dirty story. Adlai understood. He hated to buy things for his father on credit.

"Sure," Adlai said.

He filled the order, and the kid left and the store was empty. He listened for his brother and the strange dark haired girl. He strained harder to hear, imagining there would be black and vacant crying, or a struggle, or a gasping noise of love, but things were dead still. What lingered in his mind was the queer, almost degenerate animal like moaning noise his brother had made when he first saw the girl. Adlai shut his eyes and wondered if he would ever make such a noise, ever be that alive.

fifteen

Dickie watched the bloodcolored brick buildings roll by, tenements, rooms for let, then signs for grocers, and bars, then a black man shining another black man's shoes and finally at a stop, small frayed bunches of children in white short dresses and ribboned hair pushing at one another. The windows were down full in the car in the blazing heat and the little black girl's cluttering the street waved wildly at the men in the car. O'Halleron was driving., Dickie lifted a hand and threw out three nickels. He was sitting up front, Bug and Big Ed were in the back seat.

Dickie would tell anybody who asked that he didn't hate niggers. They were soldiers in the war, ran a good business, fucked their women like anybody else. The Wops he hated, didn't trust, especially that Corigliano gang, who likely wanted his guts on a stick, now that he whacked the fat kid with a pickle jar.

"Turn left up here," he said.

It was their first meeting with the Negro fella named Dewey, and Dickie wasn't nervous, more excited, filled with an unfamiliar wanton yearning. There was something dire and electric in Harlem, forbidden he thought, untouchable, and he wanted a piece of it. They stopped at the address Dewey had given him. It was a slick-looking red lounge with a broad window in front with blinds pulled tight and a beer sign hanging in front of the blinds. O'Halleron idled the Chevy, and Dickie drummed his fingers on the outside of the car door, feeling a charge of fire from the heat on the metal. The blinds snapped up, and there was a figure there, not entirely visible, since the inside of the place looked dark, and the sun battered the glass and made it all a mess of reflection. It looked like a girl, pressing her hand on the window glass, maybe wearing something red and sheer Dickie thought, catching a glimpse of movement.

"Come on," he said.

The four crawled out of the hot car and at the door to the lounge, Dickie paused, then stepped in. They strode into the joint, like they were going in for an easy game of pool. It was dim and cool and for a brief moment, Dickie shuddered and wanted to get out and in the same moment, in his blurred and stirred up mind, he saw the eel of his dream from the night before.

"He ain't here yet. Will be. Get you a drink?"

It was the girl in the window, and she was wearing red, but as his eyes adjusted to the darker inside from the fire outside, Dickie saw it was a gentler red, more a battered pink. As she stepped toward them he noticed her tits, which he decided were perfect, and her lips, which were done up to match her dress, maybe to match the whole place which was a wash of redness, and her dark hair was pulled back tight, and she was the color of milky coffee.

"Sit in back there," she said. "Beer all right?"

"Yes," Dickie said, moving toward her, then purposely, with a slight thrill running up his back, brushing against her as he moved to the table, followed by his men. She smelled of lilac, he thought, which didn't seem right or even possible for a girl like that. The place had a bar, squat tables, a pool table in back. It could have been any bar they all went to downtown, but it wasn't.

They sat, and Bug lit a cigarette. She was coming back with their drinks, coming through the dim bar, gliding, that almost pink dress clinging at her and Dickie thought:

"She's not wearing anything under that. Nothing at all."

She set down the drinks and Dickie saw she was barefoot. As she turned he reached out to grab her dress, then dropped his hand, thinking again.

"What's your name?" he said.

She turned, then put a hand to her hair that was pulled back so tight. She looked straight at Dickie.

"Eva," she said.

"That's not the right kind of name for a girl like you."

"Really."

"You better change it," Dickie said.

She let her hand trail down from her hair to her cheek, then strangely, to her shoulder, and he thought she was holding back a smile.

"Yeah?" she said.

The door up front rattled open and shut, and she turned and was sucked up into the darkness of the bar. Dewey had arrived. He was a well-built, well-dressed negro. He wore a dark suit that fit snug, showing off the arms of a boxer, and he had on a bowler hat. He came up to the table and put out his hand to shake. O'Halleron laughed a little, and Dickie stood up fast, shaking Dewey's hand.

"Brought your posse," Dewey said.

"We travel in a pack," Dickie said.

"Nothing wrong with that."

Dewey pulled up another chair to the table, and the girl, Eva, was nearby, leaning against a wall in shadow.

"So," Dewey said. "What is it you want with me?"

Dickie leaned into the table.

"Advice." Dickie said.

O'Halleron snickered, and Dickie straightened. He didn't turn, or move, just let out a deep breath, and the men were still.

"You've got some good things going on. The numbers, horse racing even the fights."

"I don't mess with the fights," Dewey said.

"You used to fight," Big Ed said, lilting forward a little.

There was a sharp movement from the corner, and Dickie noticed Eva had gone away.

"I guess I did," Dewey said.

"I recognized you," Big Ed said.

There was a long stretch of stillness. Dickie drained his beer.

"You might think, what does this scrawny Mick want? Right? What can he do for me?"

Dewey smiled.

"Bring us back some whiskey Eva," Dewey shouted.

"I know there's been trouble from downtown. Italians trying to steal what's yours, take some things over," Dickie said. "We do things fair and square. If you give us something, we give you something back."

"Like what?"

The girl, that wash of red, was at the table, leaning in with drinks, near enough so Dickie smelled that ragged obscene lilac, that fragrance stricken with sweetness and danger.

"Muscle," Dickie said.

She left.

"All right," Dewey said. "I'm listening."

sixteen

Walt had chosen a drab hotel in Brooklyn on an ugly little street not far from the Cobble Hill section. It was a dive, which is what he could afford, and more so, it was what he wanted for he and Adriana, a grimy place to be immediately forgotten, discarded and shut away as if it were part of a fleeting and horrible dream.

The room had a bed, a chair and a sink, plus a window open wide but bringing in no breeze. It was dusk. There was a restless stir of summer insects, a murmuring that Walt heard as yearning, as pain and anguish. Wide-set evening shadows crept in darkening and marring the pale beauty of the couple's youth and nakedness. It was very hot, so they'd thrown the rough sheet to the floor and lay together, sitting up, side by side on the twin bed, their clothing cast about the room.

Though they'd made love already, he was still aroused, and would stay that way because he was near her. They were not touching, but sitting close, his broad sweaty back against the wall, making a stain there, her narrow caramel colored shoulders barely touching the wall, the waves of her hair at her shoulders, her eyes open wide looking out at the coming night. His feet hung at the end of the bed, hers just touching his calves.

The couple was breathing gently, both of them, nearly in unison. The extreme heat in some ways lulled them. The ancient melody of the insects rose and fell.

"There's a hotel in Atlantic City, on the boardwalk, looking straight out at the ocean," Walt said softly. "I read there's a chandelier in every room."

She did not speak, barely stirred, but she placed the palm of her hand on the top of Walt's hard and cut-up knuckles, and he shuddered involuntarily, almost with violence, and fought a welling up, a torrent of that nameless grief he was ashamed of. He reached for his steely and hardening anger.

"We could go there for our honeymoon," he said. "We could do that."

She sighed and gently squeezed his hand.

"He's afraid," she said.

"Your father?"

"Yes."

There was a distant rapping. Walt stiffened his back. They heard the voice of a hard, lost woman from the hall, and he realized it was a knocking on a nearby door.

"He told me if I saw you, he would take me back to Argentina," she said.

The knocking grew in intensity, then the woman yelled something vulgar.

"He can't do that. He has his practice here. He's bluffing," Walt said.

The hard woman's voice, merging with a new and more cacophonous rise of the night insects, was nearly too much for Walt to bear. They couldn't come back here, he decided.

"He is a stubborn man. Cruel," she said. "My mother left him when I was young. It isn't really his fault."

Walt drew in a breath and wanted to tell her about his mother, Angie, that sameness he and Adriana shared, the brokenness of their fathers, but he was too afraid to speak. Plus Angie had left when he was very young, so he only had half-memories from Dickie, shadows of things. He couldn't always tell Adriana the things he felt, the wild rushes of never-felt beauty and joy she stirred in him. It felt like madness, these attacks on his senses, the way she tore at him without doing a thing.

"Then he won't know. When we are married, there will be nothing he can do," Walt said.

She released his hand and pulled back, and he sat up quickly, suddenly, as if she were going to get away, as if she were a prisoner running off to something violent and unseen. But instead of moving away, she curled back into him, resting the wild tangle of her dark, rich hair onto his pale chest, pressing her lips there too, then biting gently. He brought his hand down into her hair, and the tactile feel of it calmed him.

The hard woman's voice had disappeared, leaving only the trill of insects. She curled her legs to his, then nestled closer, still biting, murmuring his name and then.

"I love you Walt."

The rush of longing was too much, and he pulled her onto him, too roughly, burying his face in hers and biting her lips, his hand staying in her hair, holding onto it, and easily lifting her up, bringing her breasts down into his mouth, then hoisting her up then back down on top of him, pressing close and hard into her, knowing he had to be careful not to break her.

They made love again, and in that rush there were things he could not bear, that he battered away, a desire to devour her, images of her father and his father, then the vileness of his older brother, and at last, despite the overwhelming scent of her and touch of her pearl-like skin, he could not stop the image of the eel, and his brother's relentless dream from the night before swallowing him whole.

seventeen

Again everyone was gone.

Adlai was alone in the apartment over the butcher shop, sweating in his bunk, the hard stink of his brothers permanently soaked into the bedroom, never letting him forget their dominance, their constant yearning for things, their control. They were far more like randy animals than he, he thought. But lately, just lately, he had touched on an anger, a fragrance of his own desires that kept him up at night, made him reckless. His brothers would never acknowledge or understand his harsh yearning, would never see that it was much like theirs, that he really was of the same blood.

His desire was not violent or brash like Dickie's, nor clandestine and romantic like Walt's. His, he realized, was more rash than he had ever admitted. His was dangerous. That afternoon in the butcher shop, working while Walt had vanished in the back with the dark haired girl, he had discovered the best way to get to the Brooklyn Navy Yard. He'd asked the older men, the graying and half-deaf ones who came in shouting for sausage, men who had served in a war, who knew of sailors and adventure and escape. They told him to take the subway then get out and walk to the water and to see the ships, the war vessels, the history.

It was after midnight. His brothers were gone, his father deeply asleep. He got up and dressed slowly, then went to the kitchen and had a drink of whiskey from a bottle Dickie kept in the cupboard. He took his time leaving.

He took the subway rail to Brooklyn, then made his way out into the night and off toward the water like the old deaf men had told him, zig-zagging down ragged-looking streets, then past soft, sleepy brownstones, always knowing he simply had to get to the edge of things, to the water.

The streets were empty and not well lit, and the night's heat was stifling. There was a slight rustle of insects, and bird's wings at times, though he couldn't be sure and wondered if it might be bats.

His mind felt full, cluttered. He was thinking almost like another person, an older person, a man from the future. The street darkened and got narrow, and he was aware of a newness coming through him. He shut his eyes and stopped momentarily, struck by a sudden wave of bold, incongruous thoughts:

"These are things that I have never done. If I am stricken, if a bat were to fly at me and bite me and they found me broken into pieces and bloody on the street in the morning, my brothers would not know at all what to think. They would be puzzled, and finally, reluctantly they would simply give up, accepting that there was no answer, that it made no sense, that these were not the actions of their youngest brother. The whole death, the demise of Adlai they would say, was nearly impossible. And they would not really believe it, though they would have to believe it because Adlai would be dead."

He reached a section of cobblestone, what he believed to be the Navy Yard. It was a massive area stretching far out. Gray dead-looking ships and docks jutted out. No one around. He was alone. He smiled, thinking how he had been hot and alone in bed, the lingering stink of his brothers, and now he was again alone, the stench of river water and heat. Out in the water, there was a tug boat moving slowly, inching through the watery muck, like a bloated spider. Adlai stood still and listened for voices, movement, but nothing came.

The rush of danger, the adrenalin he'd enjoyed since getting on the subway, began to dissolve, and his weakness, the self he knew and recognized, was creeping back. He suddenly wanted to sit down, overtaken with a swift rush of hopelessness and a despair he hated to admit. He sat, and looked out at the tug boat which seemed mired and lost in the murky water. The air was heavy with that drab muddy scent of fish, of filthy water and dank things. Adlai did not like the smell, it was the opposite of what he knew from his father's shop.

There was a slight rustle, which he thought at first could be the night insects, but it became distinct. There were footsteps, from behind. Someone was coming.

The boy spoke before Adlai could stand.

"Are you drunk baby?" a voice said.

Adlai turned. The boy was near his age, dressed strangely, wearing a silk scarf, tight pants, a cap. He was thin, pale, with hair like muddy gold. He did not appear to have eyebrows. Adlai began to stand but the youth knelt down to him and leaned in close, as if he knew Adlai, as if he needed to study his eyes closely or identify a mark on his cheek. The boy's breath stunk of something lethal laced with licorice. He had very big lips.

'You don't seem drunk at all," the boy said. "You don't seem like much of anything at all."

A ship horn blew, far off, and out in the water the tug boat was moving. Adlai turned back to the boy, formulating a sentence, a scheme about being lost and needing directions back to transportation. It had all been a terrible mistake. In the distance, two ghostly figures cut into the black night, framed by the hull of a war ship, the pointed elegance of that steel giant far behind them. The boy turned and watched the men approach.

"Well here we go," the boy said, standing up.

Adlai stood too, still thinking he must tell this stranger how he was lost, how he needed help. The men were large, but young, in sailor whites, one heavier than the other. Their figures marred the darkness, as if their pale faces and pure white garb could bring light onto the bleak black waterfront. They had their hands in their pockets. They stopped not far from the boy and Adlai. They shifted their feet, awkwardly maybe drunkenly, but seemed almost gentle.

The boy moved toward them slowly, feline-like and when he reached the bigger one, he leaned in, whispered something, then put his hand on the man's pant front. He turned to Adlai and made a funny face then motioned down toward the water, off to the left, near a shadowy area leading toward a ship. The boy left the sailor and went to Adlai and briefly stared at him, then took his arm and pulled him along, down toward the darker part of the docks. Adlai could hear the men following, but he kept his eyes on the tug boat out in the water, which was moving more swiftly now. He knew the boat was real, while he began to feel the rest of this was a dream, that he'd fallen into something not real.

His steps were flagging, so the boy yanked at him to keep up, pulling him into a small corridor of shadow and squeezing his arm tightly. The two sailors came into the narrow space which smelled very wet and rotten. Adlai wanted to speak, or maybe to scream, but the boy had grabbed the first sailor and was kneeling in front of him on the harsh cobblestones. The other man had come close, smelling of beer, taking Adlai by the arms. In the scar of shadow, Adlai could no longer see the tugboat, nor the moon, nor hear the insects. He felt dizzy. The man was on him, pushing him to the ground, then yanking down his pants. Adlai felt the cold stones on his ass and legs, and he was shot through with a fear and a desire to get away, this tainted with an intense feeling of arousal and a long-felt loneliness. He watched the drunken sailor undo his own white pants, pushing them to his knees, then yanking down his underdrawers.

"Turn over, you little cunt," the sailor said in a slurred, angry voice not at all pure or young like his face or the soft white uniform he wore.

Near them, the other boy was making a harsh, rasping noise, which distracted the sailor, and in that moment, Adlai stood quickly, yanked up his pants and ran. He made it out of the hidden spot and onto the docks, then raced up and away from the water, terrified not of the boy or the drunken sailors or the blazing hot night, but of his once frail and now monstrous and dark desire that told him to stop and turn back, to go back into that shaft of darkness and find what he knew he had for so long been looking for. No matter what the cost or pain.

He reached the edge of the docks, near the street again, out to safety, but he turned and waited. He thought the sailor may chase him. He watched the dock, empty again, and watched the place the boy had taken the men. Nothing stirred. He waited, wishing the tugboat was still moving in his view, but it was gone. There was no sound, and he was alone.

Adlai shut his eyes, and in that darkness, he felt dizzy and sick, and he started to walk, eyes shut, forward, his throat tight and dry, his head pounding. He moved very slowly, his lids trembling and his tongue thick. He kept walking, blinded, slowly.

"You stupid little mutt."

The voice startled him. It was Big Ed. Adlai turned. The boorish man was standing on the street, working a toothpick in and out of his front teeth. He had on greasy pants with a rip in the knee, the sweat stained tank top, the same he always wore. He turned away and walked toward a car a few feet up. Adlai followed. Big Ed stopped and hopped onto the hood. Adlai stood near the front headlight, then looked up to notice the moon, which seemed to have appeared for the first time that night, out from some swathed veil of heat, from a dark place where it had been hidden. The moon looked like it had suddenly caught fire.

"You got itchy feet, that it?" Ed said.

Ed leaned back and seemed to be taking in the flaming moon, the lackluster city stars. Beads of sweat cast a pattern of zig-zag lines down the front of his tank top.

"Dickie notices. You think he doesn't," Ed said.

He leaned back further on the hood, then let himself flop back there on his forearms.

"He had me keeping an eye on you. I saw you leave tonight on my way home. I saw you wandering the street like some drunk fool," Big Ed said. "I saw you get on the train."

Ed was still sitting back, then he reached his arms out, the thickness of them billowing out into the night, and he strained as if he would yank the moon down on top of them both.

"How did you know I came here?" Adlai said.

Ed laughed, his arms still up, straining further, reaching. He sat up quickly, and hopped off the hood to his feet, then put his hands in front of him in a boxing pose.

"Dickie was right you are a dumb rat mutt. Out here on your own. Come on," Ed said.

He danced from foot to foot, new sweat pulsing and staining him, dripping down his arms.

"Come on, throw a punch. Come at me you stupid mutt."

Ed stepped up, and in a sharp and quick move, he slapped Adlai. The boy reeled but did not fall back. He lifted his hands into fists before him, flushed with a wild and unfamiliar anger. No one had ever hit him. He began to move from side to side, mimicking Ed. Ed tossed his hands out, left then right, boxing into the stifling night air.

"Come at me," Ed said.

Adlai threw his hands out, and stepped closer, still swaying, then he punched at Ed's belly. It was hard. The feeling of his fist hitting a man was thrilling.

"Again, come on, big man. You think you can do this? Come on."

Ed did not come in contact with Adlai, just swayed side to side, a behemoth, sweat dripping, hands clenched and jabbing. Adlai tried again, making contact with Ed's wide chest. Ed bent down.

"Harder," Ed yelled.

Big Ed was hunched now, his broad, sweaty chest heaving before Adlai who was gasping, pushing his hands out left then right. He stepped even closer, near enough to smell Ed and it was not the stink of his brothers. It was more fragrant, more alive, and he was near enough to feel the man's drizzling sweat spraying off onto his pale face. He jabbed at Ed's chest, then shut his eyes and kept punching. He hit him many times, and his knuckles shot thrills of pain up his arms, and he wanted more. One hand was raw, but he kept punching until finally Ed whispered, "Stop, enough, stop," and he pulled Adlai into him, held him close, held him in the dazzling heat under the raging moon, while the boy cried, gripping him harder and harder, until finally, Ed pulled him into the car, held him there close, hushing him harshly in the car, soothing him with his whispers and then with his hands, his lips, his own tortured history.

eighteen

The week of searing, draining heat had finally exploded in an unexpected violent downpour, long tails of rain sweeping across the city in a visibly silver drench.

It was late night, but the blackness of the storm clouds hung heavy enough to be noticed and the rumbling heavens and gashes of lightning had young, silly and drunken people scrambling. The hotel room in Brooklyn for transients where Big Ed and Adlai lay had a small bed, an ash basket, and a single unadorned window where constant, snapping whips of lightning tore into the sky view, settling only for thunder cracks and a whispering hush of rain.

There was no electric light on in the room, but the severity of the storm, the consistency of the lighting, made it seem as if a faulty lamp were snapping on then off. Yowling voices gashed through the night.

Ed took up most of the bed with his muscular bulk, leaving only a thin strip for Adlai to lie. They both were sitting up, backs against the wall, looking out at the storm and its dance of light. There was a shattering crack of thunder, and Adlai gasped. Ed threw his arm roughly over the boy's shoulder, and pulled him in. They were nude, both very pale, their whiteness making the dingy stained white of the walls seem nearly gray.

Ed was monstrous next to Adlai, over six foot tall, curves and curls of hard won muscle, fight-earned gashes, and a soft matting of hair smothering his legs, all looking wild and out of proportion next to the boy's delicacy. He had a very wide, Neanderthal forehead, a hard jutting jaw and a nose that had been broken twice. Though only nineteen, Ed was messy with life's harshness. Adlai was just over five foot tall and weighed one hundred and ten pounds. He had no marks, no visible flaws, and the gentleness of his tone was that of pearls or new milk. He kept his pale blond hair long. A softer echo of thundercame from far off.

"He would kill us both, you know that," Ed said.

Before the boy could answer, and as if in response to his own dark prophecy, Ed yanked Adlai to him, hoisting him like a featherweight package, then pulling his face close and bringing their mouths together, forcing his tongue in. Adlai was shuddering, whimpering, and Ed held him out again, studying his face, like a harmed object.

"Don't stop," Adlai said.

They kissed again, as they had been doing all night. Ed had gone gently into their love making, and briefly just once, offered to wait, but Adlai in a frail but regal way, had dominated, coaxing him, demanding of him, even with the virgin-like rush of pain, overwhelming him with his penetrating need to be touched.

There was a snap of light and a bold crash of thunder, then a hungry wind blew in the open window at the two of them as the storm revived and grew in severity. There was crude shouting from the street, and dark animal screaming, hounds and indefinable creatures, voices drenched in the new, mad rush of storm and a sudden clatter of pounding hail.

Ed had Adlai on top of him, like a thin wisp of a sheet. He held him tightly.

"What will we do?" Adlai said, his cheek hard against Ed's cheek, his lips nearly crushed into him.

"Nothing," Ed said softly.

They lay still as the storm raged on, and not moving, they slept, princes.

nineteen

Far uptown in a similarly run down room in a tenement apartment, a couple lay watching the rushing violence of the storm through an unadorned window. This place was rented by the month, not the night. The bed was lean, hard and rickety, but covered in a broad hairy striped fur coverlet that the girl, Eva, had earned on her back.

Eva was thirty five, though she would not admit this. The ebony pearliness of her skin, the severity of her yanked-back hair against the face of a long-ago goddess, this easily fooled men, who mistook her for a girl. She was supple bodied. Her breasts were large, though imperfect due to a knife wound that slashed across one nipple, down the front of her chest like a phantomsnake.

Dickie lay on his stomach, studying the scar, and thinking of his dream, that ceaseless haunting, and the recent creature there, that eel. Eva's eyes were shut.

Dickie had left the bar after the meeting with Dewey, after making a good first connection with the man. He'd driven downtown with his men, then gotten rid of them, sent Big Ed to keep an eye on his dumb-ass youngest brother, Adlai. He hadn't initially known he was headed back uptown. He was just driving aimlessly as evening came, as the heat escalated and the storm clouds threw themselves across the sky.

He had the windows down, and he drank from a beer bottle shoved between his meaty thighs. He began to think of the girl, the Negress who had purposely, he decided, tempted him, in her vulgar red dress, her tits all over the place, her black pussy and thighs making him go just a little crazy. He'd never fucked a nigger, but he had nothing against that sort. He knew guys that did, took one of them dark girls off somewhere, leaving their Saturday night sugary white virgin dates on dusty porches in lacy dull pink skirts while they ran off in the woods to fuck some wild creature. He didn't do that. He hadn't done much with girls after Mae-Ella because he hated talking to them, and that was something they seemed to need.

As he'd driven, he became more certain she was waiting for him, alone in that bar, wanting to control him somehow. He'd pulled up to the bar and stopped, and sat for a long while, then she'd come out, like she knew he was waiting. She stopped in front of the place and lit a cigarette and ran a hand through her hair and acted like she didn't know he was staring.

Then that rain started, and he knew he was saved. It ripped in and tore at that vulgar dress of hers, making it transparent, and he'd leaned out and shouted for her to get in, and she did. Getting invited up to her ratty little apartment in Harlem wasn't hard. She was quiet, all wet and dripping during the drive, then he'd said he sure could use a drink and she said sure and he went up and that was it.

She opened her eyes, and he reached up and touched her scarred tit.

"Who did that?" he said.

"A real bad man," Eva said. "You fuck like you want to kill me."

He rolled over, his body small but hard muscled, strong. He scooted up to her and they sat side by side. He was aroused again.

"You're like some kind of little bull," she said.

Dickie flinched. It was the kind of talk that made him want to hit her. Being called small or weak. He wouldn't put up with that. But there was something about this one, maybe her being what she was, maybe that flawed imperfection, that colored curse, that he didn't follow through. Plus girls always ran away once he hit them. He studied her body. This one had a way of making love that was almost unearthly, he thought, almost divine.

"You're a whore?" Dickie said, putting her hand in his lap.

"I was," she said. "I retired."

He reached over, but before he could touch her she was on him, ravaging his mouth, biting at him, taking control. He was strong enough to throw her off, but he didn't want to. She was charged up with that magic again, making him crazy, and he half thought of his ceaseless dream, then of voodoo and how she might be casting some death spell over him. He didn't give a fuck, even if they found him like this, screwing a nigger, even if they killed her and put him in jail for miscegenation or tied him to a tree and lit him afire for lying with this black sorceress.

He let her stay on top, casting her spell and getting up a rhythm, as the storm outside increased and bits of hail flew in through the open window like jewels. He grabbed onto her tit, that scarred place, and stabbed his nail into the spot, trying to tear it, wanting to see if black blood was really oily, dark and hot, or if it had snake stink in it or if it would leak out onto his chest and slice into him. If it could drip out onto his tongue and make him a real derelict.

They thrashed there, looking like animals in warfare, fighting for dominance, as the soft white bits of hail scattered across the hard wood floor, and the storm breathed its wet might, oblivious to their vacant battering.

twenty

They kept every window of the apartment open wide, scant traces of a morning breeze blowing in, but dying fast. There were scents flavoring the air, sausage, bacon, those bought at their butcher shop below, and hints of chicory from a local shop. When he shut his eyes, Adlai smelled lilac, though he couldn't be sure from where.

He was alone in the kitchen, shirtless, in a pair of Dickie's hand-me-down undershorts. They were a faded white with a rip on one side, stitched awkwardly years ago by his father. On the kitchen's window sill sat a bright yellow finch. The bird was small, but not weak, the striking shade covering his yellow breast making him royal. Its beak was the only dark spot. It was a rich brown, as if the bird had stopped and dipped it into chocolate then let it dry.

Adlai moved cautiously toward the window. He did not want to scare it off. He had never had a pet, nor anything stuffed or childish. The bird seemed unphased at the sill, as if guarding something just beyond it. Adlai waited near the window, considering how he may touch the thing.

"What happened to your arm, Rat?" Dickie said.

Adlai turned to see his brother, also in white undershorts, shuffling sleepily into the kitchen to the stove. He turned back. The bird was gone. Adlai moved closer to the window, craning out, the day's scents stagnating and multiplying as the heat soared swiftly, now odors of things rotten mingling with the bacon, chicory, lilac. He felt Dickie's hand on his head, a soft smack, which Adlai considered more a stroke, though it threw him off balance. He glanced at his right arm, a bland and graying bruise, which made him shudder and forget the room momentarily.

"You fighting now?" Dickie said, banging pots and making coffee.

Adlai went back to the table and sat, covering the bruise with his hand, remembering how Big Ed had pressed his lips there last night after holding on to him too tightly, the big man sweating and speaking too loudly his name, forgetting his strength and relinquishing his own control for a second, tarnishing that pale, previously unblemished spot on Adlai's arm. He shuddered deeply, wanting so much to touch Ed, to smell him right that moment. He had never felt so fulfilled.

"If a guy grabs ya that's not a fight. Use your fists," Dickie said, standing near the open window waiting for the coffee to boil.

The sun overhead shifted. A harsh and unforgiving line of light fell across Dickie's chest, slicing him in half, light and dark in its extremeness.

"Or was it a girl?" Dickie said, leaning into the ledge. "A mean little cat?"

Adlai did not move. His body stiffened, and he moved his hand down from the bruise, a badge of his dark reckless self, down to the raggedly sewn up hole in the undershorts that drooped long and billowed. He worked at the sloppy thread until it tore.

Walt came in, completing the triangle, he too in white undershorts, he too shirtless. It was only some long-ago inferred feminine and deep-gutted modesty that stopped the house full of men from wearing nothing to bed through the suffocating nights.

"Adlai's got a girl," Dickie said.

Walt was not listening. He did not want to hear his brother's voice. He sat, rubbing his forehead, his eyes shut to a gentle reflection of the night before.

Dickie set three mugs of black coffee on the table. The brothers sat in the chairs they always sat in at the dark and scuffed table they had known all of their lives. The table was bare, but for the three chipped mugs. Walt and Dickie were at either end, Adlai between them. He turned his chair slightly to keep an eye out for the yellow bird. He'd never seen a bird that color before on their sill.

"You're turning sixteen this month," Dickie said, slugging back the coffee.

Adlai, in the past, stayed silent, waiting for Walt to speak and fill in gaps, sensing his brothers never expected him to say much, and knowing they never addressed anything of merit to him. He had long ago stopped letting it drag him down, his otherness. He simply let his mind wander away from them. But today was different. Now he had Ed, a vile and powerful secret that gave him an unexpected vigor.

"I'd like to have a party," Adlai said.

He hadn't planned on speaking, and he paused for a moment, not sure what to say next. He often thought things, stray bold things, colorful things, things that made no sense, sometimes vulgar raw and perverse things. But he let those thoughts scatter past, as his brothers or his father spoke. The words had come though, like a torn piece of bone stuck in his throat, refusing to go down, popping back up as reflex.

Walt looked at his younger brother as if seeing him for the first time.

"Why are you so thin?" Walt said, then seeing a sudden pulling back in the boy, continued. "What kind of party do you want?"

Adlai considered this, shivering a little with expectation. His brothers were both looking at him, and he had a strong sensation to laugh or maybe sing. He felt quite possibly he were losing his mind, at last, a fear he'd had as long as he could remember, reinforced by his father's meandering decline and increasing isolation, and that man's refusal to speak of the past, of how they'd all began there, of their mother Angie. Adlai was terrified of this encroaching madness.

"It would be nice to have music," Adlai said softly. "And whiskey."

Dickie stood up quickly, and Adlai cowered, but his brother was not going to hit him, he was fetching more coffee. He came back with the tin pot and filled their cups, and Adlai wondered what was wrong with Dickie, if he were weak or ill, and as he turned, he saw, perched on the sill, the yellow finch.

"We ought to do that, have a party. Things have gone sour around here." Dickie said.

He sat, and they all three gazed out toward the living room, and beyond that, the shuttered bedroom where their father slept. He was at the shop less and less, briefly, vacantly, quietly mentioning sick headaches, vague illness, muttering and shuffling back into the soft smothering tomb of his room.

"It might bring him out," Dickie said.

When Adlai turned, the yellow finch again was gone, but he smiled, feeling confident it would return, deciding he would scatter seed there when nobody was looking. His brothers stood and went to dress, all of them scheduled to work at the shop together that day. Adlai lingered, alone again, hoping the bird would come back and maybe even fly into the kitchen, casting a fluttering blur of yellow across the room, bringing a light in that didn't burn him.

twenty-one

Dickie was in the window of the butcher shop, standing at a charred and sliced up butcher block that he'd set up like a display table. He arranged two knives, hard worn things shadowed with silver and muddy patches. Then he laid down a cleaver, thick handled, wrapped in a rag as if in swaddling. Next he set down a hack saw, stained red on its feathery thin tips. He tapped his finger on the hack saw's delicate pins to test the sharpness and suddenly thought of Eva, angry at his desire so soon, hating that he wanted a woman that much that soon after fucking her.

Dickie glanced around the shop. There'd been a meat scare, which led him to display the butcher block and the new cutting operation. A kid had nearly died from something rotten, likely due to the heat, some grizzled piece of animal not kept cold, surely not from their shop. People were talking.

It was over 100 degrees by 10 a.m. He was going to cut slabs to order, from the refrigerator straight to the wrapping. That would show customers it was good.

They were all in the shop. Pat had roused from some hunkering slumber, some dream-state akin to morphine. For reasons unknown, maybe mistakenly thinking it was Sunday, he had dressed in a suit and coat and sat on a stool to supervise. Walt and Adlai, with his newly discovered talent for wrapping packages, were at the counter. Dickie was in front of the butcher block ready to give a show.

Several snub-nosed boys peered in the big front window, one holding a greasy mutt by the neck. Dickie smiled, then curled his lip at the mutt. The boys did not move. Dickie planned to slash at manageable pieces of a carcass, an arm roast, chuck or leg.

Two fans blew around the place, hot air circling and throwing itself back and forth aimlessly. A heavy woman with hair dyed bright jangled the customer bell and stopped inside the door, surveying Pat, the boys, and Dickie, positioned in the window holding the cleaver and wearing a white apron. She dabbed her forehead, and Dickie half expected the tissue to turn scarlet.

"Boy the heat," she said.

She waved to the counter, and Dickie glanced back. Adlai, the runt, was waving at the fat woman, and Dickie wondered momentarily if his youngest brother was fucking an old cow like this. She turned to Dickie.

"What's this about?"

"What can we get you today?" Dickie said.

The woman, wearing a skirt, sweat-stained blouse, and a hat with a veil swiped backward as if a forgotten shred from church, glanced at Pat slowly, sadly, then smiled again at Dickie.

"Pig's feet. Good morning Pat," she said loudly.

"Fetch a hock joint and pig's feet Adlai," Dickie said. "We're cutting right here in the window. Straight from the refrigerator wrapped fresh."

The woman pulled her grubby little hand, which Dickie noticed had a sizeable wedding ring on it, to her cheek, her hankie dangling like an extra piece of flesh, her mouth open wide and her eyes too.

"Well you don't say. I like that."

Adlai was dressed neatly, his white shirt crisp and buttoned up, his apron whiter than the other two on the account that he'd bleached it. When his brother called for the pig's feet, he had been musing, wondering if there may be a hat he could add to the ensemble, if he and Walt could wear matching hats behind the counter.

He didn't like the new routine, having to see the animal pieces sawed or hacked. When he'd pulled smaller steaks or sausages from the cooler, set them into the wax paper, tied them meticulously, he felt it was clean. This was something else.

He hated running to the back refrigerator, the dimness and chill of it, the shelves with arms reaching out, the hooks of dangling carcasses. At the cooler, he thought he'd get it done quickly but inside, stepping further back past the cheerful light of the store and his brothers, he paused. The walk-in refrigerator's door angled back in toward him, stealing the light, the animal's feet poking out hooved and angry. He began to shake.

Dickie shouted again, and Adlai went all the way in and grabbed the thing, distracting himself by thinking briefly of the night before, that piece of himself, that touch. He moved out to his waiting brother.

Dickie threw the pig leg down on the butcher block. It was cold on his fingers. He looked up at the fat woman and for a fleeting second thought how much meat she'd deliver, how much fatter she was than the fucking pig. He hated fat women. Then he slammed the cleaver into the frail end of the leg, too hard, too fast, and the feet jumped forward nearly off the edge of the block, as if they would fly forward and dance. He halted their flight with his free hand, and the woman scrunched her face, but as he lifted them and smiled, then handed them over to Adlai to wrap, she calmed.

"That is good service," she said.

There were several more people gawking in the window now, though the snub-nosed boys had left. A blonde girl, wearing knee socks stared in, and Dickie thought how pretty she was and how uninteresting, how cold. Her pale face, the dew of sweat at her blue eyes, the slick pull back of her hair, that cheap swath of blush at her cheek bones. There's nothing to look at, nothing to get at, he thought, and he saw Eva in that dress, the same red as the stained hack saw, that dusty, lost red. Then he looked up and saw another face in the window.

It was Frankie Corigliano, the youngest of that family of men. He wasn't the leader, but he was blood, working with brothers and uncles and the rest of them. He had not been on the dock the night of the shooting.

He was Dickie's age, but looked younger, tall but wiry lean, wearing a shiny black suit and a tie and spit-shined shoes with pomenade in his curly black hair. He had two goons with him, beefy thick-headed wops with that thick greased-up hair that the gang was known for. Wild waves of black and tight button-over pants and shined up shoes, more like pansy dandies than thugs, Dickie thought. The Coriglianos, they ate at restaurants and swilled champagne and fucked big titted blondes who wore diamond earrings. That was who they were.

The three of them were staring in, watching the shop. The red haired woman went out. Pat was slumped, eyes shut in the corner, and Dickie glanced at his brothers who were idle at the counter. Dickie set down the cleaver, but it was near him. He stiffened his back, then ran his palm along the front of his apron, up and down, like he was rubbing at a stain. Frankie moved from the front of the store slowly to the door, and the customer bell chimed. Pat sat up.

"Why don't you go upstairs Dad," Dickie said.

"It's not closing time," Pat said, in a soft but urgent voice.

Frankie stepped up to the butcher block, flanked by the two men just behind him. He was known to have a mean streak.

"Your little run is over," Frankie said softly, leaning close. "We could kill the lot of you right now. That's what I say. But that's not how the Coriglianos do business. And you're not worth the mess."

There was a slight tightening in Dickie's jaw. He let his hands linger at his sides, swaying slightly.

"You want something from me?" Dickie said.

Frankie didn't flinch.

"That shit you pulled. Whacking my boy with the jar," Frankie said.

He leaned closer now.

"That was stupid. You're gonna have to pay for that you stupid fuck."

He leaned in even closer, glancing at Pat and the other two brothers, then speaking in a voice that floated out into the shop like a whisper, like he was sharing a secret or telling a dirty joke he didn't want anyone else to hear.

"You worthless piece of shit," Frankie said.

Walt was stepping out from the counter to get a look. A balding man approached the door from outside, but turned and left. Dickie leaned onto the butcher block, getting close to Frankie as if the two would kiss, then he spit in his face.

The thugs came forward quickly, and Frankie flew back, shouting, rubbing a hand on his cheek where the spittle had flown, scratching at it as if it were venomous.

One of the thugs came at Dickie and grabbed him, but Walt was in the fray, yanking the beefy guy backward, catching him off guard. Adlai stumbled out from behind the counter too, and as the big man fell back, he knocked into the boy, both of them falling to the floor. The shop was momentarily still, only the light hum of the counter cooler, whose light glowed gently. Then came the shuffle of the other thug moving toward Dickie. From the floor, Adlai could see the thug's spit-shined shoes, then he looked up to see the man go for Dickie's throat. Adlai reached out and grabbed the guy's ankle, setting him off balance. As the man threw his hand out toward the butcher block to get his balance, Dickie pulled the thug's hand onto the block and swung the hack saw down slicing off his little finger. Frankie came forward and was screaming.

"You fucking crazy butcher! You fucking nut! You're all dead you stupid fuck."

Frankie's voice was shrill, almost female, and his face was ashen. Dickie looked at him. The thug who lost his finger was wailing, blood seeping as Adlai rolled over into a corner, and Pat stood dumbfounded, unable to comprehend what had just happened, the swiftness of it all, the violence. Frankie was screaming threats, leaving with the two thugs.

Dickie set down the cleaver and wiped his hands on his apron. He turned to see his father, hovering in the corner, sweating, a gray pallor and horrified look of disbelief. The fans spit out more hot air, and Dickie thought to say something, to ask forgiveness, to try to tell his father how things were going to be. But when he looked at the man, those eyes were too vacant, his trembling hands too weak. Disgusted, Dickie turned to go lift his youngest brother up off of the floor.

twenty-two

It was still in the back of the butcher shop. Dickie sat quietly with Bug, Ed, O'Halleron, and Walt. Adlai was in a corner, watching Ed, who had on a faded tweed cap, shielding his eyes and broad nose. He had on that same greasy white tank, the one with the hole in the back. Adlai took a step out of shadow, daring the room to notice him. He realized he was shaking.

His once unblemished face was now marred above the right cheek with a jagged cut, a battle scar. When he'd fallen out of the mean grab of the Corigliano thug in the shop, he'd flailed an arm out to break his fall, his hand turning in and a fingernail slashing into his own face, as if striking himself for not fighting back.

He hadn't eaten much that day and felt lightheaded. He was overcome with waves of a strange exhilaration, a sense that he was filling up with charmed new air, as if each breath he took was soaked in lilac and infused with divinity. The hot dreamy air gave him strength. He watched Ed's every move and boldly thought, *That is mine.*

Dickie had set up a circle of mismatched chairs. Walt got up and stood near the back garage door staring out into the alley. After the attack, after Dickie had wielded the cleaver and sliced off the tip of the thug's finger, after that, Adlai felt everything was forever changed. After the attack, his father had sat, not moving for quite awhile, staring ahead, his face a fake illusion of something it couldn't be. He kept smiling looking ahead as if remembering something fondly. Adlai was afraid for him.

After the Coriglianos had gone, Walt had spoken quietly to Dickie, and Adlai, holding a rag to his face to stop the blood, couldn't hear what they said. He kept looking to his father, seeking recognition, contact, but the older man was dreaming, unable still to take in what had occurred. The thrill that shot through Adlai during the violence, and really the ceaseless excitement that had started the night before with Ed, only seemed to be escalating. Adlai felt his life was on a new path. And Dickie, too, had shifted with this latest violence.

Adlai looked at his oldest brother, as if he were a war general preparing to seduce his men to arms. He'd put them all in danger. His spree of violence would surely catch up with him, with them all. It was inevitable. That part too was like a dream, thought Adlai. But looking again to Ed, he thought, *he will save me*. As if summoned, Ed tipped back his cap, and his eyes shone, steely and firm, first at Dickie and then, darting to Adlai. He looked at him with eyes gentle and a thin curl to his lips, a trembling smile.Adlai gasped. Dickie turned.

"Get out here, Rat. Get out of the corner," Dickie said.

Adlai glanced toward Walt, who still stood, his back to the group, staring out into the alley. Adlai strayed forward. There was no chair for him, so he stood outside the circle behind Dickie, and he kept an eye on Ed, who had taken off his hat, and looked at him almost boldly. The room was dimly lit with scant electric bulbs, a trifle of moonlight coming through the back door. Adlai noticed the thickness of Dickie's shoulders, the pop of sinew and muscle, his head and shoulders barely outlined by the gray night light. He wants to be an avenging angel, Adlai thought. But that's not possible.

Adlai looked toward Walt, as if he would finally speak up and offer reason and sanity, but his brother just leaned against the wide entry way out into the alley. He was looking up at the sky, restlessly, rubbing one palm across his neck.

"Go get us some cold beer, Rat," Dickie said.

Adlai turned, but as he did he saw, curling up out the side of Dickie's pants dark,oiled and lean, a gun. He stopped and looked at the thing, wanting to reach out and touch it, see if it were hot, see if it had been fired. He was used to the mundane repetition of his brother's physical violence, his wild threats. He knew Dickie owned a gun, but he'd never seen him carry it, like some bandit from the Wild West. He looked up, and Ed was following his gaze, and Adlai knew somehow he shouldn't be noticing the gun, shouldn't speak.

He went up front to the walk-in refrigerator to get the beer. The shop was dark, lit only by the Avenue , harsh taxi lights and flares of passing horns and voices. The front window was covered with the homemade sale signs he'd drawn for beef and sausage, the pattern allowing sharp channels of light and shadow across the floor. As the cars passed, the lights changed, and Adlai watched this, something he'd done before, as a kid, alone in the shop, hiding out from some nonsense, following that dazzling play of light or in winter, the battering of snow on the window. But that was a long time ago, he thought, before last night, before Ed, before everything important.

Adlai took a deep breath and wanted to go up and touch the signs, but as another swell of cars passed noisily, he saw in the shadow a phantom figure, and he was sure it was his father. The light changed again, and he knew the place was empty, and he thought, almost aimlessly, of his mother, of she who he did not know.

He turned away and went to the refrigerator, hauling open the door and rushing in and not bothering with the small stick he usually wedged to keep it open. He didn't care if it shut and he was swallowed in the cold blackness. He made his way back to where the beer was kept as the door slowly fell inward, taking away the bareness of light, leaving him in that cold place. And for once, he was not afraid. There was an animal hanging upside down, legs hooked up, gutted and cold. It swayed as the door suddenly opened then shut completely, snapping tight, and he was in utter darkness. He turned, wanting to get out now, and he heard the whisper.

"Stay quiet."

There were big, callused hands on his shoulders then under his armpits and down his sides and he was being lifted, his feet dangling off of the ground like the carcass hanging there. He was being pulled in close to a bearded cheek, cigarette hot breath, beer. The lips were familiar and the tongue. Big Ed hoisted him a little higher, and Adlai put his arms, in the darkness, around the man, and, his arm brushed the dead thing swaying helplessly there.

He fell into Ed and moved his mouth to the whiskered cheek to taste, and he could smell the meat at his shoulder too there in the dark, the cold hanging thing emanating that musky, slaughtered scent of recent butchering and hard-gutted manhandling.

"I got you," Ed said.

His voice was raspy and desperate, Adlai thought, and it was the way he too would sound if he could speak, but he could not. Ed squeezed him hard, and a thrill shot up his back, and he knew the door could swing and a gun could go off, and he knew this was what desperation felt like and this was that thing he'd only read about, that thing called passion. Ed set him down.

"We gotta get back," Ed said, and he was gone, out through the door.

Adlai took an armful of beer and left. When he got back to the circle, Dickie was smoking, and back by the garage entrance, Walt had vanished.

twenty-three

There was a bench a half block away from Adriana's building. Walt couldn't bear to look at it squarely, so he gave himself the distance. The building, the memory of that horrible dinner, loomed in the still night, and Walt felt as if there was something literal, something palatable in the air, as if the meanness of that episode left a dreadful impression on the whole block, much like a brutal murder leaves a reek of never-vanquished emotion in the home where it was committed. The closer he was to the place, the weaker he felt.

It was late, and he hoped he might see her coming home from work. He didn't plan to stop her or even call out. He just wanted to see her physically, to match the constant wash of images that stayed with him, obsessively, throughout the day. He had no real plan. He had nothing at all, really.

He sighed and looked up at the hard black night sky. He'd come to see her, but he'd also run from his crazy brother whose reckless actions cast a layer of doom across them all. He always knew Dickie would go too far, but he presumed it would be vacant and small. He didn't think his brother was smart enough to rise above petty fighting and harmless local brawls.

He was realizing, slowly, that Dickie was more dangerous, maybe even powerful, than he imagined. And his oldest brother seemed to be gaining a warped confidence, despite the insanity of his actions. There was, Walt thought, an odd respect given to reckless and brutal men who are not afraid to get exactly what they want. That, Walt thought scanning the bleak night sky for some brilliant little star, that was how he had thought *he* would turn out, though in a brighter way. Things had gone against him.

Walt always felt superior to his brother. He was going to be a Doctor. Respected. He had been sure that, later on, he would reach out a hand to the flailing Dickie. Once that flame of wild dumb bullying had died down and he was seen as a punk, Walt would help him. That's what he used to imagine.

"I am a good man," he said softly.

She was traveling toward him up the street. She must have noticed the lone man on the bench, head cast back. He sat up and took a breath. She came and sat on the bench next to him, glancing toward her father's building, then gently placing her hand on his. They were silent, side by side. He felt close to her, yet separated by the building, that man a block away. When he tried to think of what to do, how to solve this, how to get them back to the time he was dreaming for them, there was nothing in his mind. She squeezed his hand but he felt lost, useless. Then in an instant, he thought of killing her father.

It came upon him, like a gentle and forgotten task, harmless and sincere. If that man were gone, that could offer the solution that would bring her to him completely. He knew this thing, this vile thought, was merely a remnant of Dickie's behavior. His brother was beginning to infest him. He pulled his palm away, then put his head into his hands.

She sat close, comforting him, hushing and saying soft things, but he could not be consoled. He felt as if something were being drained from him, the very life blood, the thing that made him right, and he did not know how to stop it. She kissed him gently, but even that, even that felt cold.

"When my mother died he hid himself in a room," she said.

Walt looked up. Adriana had never spoken of her mother, but the mere allusion to it brought the phantom of his own mother, of Angie, out from under a forgotten shroud of memory.

"I had an Aunt who stayed with us. She was a thin, brittle woman, and she did not care for me. She could be very hateful," Adriana said. "He stayed in there, alone for a month. Back in Argentina. I was very young, and I thought he might not come out. I'd sit outside the door of his study where he hid. I listened closely."

Walt turned to her. She was looking up at the night sky, speaking in a soft, breathy tone.

"The door to the study was made of dark, heavy wood. It smelled of what I then thought was liquor. But I don't know. It had this strong dizzying fragrance. I'd sit there for hours, days, waiting for him to come out. I'd fall asleep there, smelling that thick, drunken odor."

Walt leaned his head back again, following her gaze. There was a small cluster of stars emerging up out of the blackness.

"We were very rich. He left it all to my Aunt, his sister, that bitter woman. He couldn't stand to be there. Not even in the same country where my mother died. He gave up so much just to come here. He did what he had to do."

She turned now, her calm face toward his, her dark emerald eyes on him.

"That's what I have always seen in you Walt. You are determined to make life work."

He saw the deep green willfulness of her eyes, and past her, the scant and fading apartment building, whose lights were diminishing one by one, as residents fell off for the night, and Walt understood both what he had to do and what he could not become. His father, far off asleep, dreaming, dissolving. He would not deteriorate that way. His brother empty and violent, he would not turn that way. He was not one of them. He understood that blood was his blood, that name was his name, but the bleak, disastrous turn to despair was not his.

He pulled her face to his, the clutter of night stars just behind her eclipsing all else, her lips tight on his mouth, and he felt ravenous again. He felt her closeness, and he tasted the brightness in them both.

twenty-four

Adlai tilted a beer bottle back and let the liquid dribble down his chin. It tasted tinny and warm, like dirty rain, and it felt cool in the heat against his face. He'd dragged a chair out from of a heap of unused things and was sitting, not in the circle of men discussing dark and heady things, but just outside of it. His chair was spindly, something cast off years ago, with spider legs and a scratched childish pattern of scattered blue flowers against its back. Adlai tilted the chair onto its heels, and titled the beer bottle again.

There were stray sounds of distant sirens, laughter, and Ed let his gaze creep across Adlai every so often, a darting flicker of a look. Adlai wondered if he would be asked to do anything, to participate. Walt had disappeared, but Dickie seemed not to care.

Adlai was a little drunk, and decided he was being drawn out, this latent acknowledgement a part of the shift that had pulled him from a sickly shadow, out behind the sheath of childhood and womanly things, into the light of Dickie's world. His brother had been talking a long time about what might happen next, but now he stopped. There was a lull, the men also sitting looking toward their leader. Dickie stood up and lifted his beer. He craned his neck to Adlai.

"Come here," he said.

The men rose and held their drinks, and in a long, hot, dull moment Adlai could hear them all breathing, smell the constant stink of meat and the desperate desire of restless men that he'd lived with all his life.

"To The Butchers," Dickie said.

He lifted his bottle higher, as if to continue, but paused, as a sudden thundering rush filled the alley, casting bold yellow light into the garage area, white on the wall, then a screech of tires. Adlai stepped back as the men turned, noticing the shimmering nose of a car stuck into the mouth of the garage, and before they could move, four men stormed out, armed with guns and moving fast.

Adlai recognized them from the day before. He saw the thug who had lost his finger. There was a cacophony of voices shouting, and men were forced to the floor, all but Dickie, and Adlai who stood frozen. Frankie Corigliano, with his greased and curly black hair, was shoving the end of his long gun into Dickie's gut and screaming at him, but Adlai still only heard the roar of the car's engine, the rush of the men.

He was confused, then he fell, feeling a hand on his ankle, tumbling to the concrete floor and lying next to Ed. Looking up now, he could see Frankie and the other three men yanking Dickie away. He sat up, despite Ed's hand on his back, meant to keep him still. They were pushing Dickie into the car, then the tires screeched again, the hot white headlights slammed against the wall and then, it was over.

Ed stood up first, then the others, and finally Adlai. Bug, his face as white as his pale and freakish hair, spoke first.

"They got him. Oh fuck."

They were breathing heavily, all of them, then they turned to Adlai, looking at him looking hard as if he were the answer, as if his blood would offer some solution.

twenty-five

They were in the kitchen, and it was like that recent morning, when the brothers had eaten bacon together in the heat in their undershorts. But it was not morning; it was deep night, and a hard rain fell. There was no yellow bird in the window, though that same window was open to a slate sky and an undulating spray, as the storm blew sideways, tearing across the city.

Adlai sat in his seat, Walt in his, but Ed sat where Dickie ought to have been, and Pat lingered near the stove, that light rain reaching his one arm which hung limply at his side. There was no coffee on the table, only a bottle of whiskey that no one touched. Adlai looked across the table at Ed, his thick mass of black hair, sweaty, his same white tank, dirty. Adlai noticed that Ed's shoulders were wider than Walt's and gnarled with labored muscle. His hands big and knotty with calluses, lying flat on the table.

Adlai's feet were tapping lightly on the floor. He could barely contain himself, the smell of that man so near, the memory, like some thick serum, shot up in his veins to tempt him forever, ceaselessly. He could not look away. Ed avoided his gaze and finally picked up the bottle. There were no glasses, so he set it back down. Adlai got up to fetch glasses. He passed Pat, whose arm near the open window was slick and dripping. Pat looked up, as if at a stranger.

"We don't have any pictures of him, or anything, do we?" Pat said.

For a moment Adlai thought *this is his ghost already*. Like his brothers, Adlai could not bear the steep deterioration, the recent tortured falling of his father.

He went to the window and despite the stifling heat, pulled it nearly shut, so his father's arm would not continue to get wet, then he went to the cabinet for three small glasses. He took them to the table, standing between Walt and Ed, closer to Ed, depositing the glasses, then reaching over, brushing his arm against Ed's, taking up the bottle and pouring.

"Thank you, Adlai," Walt said.

Adlai went back to his seat and drank the shot of liquor quickly.

"Why did they take him? Why not kill him?" Walt said.

"What?" Pat said softly.

They all glanced at the man near the window. Pat lowered his head, rubbing his palms together rhythmically.

"I don't know what to do," Adlai said softly.

It was again still, save for the dull and gentle wash of the rain. There came another sound, just as gently. It was lilting, first soft then a bit louder, as if carried in on the scent of the delicate night rain.

"O-ro the rattlin' bog, The bog down in the valley-o-ro the rattlin' bog, The bog down in the valley-o."

Adlai turned to watch his father, who was singing, his eyes shut, moving one arm in the ai,r as if following the line of someone's face. Adlai somehow knew the song, yet did not, as if in another life he had sung it, or as if it was part of him. Walt turned then stood up quickly. Pat sang on.

"And in that bog there was a tree, A rare tree, a rattlin' tree, with the tree in the bog, And the bog down in the valley-o."

"Shut up," Walt said, turning completely to Pat, in a voice unfamiliar to Adlai, in a tone nearly like Dickie's, but deeper.

Pat went still, leaving only the sound of the rain, and now a wind, rising at the window.

"I don't know how this all happened," Pat said in a near whisper. "I need to figure this out."

Somehow, Adlai knew the next line of the song, and he wanted to rush to his father, to lift his head and sing it with him, but that thought was fleeting, as the brothers had banded together long ago against the man, as if he were the enemy though they knew he was too feeble for that. Still, they were in solidarity against him. Lately, though, Pat's phantasmal dereliction had made their disregard for him feel brittle and mean.

"Go to bed. Go on. I'll be back in the morning," Ed said. "We'll figure out what do then."

"Stay here," Walt said.

Pat rose and moved slowly out of the room.

"Take Dickie's bed tonigh,t Ed," Walt said.

Adlai gasped, then laughed and lifted his glass to his lips, though it was empty. Walt looked at him with kindness and concern.

"No," Ed said. "I'll be back early."

He stood and stretched, the tattered edge of his tank rising up to reveal a tangle of fine hair on his belly. He sighed and went to the door, not looking back. Walt left the room, and Adlai sat alone, staring toward the window, then toward the door where Ed had just gone, listening to the rain, and vaguely recalling the melody of that long-forgotten Irish song.

twenty-six

They'd taken the rag off of his eyes and gone at his face.

Frankie Corigliano began it, speaking to him briefly then landing one hard slap, before Mickey, the thug who'd lost his finger, set in. Dickie's eyes swam at first in the harsh light. The rush of the fist at his cheek, the sting then crushing inward crunching of teeth and skin, made his head fly backward. Mickey was a big man, broad and pulsing out of a slick dark suit. He was rubbing his fist which glinted with gold, and Dickie, through searing pain, thought, *Who wears a suit like that*, then, *Eva*.

The fist came again, more leisurely, as if Mickey had gotten the first frantic round of rage out and now could take his time. Dickie felt his top lip flip inward, reaching under his front teeth, and he again thought queerly of Eva, as Mickey pounded, of Eva, with all that red, her perfect tits.

Dickie shut his eyes, and he heard grunting, then he opened them and looked again at Mickey, his long greased black hair and his smiling mouth and teeth. The pain made him feel hot, and he thought, *Those teeth are too white, too big*, as Mickey took a deep breath, and his hand flew to flesh, and Dickie suddenly had a glimpse of that ceaseless dream, as if momentarily asleep, as the eel curled around the edge of a well and slipped down into it. Mickey's fist came hard, three times: cheek, eye, nose, snapping, then a pop and cartilage cracking.

Frankie called out.

"All right."

They were in the living room of a house, Dickie knew that much. Frankie stood in the center and Mickey stepped away. There were two other men sitting nearby at a big dark table. They were eating. Dickie was in a chair, though not tied. A large sheet of plastic had been placed under the chair, billowing out around him. He let his head tip down and saw small blood puddles and a light spray of crimson near him, and he realized the plastic was to protect the floor.

"Where am I?" he said.

"Shut up," Frankie said.

One eye was swollen shut, and he took his time swallowing, the tang of blood overwhelming and choking him. He spit out a tooth.

"Watch it," Frankie said.

"Sorry," Dickie said softly, swallowing more blood. The tooth had flown off of the sheet, landing on the hard wood floor, near an overstuffed ornate armchair. Dickie thought, *This looks like the house of an old lady.*

Through his one good eye, he noticed a big painting of something with wings. A woman, he thought. Frankie came close to him, then knelt. Dickie tried to smile, but his cheek was frozen. He was happy because he realized they were not going to kill him, and he thought again of Eva, feeling giddy and aroused despite waves of pain tearing at him. There was an odd sense of deliverance, of survival and renewal. As if he had won.

"You know why you're not chopped up in pieces?" Frankie said.

Dickie laughed and tried to sit up a bit, to show he was one tough fuck, but each movement was unbearable, and he gave into delivering only a mild, lopsided grin.

Frankie shook his head in wonder. "He gets the knuckles, and he still smiles."

There was a light tittering from the table, where the men ate and a soft cussing from Mickey.

"You have grit. You're likely a little nuts," Frankie said. "It's something we need right now. You want a drink?"

Dickie nodded. It hurt to move his head, and the ache was growing, like it had only started and was going to build to some horrifying peak. He'd never felt pain like this, and as unbearable as it was, there was a dreamy dullness to it. Frankie brought him a glass, and Dickie took it. He tried to drink, but most of it spilled out of his misshapen mouth, a little bit burning hot down his throat.

"We're at war," Frankie said.

"With me?"

Frankie stood up, and Dickie got a look at him. His suit had a soft blue pinstripe and he had on three gold rings. His face was very smooth. Frankie was grinning.

"You see, that's what I mean," Frankie said, turning to the men at the table. "He can really think like that."

Dickie raised the glass shakily again to his shredded lips and let it burn over them.

"We are at war with the Lucianos. Your piss ass Irish gang has nothing to do with any of this," Frankie said. "If we wanted to take over your two-bit shithole butcher shop and kill your whole stinky-ass family, we would. But you took out one of them. You killed Sal Luciano, which is something we didn't think of. They pinned the job on us, which got this whole war started. It isn't such a bad thing. It was destined to happen. You just gave us a kick in the ass."

Things were fading a little, and waves of dizziness had come on, but Dickie thought of that night on the docks, how he'd done what he set out to do, how he'd shot that man dead, and then with a rush of pain he thought, *Adlai was there. He's in this too.*

"So, we go by your shop to put you in line, and you come on like this bull, the fucking butcher."

Dickie was only hearing part of it. Mean, tingling pain needles crept up his spine. He couldn't keep the spittle down, all that damn watery blood, so he let it dribble out of his mouth and down his chin. Frankie had his back turned and was addressing the men at the table.

"What do you think guys? This one's got big balls, right?"

"Fuck yeah," Dickie slurred, opening and shutting his good eye, trying to stay upright.

Frankie had come back, kneeling, looking at Dickie with eyes that seemed lavender, lashes too big, looking at him too long, and he thought how he just needed to sleep; he needed to lie down. Frankie brought a hand to Dickie's cheek, and the touch was brutal and hot. But his eyes were gentle, like they were lit from behind, like fireflies had flown up inside the man's head and were shining through. He felt sick, like he might throw up. Things were fading in and out. Frankie spoke gently.

"I know a lot of violent men. Goons that will cut your insides out. Mean, evil men. But I've never seen anyone so calm as you," Frankie said. "There's a quality to that I need."

Frankie paused, as if he were searching for a radiant, saving thought. And Dickie thought, *What is he doing with me?* Frankie stood and stretched, then smiled.

"That's what I can use," he said. "That's why you and your brothers aren't dead. You're gonna work for me."

Frankie knelt back down to touch him, and the heaviness was too much and Dickie let his lids fall, that hand still on his cheek, and a voice saying something, and a smell of sausage frying he thought, like in the shop, and then just washes of red, like his eyes were open but underwater in some rushing bled-up sea, and he saw Eva, then that eel, the dream came upon him, and he passed out.

twenty-seven

When the door swung and the morning heat rushed in and the customer bell rang, Adlai was dreaming. He folded and refolded the wax paper over three fat pork sausages, creasing it gently and evenly, the way he liked it to be done.

Walt was ringing up the kid who bought the sausages, a teenaged boy who was barefoot and shirtless. Adlai let his head lilt that way, a glance at the ripple in that stomach, the dirty fidgety fingers on that boy, then he came back to the package and his dream. He was in a room by an ocean with Ed. He glanced up, as he always did when the customer bell rang, and he saw the man with the hospital face, the scarred-up ruddy bandages, then he saw Frank Corigliano.

The boy with no shirt moved over to Adlai's end of the counter and was pressing his naked stomach against the cool glass of the case and drumming those mud dirt fingers.

"You done with that?" the kid said grinning, showing a missing front tooth.

Adlai had stepped away and looked to Walt, who also had his eyes on Corigliano and the other man, who Adlai realized was Dickie. Adlai took the sausage to Walt, who got the order done and the kid out.

Dickie was moving gingerly across the floor toward Walt, weaving a little and leaning onto the counter as he went. His face was fat with messily tied bandages that were still seeping blood. Walt rushed from behind the counter to meet his brother. Corigliano was near the door. Walt threw his arms around Dickie, and Adlai thought, *Is there a gun? He has a gun here. Am I meant to go get that?*

"It's all right," Dickie said. "Rat, get us some beer. And put the closed sign up.

Let's go in the back."

Adlai shuddered, choking down a rush of terrible sadness and a sense of utter relief, realizing as he locked the door and ran for beer that he did not want his brother to die. When he got to the back of the shop, all three men were seated in a circle. Corigliano had his legs thrown open and was fanning himself with the straw hat he'd worn. He was dressed in a pinstriped summer suit, and looked like a southern gentlemen who'd wandered off the wrong train. Dickie was slumped slightly in a chair, Walt next to him. There was a seat for Adlai. He delivered the beers and sat.

"I'm gonna let him talk," Dickie mumbled.

His voice was soft and muffled, like he was speaking through a wall of cotton, like he'd aged a few hundred years over the past night. Adlai's foot was shivering, tapping the floor, and he couldn't stop it. He did not know what was going on, and he wanted to go take the bandages off of his brother's face and redo them, to fold them neatly like he did with the wax paper on the sausages. He wanted the blood to stop.

"It's good you all didn't do anything stupid," Corigliano said, tipping back his beer bottle. "First of all, this is just business. Nothing personal. We had to beat your brother up a little since he cut off my man's finger."

"A little?" Adlai said.

He had thought it, still trying to figure out how he could get over to his brother to mend his wounds. He did not mean to speak aloud.

"You're the youngest?" Corigliano said.

"Be quiet, Adlai," Walt said, sitting forward in his chair, then placing one hand on Dickie's shoulder.

"We are at war with the Lucianos," Corigliano said.

Adlai took a drink of beer. He'd never had alcohol so early in the day.

"We need maniacs with muscle. We need your brother. Plus, you work with us, we don't kill any of you for all the shit you pulled."

At that Dickie snorted a little and sat up, and the movement sent a rush of red across the bandage over the side of his head.

"What did you do, son?"

It was Pat, in the doorway, watching them. He moved to his oldest son, knelt down in front of him, and gently touched his cheek.

"We need to fix this," Pat said. "I know how to do this. I stitched up men in the war. But we need to do this now."

Adlai stood up, startled by the strong and lucid sound of his father's voice. He thought again of the song Pat had sung the night before, and he wondered if his father was coming back. If he was regaining something long ago lost.

"Help me get him up," Pat said.

Walt stood, and they hoisted Dickie up between them.

"What do you want from us?" Walt said, glancing back at Frankie.

"Get him in shape. I'll be back in a few days," Frankie said.

Walt and Pat guided Dickie upstairs to the house. Adlai stood grasping the sweaty beer bottle. He looked at the young Italian who was still fanning himself.

"How old are you?" Frankie said.

"I'll be sixteen this month."

The Italian took a drink and made a whistling noise through his teeth. "I'm the youngest too. Nineteen. It sucks sometimes, am I right? But you're a real runt."

He stood up, drained his beer and put his hat back on.

"Make sure your brother Walt understands, it's all business. We can do some business together that's all," he said, turning to go. "Don't make us do anything we don't need to."

Corigliano smiled at Adlai, and his eyes lingered for a moment, lingered a little too long, and Adlai thought, *What is he trying to see?* Then the man was out and gone, and Adlai went upstairs.

twenty-eight

They were all four in the apartment's cramped bathroom.

Dickie sat, eyes nearly closed, a little dazed, on the lid of the toilet. His near naked body was swallowed by his father's shadow, a shadow cast by the glaring electric bulb just behind them. The bulb was caked with dust, and a thin metal pull chain hung limply. Opening his eyes momentarily to watch Pat, Dickie thought, *The chain's like a girl's bracelet hanging there.*

The bathroom was the hottest space in the house, windowless and directly above the back of the shop, far from the refrigerator and cooler. It smelt of uncorked medicine bottles, and there was something feminine, something too soft and cloying in the way they were holed up in the room messing with his face. He tried to stand, but the dizziness was overwhelming.

Adlai and Walt were in the tub, the only space available, Walt standing and Adlai hunched down, as if in a creek bed bending for a drink. Dickie thought they looked like idiots and would have said so if he could move his mouth.

Pat removed the bandages, and Dickie's skin felt raw, sensitive to the air. He lifted his head looking over Pat's shoulder, glimpsing himself in a small mirror affixed to the wall for shaving. His face was distorted, as if seen through a fun house mirror. His cheek had jagged gashes up and down both sides. One eye was blackish lavender, swollen and shut. The level of bruising all over his forehead, cheeks and jaw changed the tonal shade of his face.

"You look like you been through the meat grinder," Walt said.

Walt leaned against the wall and sighed. Adlai rested against the lip of the tub, watching. Pat was kneeling in front of him, the wads of bloody and discarded bandage at his feet. Dickie shut his eyes, not wanting to look so directly at his father. There was always something a little dead in the old man's gaze. He felt Pat's chilly hand barely touch his skin.

"Wait," Dickie said.

He opened his eyes. Pat was studying him and had a soft cloth wet with some tangy-smelling antiseptic liquid.

"We got to clean this. To stop infection," he said. "Get the whiskey bottle Adlai."

Adlai hopped out of the tub, fetching a bottle of whiskey which he delivered to his brother. Dickie did not reach for it, and Adlai realized his brother was too weak. He knew the liquor would burn his ravaged mouth, but he tenderly reached over, tilted Dickie's head back and poured some liquor into his mouth thinking momentarily of Ed, that night in the back of the car, when Ed could not move and Adlai had poured liquor in his mouth. *That seemed so long ago*, Adlai thought.

Dickie shut his eyes. Pat began to gingerly dab the wounds.

"I was lucky in the war, boys," Pat said.

Dickie winced, cussing, and Pat pulled back his hand. He looked at his son, then paused, and looked over his head, as if at a detailed portrait hung on the empty wall behind him. He seemed to be studying something that was not there.

"Lucky to live, yes. Except for the mustard gas," Pat said.

"Yeah except for that, Pop," Walt said.

Dickie kept his eyes shut, blinking occasionally, and seeing his father in those brief moments, as the pain came in stabs. The liquid scalded his raw skin, and he thought, *He looks younger now, he looks like he used to.*

The pain was constant, not at all like the beating, not long solid blasts of power, rather sharp, needling jabs.

As Pat dabbed and cleaned, Dickie thought of things, distracting things, of Eva, and then he wondered to himself if people could change, swiftly, if things could come back. Pat was talking in a low, slow monotone.

"I've always been good with first aid. I mended a few of the men on the field," Pat said, his voice constant as Dickie tried to not think of the pain. "For smaller things, not bullet wounds but cuts, or if somebody got scraped by a bullet. I could work on them. We didn't have many doctors out there."

All three brothers listened closely, as if their father were reciting gospel as if he had found some new voice and light and were preaching for the first time, reborn.

"Did you save them, Pop?" Adlai said.

Dickie grunted, mumbling.

"Shit."

"I got them through it," Pat said, applying pressure to a deep cut in Dickie's left cheek.

Dickie pulled away. The pain was coming in throbbing waves now, even when no hand touched him, and he was very sleepy. As he blinked, he saw his father with a needle. He realized the man was going to try to sew a part of him, put things back together.

"Wait," Dickie said.

Pat had the needle poised. Dickie opened his eyes fully and looked at his father. Pat's eyes had gone cloudy, distant, and he was looking away.

"I wonder if we should take you to the hospital. I haven't done much of this part," Pat said, his voice slouching, rapidly losing volume. "She did it. She was better with this. We never had money then. Angie did this. I remember she did it when Walt fell . . ."

With his free hand, Pat reached up and touched his own cheek, tracing the line of a small scar there.

"Not Walt," Pat said. "I'd fallen and hit the edge of a table. That was back when, well..."

Dickie sat up and looked to his brothers, who were watching Pat intently. Pat lifted his other hand to his forehead and doing so dropped the needle.

"No," Dickie said.

Dickie forced his body up, grabbing onto Pat to steady himself, but the pressure made the older man lose his footing, and he fell back toward the tub, caught by Adlai. Dickie took in a deep breath, then kicked at the wads of bloody cloth. The mess flew up and toward his father.

"Enough," Dickie said softly. He took the bottle of whiskey, lifted it to his lips, and drank slowly before he spoke again. "I'm going to see Eva. She'll fix me."

Pat bent to the floor to pick up the fallen needle and then sat down on the tile. All three brothers were staring at him. Walt struggled out of the tub, looking awkward and foolish. Dickie glanced at his father, the day's minor lapse of disgust rushing back. Pat sat, his legs flailing open, his hand still on his forehead, as if he could pull something out of his mind, as if he could regain all that was lost.

"Who is Eva, son?" Pat said, frail but bright. "Have you met a girl?"

Dickie looked again at the man crumpled on the floor, overwhelmed with a maddening grief, forced to recall those early years when his father had been strong, when their mother had been alive, when Dickie knew that his father and mother, they, both of them were the fatal error in his life. They were what made the dream beat at him ceaselessly through sleepless nights. They were his curse.

He wanted to find some thread of gentleness in himself, to be able to reach down to his own flesh and blood, to even caress his battered father, but a wave of pain and the despair and disgust that raged through his veins were quicker and stronger, and he lashed out, because it felt right.

"Who is it, son?" Pat said.

The tone of frail hope in the old man's voice was too much to bear.

"She's a nigger I fuck," Dickie said, leaving the bathroom.

twenty-nine

Walt was sitting in their regular booth at the diner alone, long, dreary shadows coming through the front windows from a fast setting sun. It was that period of summer when fall made itself known, when night came earlier and unexpectedly, as if weeks instead of days had gone by since the last long, hot evening.

He was drinking black coffee and dreading the next month. School was beginning, and he knew he wouldn't be able to start as he'd hoped, not with all the mess with Dickie. Corigliano was stuck on a plan that involved all three brothers working for him in some way, Dickie said. Plus Pat had gone down hill over the summer, and someone needed to take charge of the shop.

Adriana drifted past the front window, cutting through those dreadful night shadows, then stepped into the diner dressed elegantly, strangely, in a silk green dress with puff sleeves and a nipped waist. She wore a hat with a small veil and gloves and briefly, Walt thought, *What is she doing in this dive. She doesn't belong here. She's leaving me. She's come to tell me it's over.*

He had these brutal thoughts often, ever since the dinner with her father. He shuttered the passing visions away and swallowed quickly, focusing on something smart to say. She had on heels and moved slowly across the floor, then at the booth where he sat, she lifted her veil and knelt down to kiss him on the lips. She smelled of lilac and tasted of something sweet. He placed his hand on the back of her head, feeling the rough fabric of her hat, feeling the soft rush of her lips. She lingered with him, letting him kiss her more. Then finally, she pulled away and sat down.

The waitress, who knew them, brought a coffee cup for Adriana and left them alone. Walt glanced again at the window, wishing things would just go black, that night would rush in and scatter moonlight and hope.

"I'm not starting school next month. I can't," he said.

Adriana drew in a breath, then reached up and removed her hat. She was wearing makeup and something pink on her lips.

"Where have you been?" Walt said.

"I had to go out with father to an event," she said.

Adriana set her hat on the table, then lifted her cup, sipped it, then set it back down.

"You can't do that Walt. I won't let you. You are going to be a doctor."

She lifted her hand and waved at the waitress. "I'm going to order pie," she said.

"It's my brother. He's in trouble," he said.

Adriana sighed. "I don't care."

He looked again at the front of the diner. Night had come on, and he felt relieved.

"I just have to wait a semester until things settle down," Walt said. "Plus I think I can make money working with Dickie and Frankie Corigliano. Money so we can be together."

She shut her eyes and brought a trembling hand to her lips.

"What have I done to you?" she said.

The waitress set down the pie, and Walt got up then slid next to her in the booth. She opened her eyes, and he forgot the silk dress, the gloves and hat, and he saw her eyes and her fear and her forgiving him for his terrible weakness, for his loving her and being so incapable.

"I can't just go to school right now that's all," he said. "I really think if I can be like my brother just a little bit, if I can push through, I'll get us past this. I'll make money and do whatever it takes."

She was smiling, and put her hand on his cheek. She leaned into him, and he knew again she was his, she was not running away.

"You'll see. I'll make sense of all this."

"But it's dangerous, what he does," she said. "I've heard of the Corigliano family."

Walt paused. He realized he'd never shot a gun, never got into a bad fight. Once when he was nine, one of the boys at school had picked a fight, and Walt had run at the kid, like he could just knock him over. The other boy had moved away, and Walt had landed on the ground. When he looked up Dickie was there, reaching out his hand, hoisting him up, and though he was smaller in size, Dickie had turned on the other boy and beat him solidly, until the child had screamed for him to stop.

"I know how to do this," he said softly.

Walt had no idea what Dickie was going to get into with the Coriglianos, or what would be expected of him. But he knew, deep down, that he was nearly lost, that the stink of frailty he saw in his father was part of him, that if he did not turn this tide he would lose Adriana. Just for now, he needed the brutality and drive of his older brother to save him.

"He's bad," she said.

"It won't be for long," he said.

She stayed with her head resting on his shoulder, and he began slowly, gently to pet her, not letting his hand shake at all, holding it steady and strong.

thirty

Eva opened the door and stared him down.

She was wearing a silky robe, tattered and barely reaching her waist. It hung open showing off her dark naked body, those perfect tits. Dickie smiled, and despite the sickness, the deadening pain, he felt aroused. She didn't shut her robe, and he looked at the scar on her breast, then back to her eyes which were dull, expectant of nothing.

She sighed and stepped aside. "Come on in."

He followed her and stood in her living room. He felt stupid, like a kid waiting for his mother to scold him or serve him supper. He ignored a harsh and driving desire to hold her, to be held by her, to smell her skin.

"Let's fuck," he said.

She smiled and laughed softly then went to a rickety wooden table where liquor bottles sat, warm and dusty. She poured two glasses then went into the bathroom. He heard water running and shut his eyes. He'd barely made it uptown, he had to sit down.

"Let's get you in the tub," she said.

He heard her voice, but kept his eyes closed, and briefly the eel of his dream flew at him, and he cussed because he did not want to pass out in her place, in front of her like a dumb Mick. She'd come back in the room and was messing around with the phonograph. A woman's voice came up, dark and soulful. "Nobody knows you when you're down," she sang.

He felt her hands on his shoulders, removing his shirt. It was stuck to his chest. There was a spot where that thug Mickey had cut into his belly with the brass knuckles and as Dickie touched there, it felt like traces of his insides were outside of his body. He hadn't been noticing that one so much, since the face wounds were so dire.

She gently peeled his shirt off, and he finally got his lids to open. She was kneeling, and her silk robe was open, her face at his feet. She was pulling his shoes off, helping him lift his leg and then she got at his pants, and then he was naked and his cock was stiff. He wasn't even sure how that was possible, but there it was.

"You're something else," Eva said, taking his hand and guiding him into the bathroom. "I've cleaned up a lot of men. You're the first wanting to screw."

He let her take him, and he thought, *Holy fuck I want this woman too much.*

But he blamed that on the pain, the ceaseless pain and what he'd been through the past few days. In the bathroom, he let himself slowly lower to the ground, dipping one hand in the tub's water which was warm. He leaned his head onto the cool porcelain of the tub's rim.

"I'm gonna pay you back for this. I'm gonna take you out for a fine night on the town," he said, letting his hand sink further into the water. It smelled like flowers and had a bit of suds.

She stood near him to test, then shut off the water, and he landed into her legs because he needed to touch her, though he was thinking, *Don't do tha;t don't grab for her like you can't be without her.* But his hands went to her legs anyway. She didn't seem to notice, just leaned down and guided him up and over the edge and into the tub.

He sunk down, and it felt hotter than he thought, and he shivered with the heat, and he wanted to whimper, but he didn't.

"This ain't so bad. You ain't been shot. That's bad. One fella I knew got shot five times." She had a sponge and was starting to caress him with it. "Somebody's already been at these deep cuts. You got another girl?" she said.

He smiled, his eyes shut for good now, feeling her hands on him. "No, no there's nobody else. No woman would have me, Eva," he said.

"Who did it?" she said.

"Frankie Corigliano," he said.

Her hand paused with the sponge, just briefly, then started up. "Oh."

He felt the water rushing all over his body, like he was stuck flat in a shallow riverbed and the current was her hands.

"But it's okay now. I'm gonna work with him. This was like the initiation."

"Yeah?" she said. "Funny way to make friends."

She brought the sponge to his face, and he winced. "Hold still," she said.

He did. Eva hummed with the record.

"Who's that?" he said.

"The Empress. Bessie Smith. She's good when you got pain."

Eva dabbed his brow gently.

"We're gonna do some big stuff Eva," he said. "I'm gonna make some real money and buy you something."

She moved the sponge down his belly, then into his crotch. She was playing with him now, teasing him. He liked it, and the pain sat separate from this, lost in this flourish of her seducing.

"We?" she said. "Is that how it is?"

"Yeah," he said.

He could barely stand it, and he needed to kiss her, and he tried to boost himself up, but it was impossible. As he opened his eyes, she was leaning into him, her lips close, then kissing him, then moving onto his cheek. She kissed the wounds, then held at his eyes, her tongue there. He sighed and shivered again and let her do that.

"Voodoo woman," he said.

"Yeah," she said. "We're gonna put you in bed for a while."

He didn't want to leave the tub, but he let her get him up standing in the water, then she helped him step out of the tub. He leaned on her to get into the bedroom. He was very tired and he kept his eyes shut as they moved, and there were moments he thought his feet had stopped and there was no sound but then he was awake again and she was lying him down, then putting a sheer womanly sort of throw over him.

"This is all I got," she said, tucking the throw around him, then dimming the lights.

He wanted to say thanks, but his lips did not move, and he felt like her bed was even softer than the water he'd been in, the river he felt like he'd been floating down, and he sunk and everything in him finally shuddered and stopped.

He woke and didn't know how long he'd been asleep. The room was dim, as it had been when he passed out. The sheer whoreish throw of hers was twisted between his legs and soft music was playing again in the other room. Another woman's voice was singing on a record and Eva singing was along. He'd been with her, fucking in this bed before, but he hadn't really seen the room. It was a decent size and had a lot of furniture crammed around. The windows had heavy velvet curtains, and there was a fat chair with fat cushions and a broken looking pedal-driven sewing machine and a big, dark wood dresser. There were a lot of things piled on the dresser: papers and dead flowers and clothes. She'd covered the walls with pictures, and he wondered if she had family and where her people were. He thought briefly of his father, and brothers, then went back to the images scattered on the wall.

All the people were black. A big picture got his attention. It was Eva, maybe a few years back, and she was on the knee of a man in boxing trunks. A big black iron-eating fucker with a bald head and big hungry eyes. His arm was draped over her like he owned her, and she was wearing a silk dress and high-heeled shoes and was laughing. Her teeth showed. He had not seen her smile.

He didn't know how long she'd been standing in the doorway, because she was dark and the shadow she stood in was dark and that gown she wore was purple and dark.

"You got pretty teeth," he said.

"You been passed out a while. You hungry?" she said.

"Come here," Dickie said.

She didn't move, then he raised his arm and held it up, and something in his movement, maybe a real scent of need, got to her, and she moved. She stood at the bedside, and he was able to pull her down.

"You're crazy," she said, then leaned into him and kissed his chest.

"Who's the big man in the picture. He looks like somebody."

"That's Jimmy Long," she said.

"The boxer?"

"Yeah. We were together."

He wanted to reach under and pull her to him, but he couldn't quite maneuver that yet.

"He was pretty big for awhile," Dickie said. "I'd like to meet him."

She looked up, and Dickie noticed her eyes had the tiniest slant. Like she had something else mixed in her, something foreign. Maybe that's what made her pretty. "You want a lot, don't you?" she said.

"I want some food," he said.

She got up. "I said you'd be hungry. I'll bring something hot in."

"Hey," he said.

She kept walking, but paused at the bedroom door.

"You're pretty sweet for taking care of me."

As soon as he said it, Dickie thought he better say something else to kind of stomp on what he just said. She might get the wrong idea, like girls did. She might start to think he was soft and stupid or that she could expect things. He regretted his words, but she turned and went out like he hadn't said anything at all, and he thought, *Yeah that's why I like this woman.*

He shut his eyes and that felt good and the pain ebbed a bit then the dream sprouted, like it had been idling, waiting to come back, trying to pull him back under. But it wasn't the eel this time, it was a big wall of white, and Dickie thought it must be the sun, but there was a scent. A real stink. Dreams don't smell, he thought nodding off.

"Hey," Eva said.

She had a plate of runny eggs and sticky fried potatoes. She sat on the edge of the bed with a fork, her robe sliced open, and her tits reaching out, and he smiled. The eggs, three big ones on a china plate, made him smile, but he didn't know why. He never ate much in the morning, and he thought, *It's not morning is it?* She scooped a hunk of egg up and held it, and the mess of it dripped on Dickie's naked leg, which crept out from under the throw.

"All right, just a little," she said.

He opened his mouth, the ache pretty brutal, and waited for the food. The pain, the white-hot dream and fast rush of drowsiness, overwhelmed him. Then he felt the heat on his lips and tongue and thought, *She's kissing me,* but the eggs slid in, and he moved his mouth with great difficulty, the pain shooting and the food good. In the white, eyes shut, now dizzy and chewing, smelling Eva too, he saw a face, stark white, freckled, thick woven orange hair, stern. She was in front of him, and he knew her as Angie, his mother. She too was feeding him, and this memory, he thought, *This memory has never existed before, so why now?* He thought, *Maybe the dream is coming on.*

He tried to open his eyes, to see Eva, to shake off the oncoming dream, but instead he saw a darker image, one he'd never seen before. There was a shadow, something broad-shouldered, a demon with an eel crawling out of its mouth, and he wanted to kill it. And the rage came, with a new ramming shot of pain, his mouth steaming with egg, and he wanted to scream out like a child, but he could not.

The sound came before the action, though that couldn't be right. He opened his eyes and saw the broken china plate on the floor and Eva, hands on her hips, looking curious not angry, her robe open in front. He'd knocked the food out of her hand.

"What the fuck you doing? I can feed myself," Dickie said, confused and so tired.

She smiled and stepped over hunks of broken china. Eva dropped her robe and climbed into bed, between his legs which she nudged open, and he was aroused. She got onto him, and he felt powerful again, still weak, subservient to his desire, but with his hand on her head, eyes open, powerful.

He thought, *I think I love her,* but he pushed that far off and gripped her tighter.

thirty-one

Big Ed was driving a new truck. It was a Chevy, something a farmer might use to haul crops to market. The hood was spit-shine black, but the cab was painted a bright green, and the back of it was a flatbed pickup. He pulled up to the butcher shop and sat idling. Adlai looked at it through the shop window, through a haze of evening, wondering about the new truck, then about Ed and shivered with an excitement that frightened and embarrassed him.

Ed was taking him to the fights, Dickie's edict. He wanted his little brother to learn about the art and violence of boxing. Adlai shut up the shop, glad to get away. His brothers had been gone lately, his father barely present, the shell of that man more and more like ash that could blow away.

It was cooler. The heat wave had broken, and it was hovering just over 85. The truck was elevated, with a runner to step up into it, so Adlai had to hoist himself with effort. He tried to do it gracefully, not wanting Ed to think he was too small or too weak to get up like a man. He glanced at Ed, the mass of that man, and he felt soft and cared for, though not through any movement on Ed's part.

Ed's hands gripped the steering wheel. He was chewing a toothpick. His face was dewy and Adlai stifled an urge to reach over and wipe his brow. He thought he should probably look straight ahead, like Ed was doing, but he couldn't stop staring. Finally, Ed turned to him, and there was a look first of fear, a trembling to the mighty lips, like a wounded hero. Adlai smiled weakly. Ed softened, smiling too, then he laughed out loud.

"We're something, huh?" Ed said in a voice a little too ragged.

Ed looked forward again, shifting the truck into gear with one hand, and with his free hand he reached off and gently petted Adlai's leg, then he let his hand linger there.

"We're going to Brooklyn. There's a good fight tonight," Ed said.

The truck window was open, and traffic was light, bringing a breeze that was softly fragrant and reminiscent of spring time. They were silent, drifting downtown, toward the bridge, and Adlai felt like he was part of something, though exactly what he could not say. There was so much distance in his family, yet a taut and required honor and devotion. But this driving with Ed—as twilight came and they passed other cars with men lolling their arms out of windows and women sitting close, children walking arm in arm near the road then a fading sign advertising peppermints—this all was something more, something good.

"Oh," Ed said, reaching into his shirt pocket and pulling out a licorice stick, "here."

He did not look at Adlai, just handed him the licorice and kept his eye on the road, swerving through new traffic toward the silvery bridge. Adlai took the black stick, and held it limply.

"What's this for?" Adlai said.

Ed put both of his hands on the wheel, cutting in front of a truck swarming with bushels of fruit. "I don't know. It's for you. Don't you like sweets?"

Adlai stuck the thing in his mouth, his way of mutely thanking his lover, as Ed's truck slowed to cross the bridge to Brooklyn. Adlai had never gotten anything from anyone. His family did not celebrate holidays, though as he began to chew the tip of the bitter stick, it made him recall the sweetness of oranges, ripe and yanked open, seeds spilling. Was it Christmas? It had been cold and bright, and there were oranges, handed down from high up, a table, his brothers, and Angie in a nightgown, and Pat. Was that Pat? It couldn't be, the image must be false, some man, strong and grinning and that sweet tang of an orange on his tongue.

"You like it?" Ed said.

"Yeah. My birthday's coming," Adlai said smiling. "This is my first gift."

Ed laughed. Adlai nearly devoured the licorice and wanted more suddenly and wanted Ed's hand back on his leg, but they were nearing the gym, and things would change again, that velvety distance would come, and he would be stranded. Though never like before, not anymore. Ed turned a corner and put his hand back on Adlai's leg, gripping harder this time.

"Dickie said you're having a birthday party. Where's it going to be?" Ed said.

Adlai hadn't decided where to have his birthday party. So much had happened since he'd asked about it, but he still wanted it, he wanted this thing his brothers would do for him.

Ed left his hand on Adlai's leg, removing it to shift gears, then placing it back again, gently and barely touching, like a confessor does on the bible before they reveal some dark secret in court. Adlai wondered how the night would end and how it would be to sit close to Ed at this thing, this fight, watching men beat at each other.

They pulled up and parked. Ed hopped out of the truck and started to move away, then he did an odd thing. He turned back, lumbered over to the door that Adlai was starting to open, and he swung it open, and he grabbed Adlai and lifted him out and set him on the ground. Then he slammed the door shut, with power that made it ring. Ed glanced to Adlai with a chaotic look of excitement and need, then crossed the street toward the boxing gym, Adlai struggling to keep up with Ed's steady and suddenly anxious pace.

"We might as well try to get up front," he shouted back. "You want to be able to see. It's hard from the back."

Inside Ed slowed down, scanning the gym. There were bleachers on all four sides of the grandly elevated boxing ring. Adlai thought it looked like a strange kind of throne, ensconced in suffocating rope, where important men would be crowned or executed. The lights were bright, but the place was smoky and very crowded, ripe with sweat brutalness, making everything feel urgent and deadly.

It was nearly all men, though a few brash, painted women lingered on the arms of slick fellas in suits. Adlai thought he heard a baby cry, then someone shouted, and Ed began moving through the throng to the front. Adlai kept up and glanced at a woman with bright black eyes in a clinging dress. She had her mouth on the neck of a fat man. Ed turned and waved, and Adlai went to him. They were on the aisle in the second row. Ed was talking to the man next to him. They were packed in the row tightly, Adlai's leg hard up against Ed's. The man next to Ed, with a shock of red hair and smoking a cigar, shouted.

"First fight, kid?" he said, leaning over Ed to glimpse Adlai.

"Yeah, his first," Ed said.

"Close enough to get some blood splattered on your face," the red head said, "sign of a good fight."

Ed reached his arm around Adlai's shoulders and patted him several times, then he took it back, but his leg remained tight, the muscles crushing Adlai's narrow thigh. The red head slapped Ed on the shoulder shouting something Adlai could not make out. He felt safe, secluded almost, cushioned by the ever-increasing throng and a palatable and hot energy indicating an escalation toward the fight.

Someone knocked into Adlai from the aisle, a tall man rushing toward the front. There was a rising wall of noise, building around them, and the air thickened and laughter mixed with shouting, and for a moment the lights blinked. Then everyone began to scream, and Adlai wondered if the place was on fire. A small, muscled man was coming up the aisle, dancing really, one of the fighters.

"That's the Cuban. They call him Baby. I have money on him," Ed said, standing and clapping violently, shouting into his cupped hands.

The smallish, dark man, Baby, hopped through the ropes and up into the ring, thrusting his arms over his head and in that move letting a cheap, shiny robe fall, revealing a sinewy body and red trunks that almost looked too big and ballooned. The noise continued to rise, as from the far right aisle the other fighter came, also dark and smallish, but wearing no robe and in yellow trunks. He too hopped up, dancing back and forth, moving to his corner, where two men waited. Baby was in the opposite corner with two men, sucking on the end of a bottle of water.

"Why do they call him Baby?" Adlai said.

His voice was lost in the nearly ridiculous din of the crowd. Ed was still standing, shouting, then turned and winked at Adlai and sat down. Ed squeezed the boy's narrow thigh roughly, then he turned and looked at Adlai dead on, bearing his teeth and sweating, his thick unwashed hair hanging into his face, his eyes blazing.

He looks like a beast, Adlai thought, *he looks like he wants to hit me.*

A spindly, kind-looking man entered the ring and shouted things, then the two fighters came together. Adlai felt momentarily weak in the heat of the room and leaned toward Ed, who didn't seem to notice. A bell rang, and the two men skirted into the center, dancing and jabbing, moving quickly, as if they wanted to avoid contact.

"Baby's a dancer," Ed said, leaning close to Adlai, shouting over the now constant roar of the mangy crowd.

Adlai could smell licorice on Ed's breath, and he realized Ed must have eaten some before picking him up. A bead of sweat flew onto Adlai's cheek from the matted mass of Ed's sweaty hair as he swung his head away and shifted his gaze back to the ring.

The fighters had stopped for some reason, retreating momentarily, before they were set out upon each other again, this time closing in, hugging tightly, then yanking away. Baby in the red trunks swung suddenly and viciously, smashing his fist into his opponent's jaw, who Adlai guessed was named Jack since that name rang through the crowd as often as Baby.

Jack in the yellow backed off, slumped, then fell back onto the ropes and Baby was on him. Adlai could see nothing but Baby's mighty back, heaving and grasping, then pummeling more gently into the flesh of Jack.

The bell rang, and the fighters retreated, and Ed turned to Adlai, his eyes alight.

"Good fight so far," he said.

Before he could answer, the bell rang, and the men were swaying around the ring's edges, both hopping, then settling, closing in, then jabbing. Adlai closed his eyes briefly, a little dizzy. He opened them, and Ed was again standing and shouting. Jack in yellow was directly in front of them on the ropes, and Adlai could clearly see Baby's strangely pretty face, and his carnivorous grimace, as he pumped his fist into the man's jaw several times. Jack's head swung out to one side, and then one more swing, and a spray of red flew out into the crowd, and the bell rang.

Adlai reached up and felt dewy drops, a tiny bit on his cheek. Ed smiled at him, and the red head next to Ed screamed in a voice filled with honor and thrill. "You got the blood, I told you, kid," the red head said.

Adlai wiped his face and stood, wanting to be closer to Ed, who was standing. The fight began again, and with the sway and momentum of the thing, Ed swayed too, his side and leg gently brushing into Adlai. The noise of the hall rose and fell, and the men plundered one another over and over, and Adlai gave into his own rising mood of excitement as he began to feel the sweat from Ed's face spray constantly down onto him, as the muscled and vibrant power of the room overtook him.

thirty-two

They stopped at the end of a quiet, deserted street in Brooklyn facing the water, looking toward the city. Ed shut off the engine. Adlai stared out at the East River and thought of the lonely tugboat, of that night when Ed had found him near the docks. He listened for the cry of insects, or voices, but it was still.

"You ever want to get out of this city, just be gone?" Ed said.

Adlai turned his body toward the man, pressing his back into the truck's passenger side door. Ed was leaning into the steering wheel, resting his chin there. He looked uncomfortable, like he didn't quite fit, like someone had crammed him into a truck too small for his own frame.

"How tall are you?" Adlai said.

"Six two. Two hundred pounds," Ed said, his voice soft and lazy. "Why? You want to fight me?"

Keeping his head on the steering wheel, he turned his face to Adlai. Clouds had scattered across the night sky, veiling the moon so Ed's face was dark and unreadable. Baby had won the fight, and Ed had made money. The evening, the overwhelming mix of smashing fists and a scalding mania, had left Adlai anxious. He held Ed's gaze, the face that seemed so much older and harder than nineteen, the hair thick unkempt and matted, the squared off jaw and wide forehead. Lately, he was fearful of losing Ed, as if their private meetings were thin, scattered remnants of dreams. Unreal things. On the days between their meetings, the debris of life began to suffocate him. He imagined he'd pass someone on the street who would casually mention that Big Ed, one of Dickie's goons, had flown the coop, had disappeared, had been cut up into pieces and thrown in the river. Or even worse, had married to a young blond girl.

"You know what your brother's becoming?" Ed said.

Ed's voice was tired, lazy. Adlai looked at Ed, though he very much wanted to look away. He had a sudden urge to get out and wander to the docks, to find that girly tart and the sailor who had tried to fuck him. Instead, he slid across the seat. Then he leaned in and kissed Ed on the cheek. Ed still had his arms and face resting on the steering wheel, so Adlai got up on his knees and leaned in to get to Ed's mouth. Ed did not move as the boy put his hands on the man's sweaty head and forced his tongue deep, tasting that long gone licorice and a saltiness. Ed moaned, and Adlai thought the man might be weeping, but that could not be true. Adlai kept kissing him, pulling away briefly to catch his breath, their faces so close, Ed's breath on him, then Ed's voice came in a shuddering growl.

"Dickie's gonna be a killer. He's gonna kill who they tell him to. And he's gonna want me to be part of that," Ed said.

Ed turned and touched Adlai's shoulder, pushing him back into a lying position on the seat. Adlai lay back, his knees bent to fit in the small space, his shoulders pressed against the passenger door. Ed turned and struggled to get himself on top of the boy clumsily forcing his bulk over Adlai, overwhelming the boy. Adlai was suffocated, seeing nothing but Ed's face and feeling the big man's hands first on his neck and face, then Ed held himself up with one muscle-strained arm, and he undid Adlai's shirt and pressed his lips onto the boy's pale chest. He was muttering, and Adlai gasped for air, feeling crushed, but overwhelmed with desire.

The street was still, and Adlai prayed it remained so, that no one discovered them.

Ed reached down and tried to undo Adlai's pants, struggling to get them down, then giving up, forcing his hands in. Adlai ignored the scraping of the seat, gripping feebly at Ed's back then going limp, letting his body be twisted to fit into the curve of Ed, their bodies all rivers of sweat and random groaning, coming together in a fierceness that summoned an image for Adlai of the fight, Baby overwhelming Jack, hugging him viciously then landing the killing punch.

They stayed on the seat after, squashed there, clothes half off, breathing heavily, fearlessly in the night. Adlai never wanted to leave Ed. This, he knew, was love.

"Do you think I'll have to do it too?" Adlai said.

He glanced over at Ed, who had one arm draped across his face, bicep straining.

"Do what?"

"Kill people."

Ed reached his arm out to get it under Adlai's neck and pulled him closer. They lay together, defiantly, knowing this was the danger, this was their fatal flaw. They could survive Dickie. This, this was something else.

thirty-three

Adlai's birthday approached as the city wilted further, summer languishing. Trees swung heavily and low on the Avenues, brittle from the long and tiresome heat.

Dickie had returned to work in the shop, patches of his skin oddly lavender with bruises, and portions of his body bandaged roughly. Walt and Adlai had been running things until then, each casting the other aside, as if he were alone, each caught in a tumult more similar than different, but completely unknown to the other.

It was evening, and Dickie had called a meeting, gathering the usual circle of chairs in the dim and lofty back area of the shop. He left the back garage door open and hauled a tall electric lamp in, as if more light was needed for an urgent announcement. Walt was in the circle, along with O'Halleron, Big Ed and Bug. There was an empty seat.

Adlai lingered at the doorway, thinking the seat may be for him, though Dickie had avoided him since returning. He'd yanked Walt aside several times, hovering in corners, using his hands to draw figures in the air. There had been mean laughter, and that had frightened Adlai, for his new life, his vile secret, felt transparent. He imagined at any time he may turn, and his brothers would be on him.

As he began to move toward the circle, a figure emerged from the back, lit at first by a red ash glow, then stepping forward in pieces, limbs, as if climbing through a wall of shadowed vines. Adlai noticed the hot cigarette ash, then the hand holding that cigarette, laden in rings, then the fancy, striped fabric on the pant leg and finally the man, caught in the arc of light from the electric lamp. It was Frankie Corigliano, and Adlai thought: *How old is that man? Why does he look so much older than me?*

And he thought of his upcoming birthday. He needed to ask Dickie about that tonight.

Dickie stood. He was wearing a muddy brown suit. It looked too heavy for summer, cut from a thick tweedy fabric and paired with a tan shirt. Adlai did not recall ever seeing his brother in a suit.

Dickie went to Corigliano and shook his hand, and all the men stood, tensing for battle, as Dickie pulled the visitor into the circle and toward the empty chair, coaxing him along as if to a friendly execution. Adlai slumped against the wall, then sat. O'Halleron grunted and took a step toward Frankie, and a dark voice bellowed from the far back.

"Boss?"

Frankie sucked on his cigarette. "We're fine." he said.

"Sit down, everybody," Dickie said.

They did, but he did not.

"I invited Frankie, can I call you that?" Dickie said.

Corigliano motioned acquiescence with his hand, smoking.

"We've sorted things out. We're gonna be working together, all of us," Dickie said.

O'Halleron, restless, rubbing his hands together, spoke up.

"The guy that tried to kill you? Now we're all fucking friends?"

Dickie sighed, lowered his head, then lifted it again. He leaned forward, toward the off-cast light from the standing lamp, so his face took on a ghastly yellow glow, his features exaggerated in the harsh light, the patch quilt of colors from the varied levels of bruising, almost horrific.

"I have at one time or another pounded on all of you, right?" Dickie said. "I've smashed a lot of heads, right?"

"That's different," O'Halleron said.

"What are we? We shake down a few small time businesses. We get a few bucks. We strut around. What are we?" Dickie said softly.

There was a silence that followed, then an odd, irritating hum that the standing lamp began to give off. The hum increased, and Big Ed stood up and shook the thing, and the bulb flickered on and off several times, intensifying the ghoulish glow on Dickie's face in a carnivalesque way. Then the lamp went out.

Bug turned in his chair, and with the loss of the illuminating light, the spot on the ground where Adlai sat was no longer set aside in a darker shadow.

"May I?" said Frankie. He stood next to Dickie and smiled.

"One of my men lost a finger. Another got a glass jar of pickles jammed into his head. We had to get at Dickie. But the beautiful thing," he said, clearing his throat and dropping the now dead cigarette and squashing it with a shined boot. "The beautiful thing is that we found a way to work together. Dickie is our new muscle. He's on the winning side now. And you're all gonna benefit. Financially."

The men sat still, looking, waiting as if there would be more to this, more grit behind this call to battle.

"What exactly do we have to do? We all going to run around with machine guns now?" O'Halleron said.

"Hey, Adlai," Bug said, pointing toward the boy, speaking in a loud, false tone as if things would be said that shouldn't be.

Adlai got up and stepped toward the circle.

"What are you doing there? What do you want?" Dickie said. "You spying?"

Adlai knew the tone, the sudden upswing in intensity. His mind swam, and he spoke quickly.

"I came to ask you about my birthday party."

From the back, a car motor started. It purred, as Frankie Corigliano lit another cigarette.

"We got a few nice places in Brooklyn. We'll throw the birthday party for the kid," Frankie said. "It's our way of making peace, of bringing you into our family. I'll let you sort this out, Dickie. Nice suit by the way."

Adlai stepped back again, wanting to retreat to the safety of the shop up front, afraid he set in motion something that could not end well. Corigliano moved toward the garage door and the waiting car, back into the shadow he had emerged from. Then he stopped.

"We can get you all nice suits, you like that?" he said.

"All right, Frankie, all right," Dickie said.

The purr of the engine rose, a car door opened and shut, and Corigliano was gone.

thirty-four

The three brothers sat in the living room, forming a triangle, each in a chair pointing toward a shabby coffee table, each facing the other, though with eyes looking away.

They had dressed as if they were young and vulnerable boys directed by a powerful, matriarchal force. It was as if the lure of this event had summoned a ghostly femininity, this force pressing at them, enforcing the fact that something special and unchangeable was about to happen, and they had to be prepared for it. As if it were a wedding or a funeral, not simply a birthday party.

Dickie wore the thick woven suit he'd stepped into and refused to get out of since Frankie had given it to him. Walt was wearing his only black suit, a white shirt Adlai had ironed and starched, and a black tie. Being the guest of honor, Adlai chose his outfit with extreme care. He wore tight, white cotton pants, tight simply because he had outgrown them, but they were the best and dressiest pants he had. He wore one of Dickie's white shirts, the sleeves meticulously rolled up to underplay the fact that the shirt was too large. He wore a shiny red tie which he'd bought himself with money saved, and he wore shined black shoes. In the pocket of his shirt he'd placed a red carnation, this also purchased and positioned with great care.

He was slightly uncomfortable in the get-up, but he was proud, giddy almost, certain he would be noticed and acknowledged. He did not know until the day before if there would even be a party, but Dickie had come through, the offer from Frankie had been realized, and they were going to Brooklyn.

They were waiting on Pat. Dickie pulled out a flask and drank, then glanced at his youngest brother, as if noticing him for the first time. He offered Adlai the flask.

"Happy birthday, Rat," he said.

Adlai took the flask, tipping it gingerly into his mouth, not wanting to spill anything on his pristine white outfit. The flask was filled with a sharp and tangy liquor which burned. He passed the flask to Walt, who took it, smiled briefly, then went back to brooding.

"Where is this joint?" Walt said. "I want Adriana to meet us there." He handed the flask, circling back, to Dickie, who took it and slugged.

"You still fucking her?" Dickie said.

Walt glanced at his brother, then looked away.

Pat stepped into the room. He had on wool pants and was barefoot. He had on a shirt, half-buttoned, and a tie looping down the front of him like a lazy snake. He had bits of tissue stuck to his cheeks which were turning red. One of them, drenched, fell off like a scab onto the floor. "I cut myself shaving. And I'm not sure how to tie this," he said.

Nobody moved.

"Go in the bathroom and press on that to stop the bleeding. Then I'll tie that for you ," Dickie said.

Pat went back into the bathroom. "We ought to have the ring cake," he shouted.

He turned the faucet on.

"Don't wet it. Just press on it," Dickie shouted back.

The faucet shut off. Pat spoke slowly and loudly, his voice echoing out of the bathroom.

"When I was nine, still in Ireland, my mother made the ring cake for my birthday. That was the last time I had that cake, my last party I think."

"Are you pressing?" Dickie said, standing, stretching his arms over his head, then yanking a gold pocket watch from his suit.

"When did you get that?" Walt said.

Adlai admired the watch, wondering how his brother got something so fine.

"She only made that cake on special occasions. She put a rag in it, a ring and something else. If you got the ring you were going to be married," Pat said, his voice from the bathroom clear and resonant, younger. "It was a very good cake too. You'd think with that rag, it might spoil the taste. It did not."

Pat reemerged, and his face was clear of tissue.

Adlai went to him. "I'll tie this for you, Pop."

Both brothers turned when they heard him address their father. For years, they had not called him anything but Pat. Adlai was aware they were watching him, aware he had done something different, set a tone in motion for the evening. He again felt a rush of giddy exhilaration. Pat knelt, so his son could get at the tie. Adlai stepped around behind his father, to tie the tie as if it were on his own neck. It was easier like that.

"What did you get at your party," Adlai said. "As a gift?"

"A gun," Pat said.

Dickie snickered, still standing. He held the flask out to his father, who took it, smiling and took a snort. Adlai had not seen his father drink, and he felt this too was a clear sign that the night was going to be a success, and he would be the driving reason for this new union of the four of them.

"We moved here the year after, but that year, when I turned nine, we were still in Ireland. And we went shooting. My father and I."

Adlai had screwed up the knot and was trying again, and both Dickie and Walt were staring at him as he tied it, but more so, watching their father.

"What do you mean?" Walt said.

"We would hunt. We were very poor. We would hunt for food," Pat said.

Adlai got the knot done, then went around to face his father and tighten it. He was looking down at him, Pat still on his knees, and this was an uncanny sensation. He had never looked down on his father, but he did now, smelling the corn liquor on his breath and catching a glint in his eyes, a surge of excitement, a rush of knowing that this was a special night.

There was a soft knock at the door, then Big Ed came in.

Adlai turned, then felt his father's hand on his back as Pat stood up and steadied himself. Ed was also dressed in a suit, his green one with a vest, tight too, and dark brown high boots and even a hat. They all glanced at Ed, and for a brief moment Adlai thought, *Yes that too is mine, this is all for me, you don't know but it is.* Then just as swiftly, as if the light had drained from the room and a bleak sheath had cloaked him, he felt a sudden terror run through him. Ed spoke, and the spell was broken.

"Happy birthday, Adlai," he said.

"You got the car?" Dickie said, offering the flask.

"Yes," Ed said. "We're ready."

They all looked to Adlai, who turned to the door, leading them.

thirty-five

They took Dickie's Chevy. Ed drove. Dickie sat in front, and Adlai was crammed in the back with Walt and Pat. Pat fluttered his eyes open and shut, nodding off at times, then waking and humming. The windows were open, and the air was hot, and it was a struggle to breathe. It was a sticky night, and Adlai was perspiring, stains gathering under the arms of his white shirt. The satiny red tie he wore pressed against his shirt and bled slightly, a dull film of cheap die creating a thin bloody line down his front. He realized nobody had brought presents.

"You are very special," Pat said, but his eyes were shut, and Adlai did not know if he was referring to him or some internal reverie.

When they arrived in Brooklyn, and climbed the dark flight of stairs to a large shotgun style apartment above a rowdy tavern, when they entered that apartment to find a noisy band of men and women all in mid-flight toward deep drunkenness, Adlai wondered if the night would really be about him at all.

They stood in a cluster at the door of the apartment, which was roomy with very little furniture, but lit with an elaborate crystal chandelier. Frankie Corigliano came forth and shook Adlai's hand.

"All right, happy birthday," he said. "There's a bar stuck somewhere in that corner. Get a drink. We got a surprise for you later, Adlai. This is my girl Mabel's place. She's in a show in the city and these are her friends here. They all know it's a birthday party so introduce yourself, kid."

Frankie went to Dickie, putting an arm across his shoulder and dragging him into the crowd, leaning close to his ear to speak. Big Ed guided them to a spot where there were empty chairs, then he went to get them drinks. Walt wandered off.

Adlai noticed there were Negroes in the room. He saw that Frankie had taken Dickie to a cluster of blacks, a pretty woman in a red dress and a tall, beefy-looking black man plus a few others. He'd never been to a party with Negroes. It was the first sign the night would offer some rite of passage.

There were a lot of Italian men in the room, most of them smartly dressed with women sitting on their legs or in their arms or leaning into them in some subservient way. The women wore flimsy things, and ostentatious jewelry, and the men had on suits. The air was thick with smoke, laughter, but no music. From the tavern below though, there was noise, a steady pounding of voices blending with songs. It crept up through the floor, mixing with the din of the party.

Big Ed came back with cups filled with a clear liquor and a young woman on his arm. She had bright blonde hair and wore a sheer dress that looked like a negligee. She had rosy colored nipples that stood out, and Adlai thought she was the most vulgar woman he had ever seen. Her face was white and fine, however, and she had very red lips and violet eyes.

"Him?" she said in a loud, shrill voice.

Then she swooped in and sat on Adlai's skinny lap and bent her head to his lips and set into kissing him violently. She tasted sour. She kissed Adlai long and hard then hopped up and laughed as shrilly as she spoke. Another pretty, but vulgar looking woman, a brunette replica of the blonde, spun into their little crowd and leaned into Ed.

"He can't be sixteen he looks so so so fresh," she said.

"She says things in threes, that's her thing this week," the blonde said, then laughed in that grating way. "Frankie told us to take care of you. And we can sure take care of this big one too. We're in the show with Mabel."

She leaned in to kiss Ed, and Ed let it happen, limply surrendering and kissing the brunette.

"Are you in a play?" Adlai said.

"Oh yeah sure, a play," the blonde said after a loud laugh.

Pat sat quietly with his arms folded, like a wax figure. Adlai hoped these women, these floosies, were not the gift for the night, were not the main thing for him. The brunette had stationed herself on Ed's lap, and the blonde sat at Adlai's feet like a lazy cat, and they all watched the party. Adlai felt a stiffness growing in his gut, a dark vile tightening of all that was under his skin, as if a brittle caste was spreading across him, within him, protecting him but making him less than human. He did not enjoy thinking these thoughts, these crazy thoughts. He normally only had these when he was alone.

He looked at Ed, but Ed would not meet his eyes, and he looked at Pat, but the man looked dead to him, and he looked for Walt, but he was nowhere, and he looked for Dickie, who was close to a black woman in a red dress. Then he downed the contents of the cup of liquor and handed it down to the woman at his feet.

"Get me another" he said in a hard voice.

She hopped up and went for the drink, and he found that odd, how easy that was, to command someone. She came back, and he drank it down. The blonde woman sat again at his feet, then turned and rested her head on his leg, looking up at him.

"Hey you're bleeding," she said.

She reached her hand up to his chest, and he noticed that her nails did not match the rest of her. They were bitten down, ugly. She flipped at his tie, revealing the stain the cheap fabric had left on his shirt.

"Oh," she said.

He looked to Ed, to see if he'd been following the exchange, but he was still watching the crowd. Adlai finished the rest of the liquor in the cup, then he dropped it to the floor where it clattered. The blonde took it up and went for more and Adlai thought, well I will get drunk. I guess that's all there is to this.

Then Frankie Corigliano stood up on a chair. He was holding a bottle, and he had taken his suit coat off, and his shirt was open.

"We got a good fight tonight," he said. "In the basement. My pal Dickie, his brother's turning sixteen today. Toast!" He lifted his bottle and slugged a drink and everyone applauded.

Dickie was coming their way with a tall black man. "Where's Walt?"

No one said a thing.

"Come on let's go see the main event. You ready, Rat?" Dickie said.

The black man, who was very large, smiled. "Happy birthday, kiddo," he said.

"This is Jimmy Long." Dickie said. "He's a boxer. We're gonna work together. Come on."

Dickie moved through the crowd, and Big Ed stood up as did the women, and they all moved away. Adlai sat next to his father, watching the room slowly empty, people jamming into one another as if vying for a seat on a bus. Pat had his eyes shut. Adlai went toward the bar, and poured liquor into his cup. When he turned Ed was there.

"Come on to the basement. They planned this for you," he said.

They both looked at Pat.

"He'll be all right," Ed said.

Adlai followed Ed down the stairs, watching his thick neck. His shoulders nearly touched each side of the narrow, dim staircase. It wasn't just that they were so wide, but the shoulders sloped so deeply, and the whole of it, that back, seemed laden with some incredible heaviness. Then Ed turned.

The staircase was empty. The voices of the crowd had dimmed to nothing.

"Happy Birthday," Ed said.

Adlai was behind him on the upper stair, but still Ed had to bend due to his height, and he did bend, and he kissed him quickly, biting the edge of Adlai's lip. Then he turned and continued down. They went out and into the tavern, then through that and down another staircase into the cellar below.

The cellar, which was the length of the building, had a dirt floor and garish electric bulbs and was crammed with the party goers. Despite its awful hot shabbiness, it took on a festive air. The entire crowd had circled around a pit about 7 feet wide by 6 feet. Frankie pushed his way toward them, then grabbed Adlai by the arm and yanked him to the very front of the pit. People smiled, and women kissed Adlai's cheek as he went, and he thought, they are going to kill us both, Ed and me, this is some sort of sacrifice. When he got to the edge of the pit he saw two cocks, and two chubby, dark, Mexican men holding the birds, and further past that, beyond a ring of people, several cages, and he heard a deafening squawking.

"You ever been to a cock fight?" Frankie said. "You want to bet, I'll put one in for you. Which one you want?"

The birds looked nearly identical to Adlai in the dim light, though one had a slash of white on its feathered back and a fuller looking comb dangling down and the other had an orange taint to him. The men were holding them aloft, occasionally shoving the birds at one another, as if they would kiss, then blowing at their feathers to reveal the under-skin. The birds had mighty heads, with bright red combs at their bony necks and lean, sharp beaks.

"What's wrong with their feet," Adlai yelled, as the crowd suddenly began to cheer.

There were small leather bracelets on each of the bird's skinny left legs just above their horn claws. Poking out from the leather bracelet was what looked like a lean blade.

"The spurs. They've been fitted with spurs. Who do you want?" Frankie said.

"The one with the white on his back," Adlai said.

"Good choice," Frankie said, smiling, then disappearing into a corner where a huge man in a suit sat with a cash box on his lap.

Ed put his hand lightly on Adlai's shoulder.

"It's all right," Adlai said softly, realizing in the noise Ed likely did not hear him.

There were three chalk lines drawn in the pit. A long one in the middle, and two shorter ones. The fat man with the money box stood up and was yelling.

"Pit your cocks, come on, quit stalling," the fat man screamed.

The Mexicans were holding the birds again, pressing them toward each other, and several of the women were yelping and moving swiftly toward the stairway to escape. The fat man bellowed again.

The Mexicans seemed to understand and stood back in preparation for the fight.

Adlai wondered what would happen, how the birds would actually fight, and he wished Ed would put his hand back on his shoulder.

He and Ed were the closest to the birds, being at the front, nearly in the pit itself. Finally the men released them. At first, despite yowls from the crowd and wild crowing from other cocks held in shadowed cages, the birds simply danced about, proudly, twisting and turning. As they circled, the feathers about their necks rose in a flourish, broadening out beautifully, like an elegant collar. They moved slowly, then flew up off their claws, one pecking the other, and with that dance and a new rising dust, Adlai thought suddenly both of his brother Dickie's recent beating and of the fight he'd seen.

As the cocks danced in the suffocating dirt and heat, he decided these riled up, screeching birds were not just dumb, raging things, they somehow were the anger of the men screaming at them and even more, the rage the thug had cast at his brother, all that slaughter to his face. Adlai had never felt a fist on his body. Not even a slap.

Ed lay his palm on Adlai's shoulder, and the boy winced as if in pain, overcome with a spiraling distance from the room, as if fighters like Baby and men like his brother were able to thrust themselves fully into the world with their fists and their violence, while he was frail and useless. He gasped for air as the cocks flew at each other now, those thin sharp knives on their legs shining.

They were rising up in the air momentarily, both birds, then stomping back down. The orange one, its neck feathers stiff, flew up and over toward Adlai, and he gasped as that lean blade came near him, but the bird flew back into the center quickly. The second bird, with the white slash on its back, kicked its claw at the dank mud floor, stirring up even more dust, this now blowing upward and clinging to Adlai's white shirt and pants.

The Mexicans entered the pit and were shouting things, lifting the birds with the wild collars, blowing at their backs, yanking the thin beaks then holding the birds close, that kissing move, then finally releasing them. This last effort seemed to have worked, as the two birds hopped and pecked madly at each other, the white-backed one rising and slicing deeply and precisely into the other mid air with the spur. The orange bird hopped then flailed. Its claw crumping underneath it, its body falling sideways. The other bird swooped, and the crowd screeched as the animal pecked mercilessly at the wounded spot sliced open by the spur, quickly, as if this window of violence could slam shut at any second. The cock's beak sunk deeper into the flesh of the other bird, as blood began to ooze, and the

Mexicans hovered, on their knees now.

Adlai was sweating, dizzy, his white outfit caked in the blowing dirt. The losing bird rolled over, then suddenly lilted mightily, flying upward for a moment, then fleeing the dominant bird blindly, the side of its body a raw open wound, its tiny insides spilling. It ran crowing toward the crowd, flinging itself at Adlai's feet, as if for mercy, as the winning bird came forth, smashing his beak into the dying cock, yanking out pieces, blood spraying now up onto Adlai's whiteness, even his hands, then cheek. Ed yanked Adlai away, but not in time.

The Mexicans were rushing to the birds, and men were crowding over to the fat man with the cash box as Adlai backed up, staring at his bloodied white clothes, suffocating and choking with the dust, disgusted by the spectacle. He turned and pushed frantically through and up the stairs, into the tavern.

The tavern was nearly empty, the bartender slouching at the bar. Adlai continued through and back up to the apartment, not sure what he was doing, maybe to get a drink, he thought, or to take these bloody clothes off which had taken on a stink of death. He was woozy, and at the apartment landing, felt he might vomit so he shut his eyes. It passed, and he went into the apartment, to find it empty, save for Pat asleep in a chair.

The animal's blood soaked several spots on his pant leg and his shirt, contrasting the milder stain of his cheap satin tie. He stopped at the bar and poured a drink, then went to find the bathroom. It was down a hallway, past a tiny empty bedroom. Inside, he sat on the toilet lid, then realized there was no light, save for what spilled from the hall. The dark was soothing, and he looked into his cup. There was a tiny bit of dirt floating in the clear liquor. A figure was approaching from the hall, and he wondered if he would have to get out of the bathroom or if he could stay and scrub at his ruined clothes.

Big Ed raised his arms and rested his palms atop the door, leaning into the bathroom and swallowing any remaining light. There was a dim glow behind him, outlining his massive frame, lighting his dark, sweaty hair.

"Sorry, Adlai, this wasn't much of a birthday was it?" Ed said.

Adlai began to unbutton his shirt, carefully. He got it off and dropped it into the sink, then he turned the cold water on.

Big Ed stayed with his arms over his head. "It's wrecked. That won't come out," he said.

"I have to try," Adlai said. He stuck his hands into the sink and began to push at the fabric, the water splashing out at him, the chill feeling good on his hands. He held the blood stains up to the gush and began to rub the material upon itself. The stain began to spread out, not dissipate so he rubbed harder, leaning into the sink, pushing into the fabric, breathing deeply. Finally, he began to cry.

He felt Big Ed's arms on his shoulders, then cradling him and coaxing him

away from the sink. He lifted Adlai's face to his, and as he did, just as Adlai knew
a kiss was coming, as he felt Ed's breath and whispered lightly and felt the lips,
salty, he saw over Ed's shoulder into the hall.

It was Frankie Corigliano, watching them and another man behind Frankie,
in the distance also seeing them, but Adlai could not tell who that man was.
Adlai yanked away and rammed against the sink, that water still gushing and
everything slowed down. The sound resonated for him, the water, but he could
not see clearly. There was a sudden blur, a dizziness, and his head swam. He
gripped the sink to steady himself, to try to think clearly, but the terror of being
discovered was escalating. Ed stepped forward, his mighty chest heaving, animal-
like and ready. Adlai felt his breath quickening, his hands trembling struggling to
hold onto the sink.

I am going to fall, he thought. *I am going to fall over here.*

He saw Frankie's lips move, and Ed stepping out, but he could hear nothing
but the gushing sink, and a hushed white haze came forth to cover his eyes, like
a misty silk veil falling. Voices shouted, and Frankie pushed past Ed and came to
Adlai and gripped his face, squeezing it violently. Adlai tried to breathe, and he
let go of the sink and was held up by the man, seeing his black eyes raging and
those lips hot and moving speaking and coming close like a vile kiss, but with no
sound other than the gushing sink.

Adlai thought, *If I could put my hands in the cold water I could wake up.* And he
thought too, *He is going to kill me now, and maybe that's better than Dickie doing it.*

Then Frankie was yanked away. But it was not Ed. It was Pat, his father, who
pulled the man off of him, who had seen from the hall, who was staring at Adlai
now. Adlai noticed his father's eyes were a new strange watery blue, milky almost,
as if they'd been scorched by a sudden sun and faded to a color of his past.

"I'm sorry," Adlai said in a child's whisper.

Then Adlai began to fall, and all white-winged memory came, flying. As the
cold, tile floor met his cheek and his head smacked hard, he saw above him, Pat,
as if through water, wavering, young and pale and Angie, his mother, red-haired
and fiercesome, and she looked at her youngest son's frailty, and she spat on the
floor, and she said "He will fail you. This one will fail you surely, Pat."

As Adlai embraced that hot white dream, Pat's blue eyes were on him, sadly,
saying. "I've got you."

Pat lifted his son's head off the floor, cradling him, and it was not a dream
because voices shouted from the hall, Ed and Frankie, and was it Dickie coming
up from below? But Pat, those clear, conscious watery-blue eyes and ragged lips
moving now, with a song he knew from long ago. It was an Irish lullaby.

"Rest tired eyes a while," Pat sang cradling, preacher-like. "Sweet is thy
baby's smile. Angels are guarding, and they watch o'er thee."

To Adlai, the gentle voice of his father stayed low but ragged, like a distant wave crashing on terrible rock. Pat turned away then back, casting those eyes down at him, and Adlai was afraid. His father seemed burdened with a wild and heavy yearning, as if something were crawling up from within him that had died but was reborn. Adlai felt cold water dripping from the overflowing sink above him, a latent baptism.

Adlai tried to listen for the lullaby but fell deeper, away from the soothing voice and the voices in the hall and the sound of water, gushing, still gushing, its drops touching his forehead like God's gentle fingers.

Part

Two

The night that had meant to be his, to chase off a weak and dawdling past and bring forth the new Adlai, had turned upside down and left him in bed with a lump on his head.

Something, however, had changed. His father had come out of hiding.

Adlai woke slowly. He had been dreaming of water, velvety blue, and he felt happy and safe. Then came the pounding in his head, a long, slow throbbing, and as he tried to sit up, he saw his father in the chair by his bed, holding a satchel in his lap. A gnashing was at him. Adlai reached to touch the welt on his forehead. He could not meet his father's eyes. They had seen. They had witnessed the kiss. They knew. Adlai felt a tightening in his throat and a hot terror over his body. He could not breathe. This was surely the end of him. He wanted to crawl back into the dream, the watery place, to disappear. He knew he was vile.

"You hate me," Adlai said to his father.

His father reached a hand out toward the bed, and touched Adlai's arm. Adlai did not recall the last time his father had touched him. In the dim light he could see Pat was holding a rosary. Its tiny beads were a white-burned blue, nearly like his father's eyes. The crucifix was tarnished and the clasp connecting the beads to the cross had broken on one end, so it dangled loosely.

He's praying for my soul, Adlai thought.

"How can I hate you when I do not even know you?"

Pat leaned in, and again Adlai thought of his father as a priest performing last rites. Would he ask for his confession? Adlai thought to speak, to reveal his transgressions, but then his father began his story.

"This was your Great Grandfather's rosary," Pat said, pressing the rosary into the boy's hand. "He gave it to me. His name was Cahal. He was a very bad man."

Pat had never spoken of his father, or grandfather. It was as if they did not exist. Adlai noticed the satchel on his father's lap. It was fat, old, the size of a book. It was covered in some sort of animal skin.

"Cahal was a traitor to our family," Pat said. "My father, Aengus, he called him demon."

Adeali was tired, his head aching. He glanced at the rosary, at the tiny naked lithe Jesus on the cross. He did not understand what was happening to Pat. He did not sound at all like himself.

"Last night, when I saw you, it was like watching a stranger's son, someone I never knew," Pat said. "I was drunk, but I understood what I am. A traitor. I have abandoned my sons. I failed you."

Pat shut his eyes, his lips trembling. Adlai was used to his father's odd ramblings, that soft but harmless madness. But this was unsettling, this was new.

"That is not who I want to be," Pat said.

At this, he set the satchel on the bed next to Adlai.

"I want you to understand your family," Pat said. "Read this. It was written by your Great Grandfather Cahal. Then I have something to tell you."

Pat stood, leaving Adlai with the strange blue rosary, the hairy satchel. Before he turned, Pat reached his hand down, as if to pet his son's forehead. But he stopped. He did not touch Adlai. He turned and left, and Adlai was alone, and the fear came back. He did not know what Frankie had or had not told of what he had seen. He did not know what happened between Ed and Frankie or what Dickie knew. There was no knife at his throat, however, at least not yet.

He examined the heavy satchel. It was made of some hide, cracked and old but still furry. Adlai held the thing for a bit, sniffed at it. He couldn't decipher what the hide was, why the splotches of fur on its front were so coarse. He turned it over, felt its weight. There were wide cracks on the side, attesting to its age, and Adlai thought of his own age, and wondered if he would make it so long to have cracks in his face. Or would his brother steal in at night and murder him? He clutched the rosary in his palm. It was cold, lifeless but comforting. A string dangled like some ancient umbilical cord on the front of the satchel, wrapping three times around a metal fastener. Adlai undid it, then pulled out the innards.

It was a written document. The paper was strangely thick and yellowed and had the scent of things dead and rotten. The ink was still dark, though, and the writing wild, big and furious with many flourishes. He could make it out, but as he held it on his lap, preparing, there was a rush of something terrible and joyous, as if a window had torn open and a wind blown in, laced with some horrible reckoning. He looked at the paper and knew the room was still and all was well, despite his trembling hands and a distant ghostly voice that he'd never heard before, but somehow knew.

JANUARY, 1886, NEW YORK CITY

I will write it plain. But Lucifer be damned I will write it!

For my son Aengus, and for his young son Pat—they both surely seeing me as the devil, the traitor. I know Aengus may burn these pages unread, unheard. Still I write it for him in hopes that he reads it and knows of me. It's no plea for forgiveness, as there is no way to make up for wrongs done. It's a vain cry for something less than utter disgust from a dark and lost man.

I may go off rambling in this ragged spilling, for I'm no word man, no poet, not able to tell of no terrible beauty being born. I leave that work for them that can. But I've read my Yeats, I've spun a tale. I am an Irish man through and through, so I will tell it. And I will dream that my son, and his son after, may somehow not hate me.

It is cold, and I am alone. They will arrive by morning, my brother Brandon, my son Aengus who is now a man of 26, his young son Pat. They have promised to come. They do not know I plan to give them all I have, even this very butcher shop where I sit now writing. This place of slaughter of dead animals, of things rotting. That suits me.

But I ramble. Already I ramble! The candle flickers in the wind, and my heart too fails, but damn it I will get this done, writing with my own blood if the drasted ink well fails me.

I had first thought to tell it face to face, like a good man should, to beg forgiveness, to look in my son's eyes. But I am not a good man. I am weak, a coward, a drunkard sure. And I know my voice would fail me, and I would be lost, and it would never be told. So I will write it this night for them to have and do with what they will.

Mist catches me, and dreams, ragged, come at me even awake. Dreams of Doolin, my home, of the mist and the green and the burren and the ocean and her hair, you Claire my love, though dead these years, who will never read this. You, whom I wronged most, leaving you alone some 16 years ago with a son, the young Aengus to raise, you thinking your husband perished in that terrible water, on that coffin ship to freedom to escape famine.

So I might best start there, on that ship that took me away from you all, with a promise to send for you, to rescue you from the famine hunger that came so regular, it just was. But would you have wept as I sailed off if you knew how I'd discard you and never look back? And a God-fearing person would now say "How can any man be so evil, so dark, to abandon his family like that?"

The fires await me sure as sure, and Lucifer will take care of that, you can count on he, and this plea will not change any of that, nor the blue rosary here by me, but still it must be told. My bottle is full, so my courage will stay. The candle is tall, the night long. I must hurry, before the devil himself swoops in, or my weak, putrid heart gives out.

I recall so clearly my last night in Doolin. It was 1870, the second period of Irish famine years. I should have known then what would come. My brother Brandon, poor mad soul, had wandered off again late, as was his way. I woke, haunted by my dream, that dream all us men of our heritage must live with, our lot.

I reeled with the scent of the ocean, that heady smell that was part of me, and I wandered out into the cold, drawn to the rocks, where I knew lunatic Brandon would likely be. He was want to go out, poor lout, even more those nights leading to my departure, drunk, to the rocks, where he would yank off his clothes and lie on the rock. He did not lay with women, he, like a priest. Why, I dare not ask. The mad offer nothing but nonsense.

I did find him there, but no madness that night, no wild writhing on the rocks like a fool. He sat still, looking out, knees drawn up like a boy dreaming. He spoke before I reached him, like he'd been waiting on me, like his eyes could see backwards.

"You ought not go brother," he said. "There is no good in it. You will never return."

I hear those same words now, alone in this shop stinking of animal flesh. No liquor will warm my gut enough to forget the sound of his warning. The wind came up hard at me that night, and I swear there was a screaming voice in it, but my mind was not all with me. I was unsteady.

"You think I'm to die on the coffin ship?" I said to him.

He did not answer, merely stared out at the dark horizon.

Most did die, it was told, on those wretched ships taking our people of Ireland to the cities of America where life was good. But some made it, some ran through the diseased and foodless rocking trip. Some did, why not me, I thought.

Brandon, when he was not drunk, or mad-rambling, or playing music on the fiddle, which was his incredible and unique talent, he could say queer things that would come to be. Some said he had magic in him. Some said the way he stroked the fiddle was from God, but others said he had the pure devil in him to play so beautifully and to be able to tell the future. He was, truth be told, a soothsayer, and that night he indeed told the truth. He knew, damn him, he knew. But I would not hear him then.

The first night on the coffin ship, the wretched vessel lived up to its name. Two were ailing within a day. Drinking water was lacking, and I hid the meager food things my Claire had sent with me. I slept below amongst many. Rough waters sloshed my brain, rocked me through the night. And the dream I'd had nightly all my life, since youth, that dream which had hence been filled with wind and rock and a song so sweet, that dream suddenly changed.

This new dream, the dream that has since stayed with me, it showed me nothing but a field. The sky was white, and the field emerald green and rich. There was one sheep, which I knew was right, since we kept sheep, herded them in early years, my father's father.

But the one sheep was marked with black on its back, not red as was our brand. The animal was standing still, and as if an invisible wind with teeth gorged him, his side sliced open and the blood gushed hot but in that rushing blood came infants, three. Three boys spit forth. They somehow stayed white, floating in the animal's blood. But they did not cry as infants do. They were still as death.

I'd fall off to sleep, and that same vision would come over and over. And I knew then something had gone black, had changed, but I wouldn't believe it yet. What was told to me by my brother, this new dream he surely forced on me, came to pass in ways now irrevocable.

The candle is shrinking. I must light another. I wish I could but stop here. Do I need go on? Is it not enough to say I am doomed, a worthless sinner. Trickery! Devil! How weak I am! More whiskey. I cannot escape this amends. The church clock nearby has struck twelve, but no three ghosts will come to me. I am alone, and I must forge on.

I found cheap lodging at a room above a brawling spot for drinkers and Irish men like me. It was in a sordid and ugly part of New York City, but it was the first I came upon, and I was sore glad to be off that reeking death ship and on dry land. My funds were meager and my strength lacking. The room I secured had a cot and no window. That hit me hard with despair. We too suffered in Doolin, the famine and our lot, but we had the endless green, the ocean, the air. I think now, knowing all that took me down, if only I'd turned away that night. Left that place, run back to Doolin. But I will not bog down with regret.

That first night, I went below to the dark and wild saloon and found lively company, other Irish men and also dark swarthy men jabbering in other languages, and women loose and ugly, thrusting. I had a drink, then a man bought me another. He sat with me. He was big, red in the face with a wild shock of blood-colored hair and a mighty frame. He shook my fist like he would twist it off.

He called himself Tom, from Dublin, God bless him. He had been in the city awhile, and was free with his money and was a bright spirit. It wasn't long before I was drunk. I'd eaten little, and my body ached from the long trip. He had women at us soon, girls loose and bad, and one wearing a cross around her neck, as if taunting God, himself.

Thinking of that girl, that cross, I see my blue rosary that now sits before me, and I wonder, dare I pick it up? Dare I pray? Or would the thing scald my hand? Would God strike me down? I will refill my glass and find my strength in whiskey.

I don't know why I didn't crawl away from Tom and his lot that first night. Up to that sordid little room and to that cot, to dream, and maybe to dream of Doolin. But I did not. The heat of the liquor, the touch, it brought me down, and I lost myself. Soon a girl was at me. Her name was Bridget, and she from Dublin. Tom was staying upstairs, and we all made quite a mess and carried on and talked of many things by night's end, and I think at one point I wept, and Bridget held me.

I did not dream of Doolin. Only the sheep, the blood, those infants. I had set in motion what would become a wave of constant happening. And I woke to Bridget dressing.

"I ain't no whore," she said.

My head ached so, and I shuddered seeing that cross on her neck, God's brutal eye blazing at me. She left me there, aching and lost on that cot. But Tom was pounding soon and coming in like we was brothers. He had work for me.

I got up because despite how I felt, I knew not to say no to work and money. Maybe I could still be saved, I'd thought. Fool! But at the time, it was partly like God's miracle that I'd met Tom, that he had work, that I could remember why I came, for my family.

But what came next only sent me further to the flame.

Tom took me off to a part of town where they bled animals from slaughter to butchering. I thought he might be getting me work in a shop sweeping or scrubbing bloody floors. We met with some worn out looking fellas in a big, cold room made of wood, hung with carcasses. I suppose you may say it was fated, since I ended up here in this butcher shop, this place that may offer up my only amends to you my son Aengus, if you will take it from me.

But that day, stepping into the cold there, those animals skinned and headless hanging, I felt a dark chill of disgust. We'd herded sheep back home, sheared them for wool, slaughtered some, but that was amongst earth and air and sky. This place, with rows of meat hanging, in such a drab and barren room, it hit me strangely.

There was a fat man in a tweed suit smoking a cigar, and he looked to be running things. I recall Tom telling me to stay in back and shutup, or some such thing. I think the fat fella had been telling the men what to do, assigning them things and shouting out orders. I was hoping something in all that jabber meant work for me. I recall the loud bellow of the man's voice that day, shouting at me in particular, calling me a lout or a big fool or something. Tom told him who I was, and I'll never forget what happened next. He told me to take off my shirt. I stood like a dumb oaf until Tom nudged me. I slowly took off my shirt, feeling like the only ass. The fat man, sucking on that cigar, stepped over and punched my chest.

"Show them your arm!" he shouted.

I lifted my arm, and he pressed the bicep. He started yelling at the men that they ought to be big and brawny like me. It's true, I was a big man, full chested and hard from good work, but not anything special. Then the fat man told me to lift one of the carcasses off of its hook. He said he'd give me five dollars if I could do it, so of course I did.

I moved to the hanging animal and wrapped my arms around it like a lover. I remember how cold it felt, as if it had never breathed life. I'd hoisted and carried sick sheep when I had to, but never felt anything so lost and bloodless. Lifting the thing up and off the hook wasn't easy. I had to hoist a few times, but finally the honkering thing leapt up and off and nearly knocked me on my back. I held it there, and the men cheered, and the fat man patted me on the back and shoved four bits in my pocket, as I dropped the mighty thing.

"Take him to Bernadette's," he said.

I didn't know that day what I was in for and how it would change me forever.

The night is black, and I hear a long sad howl in the wind, urging me on. But how can I? This would be the point any sane and Godly man would say, what kept you from writing your family? What threw you so far off your goodly path? There is no ready answer, and my mind now, liquor soaked and empty of anything pure, can yank out no redemption.

I do know I was a young man and a fool. As if that's any excuse. But the fact was that I'd seen nothing but the land, the town, my Claire. The lure of this city, all that coming on me so fast, I think it snaked me under. It made forget who I was and those I loved. It seduced me. My soul was loose and easy to yank at. I told myself, I swear I did, that I would save money and bring them to me. But as time went on, as the cast went dark, I knew it would never happen. I knew I was lost.

I'd never seen a place like Bernadette's!

I will forever remember that first night. The house was gleaming and regal, gold and velvet and women with faces like white glass. But I knew as sure as St. Patrick that it was stinking with the darkest blood-sin one can imagine. No diamond lacing can diguise true evil. Plain and simple, it was a whore house.

I see clearly now how this began my real fall from any grace. If you, my dear son Aengus, may be reading, I warn you, do not hate me too much, though nothing can get better from here, as the devil surely flew close to me laughing, forked tongue so fierce. I ache now in the dark night, drinking, remembering Bernadette's. Putting the ink to paper is like a blood-letting. I want to wipe away those years. What happened to Cahal that once loved a family, that loved my dear stone cottage and my mad brother Brandon and wife Claire and son Aengus? I ache to leave him dead. But here writing, hands trembling with disgust, I am committed to tell it, to tell it all. And God forgive me, my son and his sons forgive me if you read on.

That first night at Bernadette's, I was awe struck as a babe. Never had I seen such richness, the women white and pure it seemed, all sewn up tight in bright dresses and so much grandness, the crystal chandeliers, the wood and oak, the scent of chestnuts and fine whiskey and a crackling fire and men in fine tweeds. I recall it all now as clearly as I do the scent of the ocean breeze in Doolin.

I was told to stay near the door and be ready if they needed me to deal with louts or troublemakers. The lady owner, Miss Bernadette, her voice lingers. She had a dark, throaty laugh that you could hear all through that house, and she was a mighty woman, big and hearty with a chest larger than I'd seen in my days. She winked at me whenever she passed, sucking on a cigarette in a long fancy holder.

The place had three floors, a main parlor with a piano with a man playing loud and bawdy music. I stayed near the big double door entryway, waiting to be told what to do. It was at that time I still had it in my head that I was making honest money, that I'd be writing to Claire soon, that I'd in time send money for them to travel.

But standing there all night, watching the fancy men pass, the hard women flit about, there was a dark spell setting over me. I knew I had no business being in this den, but it was warm and dry, and there was promise of pay and even shots of whiskey from Bernadette to warm me up.

As dawn crept in, there were still a good deal of men about, but things had gone quiet. The piano player left.

The first scream came so quick and fast, I thought it might be a high-pitched laugh. But the second scream was shrill and harsh. Like a sheep to slaughter. Bernadette was at me, calling, and I ran to the upstairs following the sound. The door was locked, but I knocked it down with a few good thrusts and inside was the scene.

The girl, Tessy they called her, was near the window, naked and pale, holding a razor knife, and the man, a burly one, shirtless but in his pants, was holding his cut up arm, leaking blood and cursing. He was moving toward her with mighty fists and I ran and grabbed him from behind, yanked his arms back and threw him down holding him there still. He was big, but flabby and weak under my grip. Bernaette was there, as Tessy wailed about how he'd tried to kill her.

I hoisted him up, thinking how much easier this was than hoisting that carcass that afternoon, and I took him downstairs and out the door. Bernadette came down, all broad painted and man ugly, smiling at me. She shoved money into my hand, and turned and left. I made my way out into the bright, cold day, feeling somehow Cahal had gone and died forever. I was lost.

The winter came on, and work at Bernadette's was steady. Not always so raffish and dark, some nights I'd do very little but keep an eye on the door and let my mind wander off to Doolin and home and the burren. Now I see clearly how I was dreaming of home, but really avoiding it, letting myself get further away from what was right and good. I was blind to the truth of my intentions and moved like a half-ghost, neither fully in the city, nor taking any action to bring those I loved to me. I had written nary a letter. I refused to see the blackness growing fast and furious in my shriveling heart.

It was a sweet, clear Sunday, a few months into my stay, that I was taken completely to my knees. I was out for a walk having a day off. I wandered uptown, away from the brass and clang of Mott Street, the hard and hawking vendors, the color and emptiness of Bernadette's.

I passed fine looking people, men in hats and coats with fine fur collars, women cinched up and respectable, and the further I walked, the darker my heart sank. I realized I'd not written a word to my Claire or son Aengus nor brother Brandon. And worse than that, I realize I had thought very little of them. I blotted out how I'd come to build a life and bring them forth. As I say, I'd been seduced by whores and drink and looseness and money.

The sky was clear that day I think, but the wind icy and strong, and I thought of that night on the burren, and how Brandon had issued that cursed warning that I would leave and abandon them all. My body shivered, and my heart raced as I felt the eye of God staring me down, sure to slay me right there on the street.

I turned a corner, and looming before me was a cathedral. Some of those finely dressed folks were going in, tipping their hats and smiling, and I stood near it, clutching my raggy coat to me, hearing the tolling bells and choking up. Once they all went in, and things got quiet, I inched over toward the giant doors. Up the steps I went, but at the door, it was as if that cold wind had froze me and held me in purgatory.

I told my hand to reach out, to grip the handle and go in, to kneel, to pray for forgiveness, to find my way back. But in my mind, rushing at me, were all the nights at Bernadette's, the bleak and vile lost women I protected, the men seeking to feed their own blackguard souls. I felt the blood racing through my veins go boiling and turn pitch, like the devil's tar raging. I lifted my hand slightly but was sure the handle would sear and burn my wretched skin.

The sound of a grand organ began, and to me that was the angels nailing the lid to my coffin of doom, singing forth and telling me that I was lost. I had flown far off the cliff's edge and had no place to land, but the fiery pits of hell.

I ran from that place, ran as far and fast as I could, then finally stopped, exhausted, sweaty, near mad. I fell to the street, sitting down like an ugly beggar. Looking up, I saw I was in front of a saloon. The voices, cheerful and empty, swept out at me, and with a resignation as deep as I'd ever felt, I took myself in there, accepting my fate, abandoning my family and worse than all, resigning myself to a life filled with evil, lost to anything good and pure.

Adlai held the strewn pages in his lap, like dead leaves preserved and blown from some dark and terrible storm. He'd fallen out while reading, and woke with the furry sachtel at his side, the drab scattered manuscript filled with his Great Grandfather's messy little tale.

He sat up in bed, the room soft and dark. It must be evening he thought, then reached up to touch the throbbing bump on his head. He pressed it lightly, and it was soft, and he wondered if he pushed on it, if it would burst. Would blood and visions and strange infants gush forth?

He'd never had a special dream, never been tormented like his brother Dickie, like these Irish men before him. Like poor Cahal. He wondered if his father had the dream, that family curse of vague visions that to Adlai meant nothing. He wondered if his father had read this story, if he'd met Cahal, his grandfather. He must have, since he said Cahal gave him the blue rosary.

He did not know why Pat had given it to him to read, but he decided it was to make up for the loathsome birthday. Maybe he would begin to be seen afterall. Maybe Pat would not hate him for who he was.

The door rattled, and he heard footsteps coming into the house, then stop. He looked down at the splayed history in his lap, and wondered again why Pat had given it to him, the least of the three. Why not Walt? Why not Dickie?

There was the sound of someone coming toward his room. The footsteps were animal like, heavy, but punctuated with pausing, as if the walker were a bandit, stealing in, creeping toward what would be a wild and violent stealing. It could be Dickie. Looking down again at the papers, Adlai thought how right it would be if he were to get gouged by his brother, blood covering and diminishing this tawdry history written by some long ago lost man. As if Cahal's wrongs could ever be equal to what he, Adlai, was all about. His sin. The steps continued, then the door opened, as if with a slow, dooming wind.

It was Big Ed. He was in darkness, but his shadow, the wide yank of his shoulders sloping, the thickness of legs, the hard wild curl of his hair, was all like a second skin to Adlai for he knew it as his own.

"They don't know," Ed said. "I don't know why, but Corigliano didn't say anything. And your father has been quiet too."

Ed moved toward the bed, his shadowy outline thrusting closer to Adlai. He sat on the bed, crushing portions of the manuscript. Adlai could see his face, the eyes still as dark and wild as he'd seen them the night before, a fiercesome resigning. He reached a hand to Adeali's head, barely touching the wound, then he moved a callused finger to Adlai's lip, inside to the teeth, then he bent his head into the boy's lap.

Adlai petted the man, running his fingers slowly, deliberately through Ed's hair. From the distance, there was the tolling of church bells and for a moment, Adlai thought of Cahal, that man, and wondered if it were all real? Ed sat up, then shoved a slip of paper into Adlai's fist, holding it for a moment.

"Meet me at this place tonight," he said.

Ed rose and turned and left, not looking back. Adlai put on a lamp and continued reading.

Years passed, and I became more and more a drunkard. My own stink, the reek of cowardice, that fear mixed with my shame grew month after month, year after year, working the whore house, stuffing away money, drinking late into the night, losing my soul.

I could not look at myself in the mirror any longer, and I told myself I was sparing those far off, my Claire, my boy from having to see what I had become. They were better off without me.

In drink, late, dawn at me, I'd sit alone outside, on barren alley rock, not feeling the cold, thinking of my brother Brandon, those nights when he was lost and drunk on the burren. I wanted the past to disappear. As time goes, any man can forget anything, even those things that were once so dear.

I did well at Bernadette's. I kept things in line, stopped a good many fights, saved a good many girls from dumb louts who'd want to use their fists or worse. I became stronger physically, despite all my drinking. Tom got me into boxing, the only Irish sport he said, and it did help me on Sundays to go a few rounds with him, to feel the snap and twist of my muscle and get the rage of the oceans out of my whiskey-slogged head.

There were two things that happened, that changed my life for good. And both, both God help me, were rotten to the core. Though by the end of this tale, you will see how I set out with all my last heartbeat, to make it right.

The first happened late one night at Bernadette's. It was winter, and the city was bleak and shivering. An ice storm set in, biting slags of hail knocking about at the roof and windows, loud even with the bawdy playing from the piano. The place was busy as always, but that storm put everyone on edge.

Sitting at my post, the constant smash of hail and the frightful wail of the wind brought me back to Doolin, to the weather we had, the hunger we felt. I usually stayed pretty sober during working hours, but the storm and the nagging thoughts of Doolin sent me sipping at the bottle a bit extra that night. I felt a whisper of doom too, in my bones I did, and it was likely my soothsayer brother Brandon was hovering in the shadows somewhere, telling me to beware.

The trouble had to do with one customer I never did like. He was a tall, thin and brittle looking type. Not so old, but wiry in body, thin, yellowish hair, tiny spectacles that slid off of his nose and a fine tweed suit with a dangling, gold pocket watch. Funny how I remember that demon so well, in detail like he were a painting living in my mind. While the color of my own Claire's lips have faded from memory. The scent of her hair, gone.

That spectacled fellow was always put in a special room upstairs and treated like royalty on account he was in the government and from some highfalutin family. When I saw him pass, I always got a shuddering chill, like he had a bit of the devil, himself, swimming through him. I'd heard the Madame whispering more than once about his "special needs," which he more than likely paid through the tooth for. I never had much to do with him, until that fateful stormy night.

I was watching the door, and like I said, I'd a bit more than usual to drink. The Madame came to me and gave me that nod of her head that said a "mess: needed to be cleaned up. " She took me upstairs, to that fancy room that fella always had. When I stepped in, and she quietly shut the door behind us, I felt sick.

I think maybe if I'd been sober, maybe if it had happened a few years earlier, before I'd fallen so far, I may have turned and run. That tall skinny fella was standing, still in his underdrawers, near the window. The wind was pounding outside. He was quiet and didn't seem upset, more like he was going to settle in for a good night's sleep. On the bed was the girl, Rosey. A particularly young and sweet little thing. She was naked, pale as a ghost, lain out looking mighty peaceful. But there was a long, leather string tied around her neck, her eyes were stuck wide open.

"She's dead," said Madame Bernadette in a soft and horrible voice I'll never forget.

The thin man tilted his chin up, almost like he was going to shout out an order. I noticed he had those dumb-looking spectacles hanging off his nose. The rest of the night is a muddy blur, but I remember what that cad said to me.

"Clean this up," he said,as if it were a bit of broken glass scattered on the drug store floor.

I recall one other thing that evil man said, too, the thing that indeed came to pass.

"You'll be taken care of," he said before he left.

I learned later, exactly what that meant.

It was spring of that year before that late-night promise from the evil spectacled man came to light. With that horrible duty, that death, all hope of writing my family was lost. I had abandoned myself to the drink and to stashing away money from the work at Bernadette's. I figured some day, some how I'd get the saved money to my Claire, my boy, Aengus.

One night Bernadette sent me out on an errantd with Billy. Billy was the kid who drove the carriage and did odd jobs at the whore house. He was the boy who'd driven us that fatal night to get rid of that sweet, young girl, Rosie. I went out with him, and we went across town. He pulled up in front of a butcher shop. There was a closed sign in the door, but I could see inside the big window fronting the place. That murderer with the spectacles was sitting in a chair.

"Go on," Billy said.

I stepped on the sidewalk, and he drove off. The man was waving me in, so I went. I felt a sour sinking in my stomach. He sat there all dressed like he was going to a party. He pulled out that gold pocket watch he wore the night of the murder and was staring at it. Then he started tapping on it with a skinny finger, like it had stopped working.

"I'm going to give this shop to you. You will own a business. Does that appeal to you?," he said.

I didn't quite follow what was happening, so I just nodded.

"You can keep it, sell it. But it's yours," he said. "Everything will be taken care of then. I owe you nothing else. We are even, as they say."

I stood there for a few minutes, then figured I was meant to leave, which I did. I walked back across town to the whorehouse, not sure if God was smiling on me, or if this newest twist was just another trap.

I had that butcher shop; yes, that was mine. Bernadette explained that it was their payment for my wicked silence about that poor dead girl, Rosy. It took awhile before I saved money working at the whorehouse to run the damn thing, and it took me, dumb mutt that I am, even longer to figure out why the damnable place was really given to me to begin with. Nothing, as they say, comes without a price.

This spot where I sit now, in the very back of the butcher shop, it feels like the devil's black heart. There is no light, but for the dim slice of moon crawling in from the back alley. There be nothing pure here, just dangling hooks for dead things, that stink of animals gutted and gone. It is a place for dark deeds.

Once I got the shop up and running part time, the men who gave it to me started stopping by, dropping things off, having meetings. Seems all along they wanted it to appear as a reputable business, while they used the back armpit of the place as a late night den to fulfill their bloody deeds. These hooks swinging near me now, they've felt more than bison and calf hanging from them. I shudder to think.

But it was my place, and it did all right since I'd given up any hope of doing the right thing in my life. It was not until the night of the famous mist that I saw my way out, I saw my chance at redemption.

It was late spring, but there was a bone winter chill in the air, a chill that always brought me back to Doolin. A heavy, misty fog swept in, something strange and unusual, even for this city that had seen it all. Folks talked about it for weeks after.

Having a night off work from the whorehouse, I was getting dead drunk on sweet Irish whiskey. I'd wandered off that night alone, exactly to where I cannot rightly recall, but I can still see that ghostly mist, the thick cruelty of it, for me at least, since it kept calling me back to my homeland, to the burren and the rocks and the wild tangle of a dark ocean.

I think I was near the river on the city's West side, seeking some company, some music. The fog got so thick, it was like walking through a series of curtains to find the next corner. Of course I was far gone on whiskey, so to another man it may have not seemed so dire.

Then it happened. The song came at me. I still wonder to this day if it was real, or some lost angel trying to save me, whispering in my ear. It was a song I knew, a wild jig, a joyful bit heard at holiday time or for weddings back home. I stumbled through the mist, hearing it, believing then it was calling me, which now I see, it was.

I saw a light in a saloon and people hanging out the door. It was a fiddle, a loud sharp player making music, and I heard men hooting and the sound of dancing feet. I pushed my way through, mixing in with a drunk and slovenly crowd, moving toward the fiddle, a bit crazed by that point, as it took me so close to my home, yet tore at my black little heart. Finally I got close, and I saw the man sawing away at the instrument, sweating and moving with loose joy.

And in my stupor I swore it was my dear brother Brandon, who as I said was a master of the fiddle. I pushed closer, making no friends with the crowd, now yowling his name, for Brandon was the best fiddler in Doolin, and I was more certain it must be him though part of me knew that was near impossible. Finally, they got sick of me yowling and pushing and a big man near threw me flat up to the edge of the puny stage where the fiddler played. Looking down at me, he stopped the music and a hush went over the room.

I looked up and I shall never forget the look on his face. His eyes bright and lit as a baby's, his cheeks, red as a rose, and a smile, broad as a river.

"My brother," he said.

I sat at his feet drunk and dumbfounded. It was not a dream. It was dear Brandon. My brother had come to find me.

Is that dawn creeping, or be it the light of an angel come to save me? I can smell my own stink, my own sweat. The bottle is nearly gone, my will weak. They will arrive soon, or at least I hope. My boy, Aengus, who I have not seen since he was small. Now a man, he, and his son too, Pat, my grandson. Will they come? Brandon has promised to get them here, even if he had to do it by force. Ah Brandon, my brother, my saviour, the only one in this world who cares two shakes if I live or perish.

That night I heard him on the fiddle, saw him on that stage, drunk and foolish, I thought it a dream up to the very moment he touched my shoulder and said:

"Brother, I have found you."

My memory beyond that is foggy, though I know I told him all, all of it, as if he were my father confessor. I spilled it there at the bar, me still drinking, Brandon sober and listening, and strangely, quickly forgiving, never blaming despite all my wickedness. It's as if he already knew what I'd done, and be sure he may have, him being the soothsayer and gypsy-type that he was.

After I'd told him my long tale, of drink and murder and whores and how over the years I grew afraid to even think of my family, he let me know about my poor dear wife Claire, how she'd perished in the famine, how she'd gone.

I sunk even lower then, realizing how I'd rattled on about my own fate and never even asked after my first love. How wretched I felt. But God bless Brandon, for not spitting at me and running.

He stayed with me that night and beyond. He told me how he'd never given me up for dead, though the rest had. He told me how he dreamed of me running blind in a field, carrying a scathe, trying to slaughter sheep that were not there. It was Brandon too that cooked up the scheme to bring my grown son Aengus and his son Pat here to America, to try to repair all the damage I had done. It was then also I knew I'd give the butcher shop over, give all I had over to my son Aengus and his son Pat, if they'd have it. I don't know how Brandon managed it but in time he did. He promised to bring them here to see me.

I do not know what will happen when my son and his son appear. But the light is no angel's light, the dawn is here, and soon they will arrive. Will they come with guns blazing to kill off this wretched traitor? Or will God be merciful? May my son take pity on me as my dear brother did. And what of the boy, young Pat, what was he told of his grandfather? Oh, God be merciful is all I ask. And if they will not talk to me, I have this document written and ready to hand over. So that someday they may read it and understand my actions.

The bottle is gone, the candle out. I wait now, as the sun rises. For there is nothing more for me to do. Nothing else but face my fate.

Adlai woke slowly, still shaken by a fading dream. There was a sheep, pure white, fleeing across a field. It ran at an unnatural speed, its fleece, that thick shearling stuff, flying endlessly. By the dream's end the animal was only skin, ugly, naked, purplish skin, like a still-born infant.

He was in bed, surrounded by the pages he'd read, the hairy satchel. Pat was at his side, in a chair.

"I had a dream," Adlai said, struggling to come back. "Like Dickie. I've had my own dream."

"Yes," Pat said softly.

As he sat up, Adlai felt the throbbing in his head, that wound, and recalled the night of the kiss, that horror and revealing.

"You read it?" Pat said.

Adlai wondered what time of day it was. He'd nodded off after reading the document. Had he missed the meeting with Ed? Was it the same day?

"You see why I gave it to you?" Pat said.

Adlai thought, recalling bits of his great grandfather's desperate tale. "No. What happened? There is no ending to it?"

Pat sat up. He brought his hands together, lacing the fingers. "I'm not much good at this," he said. "I don't know how to begin."

Adlai waited.

"Well, all right then," Pat said. "I was a boy. You know that?"

Adlai did not reply. He let his father take his time.

"The memory then is a boy's. It's scant, uneven. It was the shop, our shop below. You see? My father, Aengus, your grandfather. He was a..." Pat looked down at his lap. "I don't know if I should do this," he said.

"It's all right, Pop."

Pat looked up at his son and sought his eyes. "My father was cruel. He lost his mother early on. He lost his wife, as I lost mine." Pat smiled strangely. "But that you know. About your mother."

"No. You've never told me," Adlai said. He could see a softening to his father's face, and those white and wet blue eyes seemed to register things not brought forth before.

"Well Dickie then, he knows that," he said.

"Just tell me the end of the story. Did you go to the shop to meet Cahal?"

"Oh that, yes," Pat said. "We went. But my father, he'd have none of it. I think he only went to shame his father. To spit on him. He said very little, some old Irish curse, and he left. But my grandfather, he held me back, and he forced that thing on me."

Pat swept his arm across the bed at the madly scattered pages.

"Did you read it?" Adlai said.

"Alone, hiding, in bits and drags," Pat said. "My father was a violent man. I was afraid of him. I did not tell him I had it. Strangely, I felt closer to my grandfather in ways. His words, there, I read it over and over."

"And that's it? Did you see him again?"

"Never. But when my father died, young, did you know that? He died of Scarlet Fever. Well, when he died, Cahal gave me the shop. Brandon saw to that. So I had that. Well, we still have it don't we."

From the living room came the sound of a door thrashing open and shut violently as if someone busted through the wood.

"That would be your brother Dickie, don't you think?" Pat said. He was smiling, leaning down closer to Adlai, almost mischievously.

"Best gather that up. Put it away. Your brother would not understand it. But I think you will in time," Pat said, then got up and left the room.

Adlai gathered the pages back into the satchel. Lying under it was the broken blue rosary. He clutched the old thing in his palm, folded it there, so it fit hidden in his fist. It felt cold and rich, secret and his. He would keep it.

He waited to see if his brother would come into the room, but he did not. Lying on the bed was the scrap of paper Ed had given him with the address where to meet him. His head was clearing, and he knew it was indeed the same day. He would get out and meet Ed. He would keep the rosary with him.

Part

Three

They sent him to Sheepshead Bay for his first job, and Dickie thought that was pretty damn funny. He decided maybe Frankie had a fucked up sense of humor.

He sat alone in his Chevy. Twilight had come and gone, and he'd smoked most of a pack of Chesterfields that Eva had given him to hold, then forgot about, the night before at the birthday party for his kid brother. He'd been waiting a few hours in a lot near a spot by the water where some ratty, and a few slick looking, boats sat. There was a joint called The Hatch, that served fried flounder and beer.

Dickie didn't like waiting, didn't like where it sent his thinking. The name bugged him. Sheepshead Bay, he kept gnawing on that. "Here I am getting away from the damn butcher shop, and Frankie fucking Corigliano sends me to Sheepshead Bay."

The vision of a lone head of a sheep, jagged and blood-soaked, fly-ridden and lost, made him laugh in an uneasy way. He couldn't get the idea to scram. It was the damn waiting. He lit the last cigarette in the pack.

Night was on full, and his Chevy was in shadow. The only near-light was that from the fish joint. He was hungry but had to sit still, had to be patient. They didn't tell him the guy's name, just the car the dope would be driving and that he was real, real tall and liked wearing bright clothes. He was a Jew, Frankie said, like that meant anything. And he'd have a fishing pole. Somehow they knew the guy was going night fishing. Dickie figured he must be looking for bass. What else would you fish for at night? Poor lout wasn't gonna catch anything.

It was Dickie's first job for Frankie. He'd leveled guys with his fists before, left them half-dead, but nothing like this. So it had to go right. Clean and simple. He sucked on the Chesterfield, wishing Eva was with him. That musky scent she carried on her, the way her slinky dress hung. The gentle push of her nipples. He was getting hard, which was good. Anything to pass the time. Anything to stop him from thinking of a bloody sheep's head or how something could go wrong.

He knew this wasn't smashing some kid in the skull with a pickle jar. He didn't quite know how it would play out, but he knew his part was to nail the guy, get him in his boat, untie the thing and scram. Frankie had the second half planned. He kept telling Dickie to do it exactly as he told him. He said that over and over, getting real close up, talking slow and low like Dickie was a retard.

An old guy ducked out of the fish joint dumping trash, then went back in. Dickie thought how good a fish sandwich and a beer would taste. Or a steak. Frankie told him at the party that once he showed himself as useful, he'd start to see money. Real money. Dickie had heard about gangsters getting away with things, making a load of cash, living high. Frankie said this job tonight was all figured out, and there was no way Dickie could get caught. He was just the button man.

The cigarette burned down and he thought again of Eva. He'd go see her once this was done. He'd get her in the tub and just lay around drinking with her on top of him. Them, like that together; he was hard again.

A car was coming up the road, idling past the fish hut then pulling into a lot near where Dickie sat. It was a Cadillac roadster, slick and blue-silver and shining even in the dim of the cloudy, moonless night. Sweet little ride. That was the guy. That was the car, like Frankie described it.

Dickie sat up. A fellow hopped out legs as thin and long as a spider's, wearing yellow pants and a yellow shirt. He had to be over six feet. That was him. Dickie was still hard, and he couldn't stop thinking of Eva, of how he'd take her once this was done, and the horror and thrill of taking a life was on him, getting at him, under his skin, and he was riled up. He knew it was a bad thing, this way he felt, knowing what he had to do, but he was starting to sweat a little and smile in a stupid sort of way.He got out of the truck, and he walked toward that guy with the long, spider legs. Then a kid got out of the car.

The kid had red hair and a fishing pole and wore a hat. Dickie stopped. There was not supposed to be a kid. This was supposed to be simple, easy, his first job. The guy would go to the boat, he'd shoot him, he'd unhook the boat to float off a bit. Corigliano said that was it. The place would be deserted, Frankie said, and he'd shoot the lout and that was it. Nobody said anything about a fucking kid.

The spider leg guy was bending down and talking to the kid, then he touched the kid's cheek. Then the kid went into the fish place. Dickie moved fast. He had to get to the guy before that kid came back out. He was sweating a lot, and water dripped onto his arm, and he thought it looked black, but he knew that was his nerves. He had Eva in his head and the gun in his hand. The guy moved out toward the boat, all yellow like some queer bit of sunburst at midnight, some fiery hand of God looking down on them, and the water was black, and things were quiet.

Dickie moved fast to get this done, before the kid came back. He was drenched in his own stinky, black sweat, and he had the gun up aimed safety off and he would do this easy. Then that tub with Eva and her tits, and he was a little hard again, and the gun was high and he came right up to the guy. He thought he heard a door. The kid. The spider guy was turning now and Dickie was shaking all over with excitement and a sickness as he turned to look back toward the fish hut. He couldn't shoot the fuck with his kid watching. He looked, and there was nobody there.

The guy was stepping backward in fear, away from Dickie who was going at him, and he knew from the wild mockery of a disfigured gape-mouth, like a fish screaming, he knew the guy was gonna yowl, so he quickly smacked the butt of the gun into the guy's forehead. The tall man fell. There was again, that hush of a door. Dickie turned. The kid was there this time, moving toward the car, twenty feet off, looking around. He had a bottle of orange Neehi soda.

The tall guy fell out of sight, since there was another car blocking the view between where the kid was and the boat. The kid kept looking around. Dickie knelt, and the spider guy was coming to, blood seeping out of the wound on his head, but his eyes open too wide, seeing him, his mouth all fish-like again ready to yowl, and Dickie knew he couldn't shoot off the gun, or the kid would run their way. so he pressed his thumb, quick and deep, into the guy's eyeball and wrenched it up and out, and with the other hand, shoved his fist in the wanting-to-scream mouth, and nothing but a gurgling strangled cry came forth, and the guy passed out. Dickie, hunched down now, could see the kid was going back to the fish hut. There was nobody else around.

Dickie hoisted the skinny guy up and over and into the boat, and he held the gun close, one shot in the skull, echoing into the night like the sound of some mad hunter. Then he untied the boat and shoved it as hard as he could and sent it off. Drenched, wet and stinky of blood and fish guts and his own mean bad ugliness, he marched back to the car, keeping his mind on Eva's tits.

At the car, he saw that dumb ass kid come out and look at the boat that was starting to drift a little. The kid looked confused. He went back into the fish hut. Dickie started the engine and got off. He did his part. He knocked the guy. That's all they asked him to do and he did it.

When he hit the highway the moon came out more boldly, lustfully, he thought, but the glare of it through the putrid and dirty windshield cast a dark glow on his steering arm, and the flutter of that glare seemed black to Dickie, his sweat smeared with dark and oily earth.

two

Dickie lay on the wood floor at Eva's place. He liked the feel of the hardness against him. He was naked, and the wood felt sticky on his back, because he was perspiring, and the wood had that grit to it. He could hear Eva nearby, which comforted him, and for a moment, lying there, he felt as a boy might, safe and cooled by a nearby metal fan blowing, but the image of another boy, the child of the man he'd killed wouldn't get out of his head. *Damn stinky-ass runt,* he thought. *Trying to ruin everything. This is my chance, you fucking runt.*

He heard the fan's mad rattle, which was consistent with each turn east, then it quieted, then it rattled, and he also heard the soft pawing of Eva's feet on the floor and a hush of fabric against what he guessed were her thighs. His eyes were shut, and the thought of that fabric touching her skin, that scent and sweetness came together and the image of that damn-ugly runt flew apart into a bunch of jigsaw pieces.

There was the kid's eye, an arm, all going, then finally, Eva was over him and there was nobody there but her. He looked up at her, the majesty of this black witch, the smooth caramel and those tits, holy fuck those tits. They could wash anything away. He could see straight up that flimsy pink dress, up into her. She was something special.

"Come on," he said.

She wavered there a moment, like the heat, the way it came in hard, irritating waves through the evening. She bent, then lay beside him; he rolled over on top of her, grinding and she pushed him off hard, but laughing.

"You ain't afraid of me?" he said, getting back at her, hovering over her now.

Her hair waved out against that sticky dark floor and her eyes looked cat-like to him. "You think you're mean?" she said.

His arm muscle strained, as he balanced himself over her. He liked looking down at her, the edge of her jaw and the lilt of her shoulder. The burn felt good in his arms. She reached up to touch his fast fading scars. "You heal up fast. It's the devil in you," she said.

He felt a little dizzy, still holding up there, and he realized he needed to eat.

"You think I'm mean? You think I'm bad?" he said.

She smiled and showed her teeth, and he noticed her lipstick was a strange purple. He had barely noticed it was there, but a fleck of it got lost on her front tooth. A marring speck. He let himself down slowly, feeling the arm muscles burn again, and he flecked his tongue at that bit of grease on her tooth.

"I've known worse," Eva said.

Down there, closer to her, hot now, he felt again comforted. "You think to kill somebody makes you evil?" he said softly.

She turned her head away, so one cheek rested on the cool floor. "You killed for money. Lots of men die because of money."

He pressed into her, and with one hand, pressed away the sheer fabric that was in his way. He needed to have her now.

"How you know about that," he said.

"Word gets around," she said in a whisper. "They call you the butcher. A man can become known fast. I like men who are known."

He felt his way closer onto her, and he sighed then made a ragged little cry, letting the pleasure seep all over.

"You sure you're not afraid?" he said, dizzy and losing some part of himself.

He went at her harder, and she gripped him, and they swam in the heat on that sticky floor, and she moaned a little which made him even crazier, and he said it again, but louder. "You sure you ain't afraid?"

"I'm a hard woman. I don't scare like that."

That was all with the talking, they both knew, and they both knew really, there was no need for even that much talking because they knew one another, just sweating on the floor quiet and hungry, they knew one another.

three

Adlai had only been to the ocean a few scattered times. He did not swim well at all, and as a child, he was certain the relentless and beating surf would swallow him whole, and no one would hear him scream. His brothers were excellent swimmers, Walt even certified to be a lifeguard. At the beach Adlai, never quite warm even in extreme heat, sat under a tattered blue umbrella, while his brothers ran recklessly into waves.

He met Ed downtown on Hester Street, the location written on the paper scrap. He got into Ed's car, and they drove silently, and Adlai did not ask where they were going. The two had a harsh and silent bond, now that they had been seen, now that they could be hurt. They both looked out the front of the car, along stretches of near empty road, until Ed pulled up near the tip of the Brighton Beach boardwalk. He got out, and Adlai followed thinking that Ed may be taking them to a hidden dock where a magical ship would take them far off, away from all their torment and disgrace.

There was an entry to the beach scooping under the boardwalk, where the dull, hot night pavement stopped and the still, hot dead-looking night sand began. It was like a dim, little tunnel moving from the real world to the ocean, leading away, thought Adlai, to safety. The passage was very dark, and Ed stopped as Adlai caught up. Before he could pass, Ed grabbed him roughly, like yanking a box off a passing cart, grabbed him by the thin shoulders and kissed him with a black urgency. Before he pulled away, his oafish teeth scraped Adlai's lips, which cut slightly.

"I can't stand not being by you," Ed said.

Ed pulled away and moved out of the passageway straight onto the empty beach, that distant lull of constancy, the ocean's roar blotting things from Adlai's feverish mind. Adlai half expected to see a freighter, the type of dark and battered ship that broken sailors boarded. But the horizon was clear, the beach vacant, and as they neared the ocean's lip, Ed stopped. Adlai let himself be soothed by that rocking motion of sound, the waves, the only constant, since there was no breeze in the heat.

He stood by Ed and briefly, oddly, he thought of his Uncle Cahal, that strange confession. Cahal had stood with his brother Brandon on the burren before he fled for America. He thought of telling Ed about what he read.

"Frankie kept quiet," Ed said.

He was staring out at the beating waves. He stood very still.

"I don't know why, but I don't trust him. I don't know what he wants," Ed said. Then he turned and faced the boy, towering over him as always, and his handsome but anguished face took on the tragic look of a fallen hero.

"We can leave. Do you think we should go away?" Ed said.

Adlai could not look away from his lover's face. It was not like Ed to ask things. He normally stated things.

"I don't think we can run away. That never works," Adlai said.

Ed turned away again, then began to remove his shirt. The sky was clear, mostly starless, the moon sickled. As Ed quickly undid his pants, and yanked at his shoes, Adlai stepped closer. "Ed?" he said.

Ed had gotten stuck wrenching violently at one shoe, and he tumbled backwards into the sand. He finished with his shoes, and awkwardly yanked at his pants, naked on the grayish night sand, the lost, black ocean behind him, the scattered beat of the waves. He looked like he may continue his ascent and lie backwards, give up, thought Adlai, let his wide, beastly back roll into the sand, his thick legs sink, but instead, he knelt forward.

"There is no law says two men can't go swimming on a hot summer night," Ed said.

He got up and ran toward the water. Adlai gasped, caught in a rush of lusty fear, watching the herculean back of the man, the muscularity and broken refinement of a flawed Greek, knowing that he, himself, could not swim, could not follow safely.

He began, regardless, to remove his scant clothes, his cotton shirt and dungarees, folding them and lying them in a pile on the sand, hoping Ed would come back, wet and happy. Instead, he saw Ed waving madly at the water's edge, calling him in. Adlai moved slowly across the still, warm sand, glancing around at the empty beach, wishing there had been a phantom sailor's vessel to take them away. Ed was in the water, waves knocking at his thighs, his hair already splashed wet and loose, like some grand and mad sea creature. Adlai dawdled at the first touch of the water, then shouted.

"I can't."

Ed was smiling, waving in the pale flare of moonlight, and Adlai stepped closer, moved to just knee level, wanting to reach him and explain. He saw the wave coming and froze, hoping it would pass over him, and he could then flee. As it hit, he fell, and felt his cheek scraping on sand and his feet flailing as if in a wind storm. But the warm lick of the water felt good and once the wave rushed back, he was in shallow water again, on his ass, drenched. Ed was over him, pulling him up.

"I don't know how to swim," Adlai said.

A surge was coming, another night wave., Ed pulled the boy close to his chest, lifted him, and Adlai straddled him like a child, then flung his arms around Ed's meaty neck, and in the moment, the wave rushing, he felt he had found that thing he knew would last, that place he would need to go.

"Don't let go," Ed said.

He held the boy and was moving further into the ocean, the water still shallow, only up to his waist, but the relentless waves were battering, and he was laughing, which Adlai found unsettling, though the waves did not throw them over. Adlai held tighter, then brought his eyes to Ed's and his lips close, too, and they kissed like angry beasts, chewing at each other, Ed their anchor in the waves, the moon their only witness.

four

Walt was agitated the entire day. He drank too much at the party, slept too late, and was haunted by the scent of Adriana, which was false, as she was not near him. He woke several times, some dream fleeting, smelling her, the lilac of her, that indiscernible sweetness he caught when she came near him. He thought of her and how the night before, she had asked him to meet her father again.

What he found so odd, what made him restless, was that she said it to him at the end of the night, after they had kissed, after giving him that smoky, succulent and lingering scent. As he had turned to leave, she was at the door to her building. She called to him, and framed there in the doorway late at night, turned half away and half to him, looking as still as a painting, she spoke slowly and simply.

"Can you meet my father tomorrow at nine at the Hickory House bar on 52nd street?"

"Of course," he said.

He'd begun to move to her, but she'd continued her fluid movement, giving him her back, as she drifted into the building and away. He'd waited there, fairly drunk, wavering in the hot night air under a bland, sickle moon. Waiting, as if she may reappear. But she did not.

He wore his best blue suit, which was not much, and walked to the Hickory House bar. It was a clear evening, and his spirits began to brighten as he passed people on stoops, drinking and laughing, children traipsing past, up late. He had a sudden urge to keep going, all the way to the Hudson River, to see the movement of the water, the hard elegant force of it. But he knew that was ridiculous. He could not be late. Then it suddenly struck him that this could actually be the moment when her father would succumb. Maybe that is why she did not say anything. She did not want to get his hopes up. She knew things were turning their way.

He quickened his pace, and for the first time that day, he felt strong, energetic. Why did this not strike him earlier? It had to be the case. The old man was softening, realizing he could not fight the inevitable. He had even chosen the West side of town where Walt lived, not the stuffy East. He approached the bar front, stepped in and lingered in the doorway. It was crowded. He was taken with a wall mural across the room, featuring a large, oafish football player running at another player, and several men scattered, beaten at his feet on the field. The mural was one of several in the place, but it struck him as odd for a fairly pleasant spot to have a picture so brutish. He had a rush of anxiety, upset by the strange mural, suddenly strained by the idea of facing this man without Adriana at his side.

He saw Adriana's buttoned-up father, turning toward him, as if he had been announced. The Doctor was under the mural, just below the hard looking football player.

He waved him over. There was a bright cabana-like awning hanging over the main bar and elegant, thick-bulbed hanging chandeliers. The place was a mix of raffish and elegant, and then there was the mural. The Doctor did not stand. He smiled but did not show his teeth. He wore tweed which seemed ridiculous in the heat. A waiter was near, and Walt turned, awkwardly, nearly knocking the waiter down.

"Scotch and soda," Walt said quickly.

Finally he sat, cramped in the small wood booth, facing Adriana's father. There were images of film and theatrical stars lining the walls, and a rude and rattling metal oscillating fan near them, passing its breeze over then back again, ceaselessly.

The Doctor had a tumbler and lit a thin cigar. There was a purple-shaded carafe on the table, giving the appearance that he was in a sitting room, not a public bar. He did not seem unpleasant, but Walt felt very odd. He briefly sensed that he was an animal in a cage being considered for an experiment, or perhaps slaughter. He cleared his mind as the waiter sat down his scotch, which he gulped. The Doctor refilled his tumbler. The old man's eyes were luminous, almost cheerful, yet Walt felt something was not right.

"I'm surprised you came," the Doctor said. There was the mildest slur. The man was drunk already. He had an uneven grin. The Doctor sipped dark liquid.

"Why wouldn't I?" said Walt. He felt bolder now, understanding the intoxication, the possible uselessness of this whole scene.

"You dress like a pig farmer. But then that's what you do. Butcher things."

Walt waved to the waiter for another scotch. He wouldn't put up with this old man's belligerence. It was time to set things straight. He would marry Adriana with or without a blessing. "Listen, Doctor Scola—"

"Is that how you think this will be?" the Doctor said. "You really are so very young."

Walt noticed that the Doctor was wearing a diamond stick pin in his tie that shimmered when he shifted in his seat. The old man laughed, then waved to the waiter for an ash tray. Settling his cigar in the delivered circle of glass, he began: "My wife was an aristocrat, which I think forgives certain things. I was younger then, and like Alexis in that greatest novel of adultery, I sought to forgive her vulgar transgressions, but she was not interested. She pitied me."

There was a mild commotion at the canopied bar near the front. A woman was singing loudly, until her friends quieted her.

"I don't suppose you've read that book. No," he said. "Quite simply, she left us. Abandoned us. Adriana and I. I've grown to hate her more than anyone now. But it took years to cultivate that hate. You see I fled. I gave up so much and came here. But now I see the flaw in my choice."

Walt was waiting for an opening. He thought the old man was drunk and rambling. The Doctor continued. "I know now that you can never flee. There is, in essence, nowhere to run. And now, you have come."

"Yes," Walt said. "You need to know that I plan to marry your daughter."

"Yes, I know." The old man filled his glass, but left it sitting.

"I brought us here," the Doctor said. "This city. Dear God. What a place. I thought I could protect Adriana here. And what does she want to do? To go live with a dirty, uneducated Irish butcher. To sweep up pig's guts and clean out basins. She wants to leave me, abandon her family, her history. That is impossible. She would be miserable. It will never happen. I will not allow it to happen."

The Doctor reached for his glass, and drained it. Then he stood to go. Walt began to speak, but the old man stopped him and spoke slowly, clearly not looking at Walt, but off toward the front window. "We are leaving, she and I. We are going back to Argentina, our home, which we should never have left. Don't you think it's all ironic? Like a circle?"

He leaned into the table, drunk, and for a moment Walt thought he may topple, but the Doctor regained his composure.

"But that's it," the Doctor said. "Goodbye."

He turned and left Walt alone in the booth, left the thin dwindling cigar, the empty glass tumbler. It had all happened so quickly that Walt did not know what to think. But he knew he would need to act fast, to get Adriana away. To stop her from leaving with her father. And he would need Dickie's help.

five

They met with Frankie in the late afternoon at a men's social club in Brooklyn. Adlai could not help but think of the last time they, along with Pat, had been with Frankie in Brooklyn, and what had been seen that night.

It was a clear, pleasant day, though a terrible thunderstorm was said to be on its way. Frankie brought the three of them to the back of the club, to a bocce ball court. Adlai had heard of the game, but never seen it played. The court was long and narrow, dirt filled, boarded on all sides with a low wood barrier. The yard was set off from an area where men sat playing a card game under a wide canvas umbrella. There were wooden slat chairs near the bocce ball court, and a table with a pitcher of beer and glasses.

Dickie set the meeting up, revealing very little to Walt and Adlai, telling them it was business, and they were part of it. Adlai, the lump on his head now a faded lavender reflection of the night he increasingly saw as insane or nearly ridiculous, was each day feeling that he and Ed may be safe. Frankie was dressed in a flashy suit. The three brothers huddled near the table where the beer and glasses sat.

"You play?" Frankie said. He had the bocce balls, one small and white along with larger balls that were black, green and red. The brothers did not know who he was addressing. Walt and Adlai looked to Dickie.

"Come here, Adlai, I'll show you how to throw," Frankie said. "You Irish don't do this right?"

Dickie turned to the table and poured beer into a glass. "A little billiards, sure. Not this shit," Dickie said.

Adlai stood still until Dickie swatted him on the back. "Go on, Rat," he said.

Adlai went to Frankie, who looked like a dandy in a Hollywood musical. His hair was slicked tight to his head, and he appeared young and strangely innocent to Adlai. He held out the small white ball.

"Fits in your palm," Frankie said softly. His face revealed nothing.

Adlai felt sweat in his palm as he held the ball. He wished Ed was there. He decided that Dickie and Walt knew nothing. There was no way Dickie would stay quiet. He didn't know Frankie's game.

"Throw it out, underhanded. Get us started kid," Frankie said.

Adlai glanced back at his brothers. Dickie was drinking and watching closely. Walt sat down, and had his head down, almost sleepily. Adlai tossed the white ball and it landed half way down the court.

"We all throw the colored balls now, see who gets closest," Frankie said.

He handed out the colored balls, and Dickie threw first.

Adlai went and sat next to Walt, who lifted his head and poured himself a glass of beer.

"What are we doing here?" Walt said. He looked at Adlai, as if the younger could have an answer.

"Dickie's always got a plan," Adlai said.

Walt looked directly at his younger brother. His eyes darted and widened and to Adlai, seemed to swim, as if he were being forced to see through water.

"I don't know kid," Walt said very softly. "I don't think so."

Frankie was patting Dickie on the back. As they drifted over, Frankie finished what sounded like a longer story. "...fucker brought the kid on purpose. Thought that would protect him." Frankie rested a hand on Dickie's shoulder. "You did the right thing. I knew you'd do well."

Frankie winked and turned back to the court, "My turn."

Walt stood up and went to Dickie. "I need to talk to you about something," he said.

"Yeah, sure," Dickie said. "Later."

Frankie finished his throw and motioned Walt over. Adlai was left alone with Dickie.

"So you're a man now, huh kid?" Dickie asked. "We gotta get you out to fuck. I'd bet odds you haven't had a good fuck yet."

Adlai felt a chill run through him despite the heat, that all too familiar yearning to dissolve everything near him, to flee the moment. "Why are we here?" Adlai said, echoing Walt.

Dickie spun, the glass in his beer sloshing out the top, wetting his pants. He leaned close to Adlai."You shut the fuck up. If Frankie wants us here, we're here.

Don't fuck this up for me runt."

Frankie returned to the table with Walt, his hand on Walt's shoulder. "There is a place for you. All of you, even the young one."

"Yeah, he saw a cock fight, now he's gotta get fucked," Dickie said, refilling his glass.

Adlai took up a glass of beer. Frankie and Walt each did the same and raised to toast.

"To new friendships," Frankie said. "You each have something to offer my family. If you can trust each other that is. To me family loyalty is religion. Trust is sacred. There is no betrayal. Not even in death."

They held their glasses in mid toast, but none touched, and from the distance came a gentle roar, a chaotic but soft thunder.

The three brothers held themselves steady in that long, still moment, keenly noticing each other, the nearness of one another, the bright scald of the sun on each of their young faces. Their arms remained raised and at equal distance, Adlai's hand trembling slightly as he tried to keep the glass aloft. It was as if Frankie had suddenly and without warning forced something on them, a new thing none of them could or would recognize. They would not acknowledge the dark, visceral and strong probability of betrayal.

Dickie gave up on the toast, snapped his arm down and drank his glass full in a swift shot. Then he turned away and looked to the sky. "They said it would rain. I don't see it coming."

"No, you don't," Frankie said. "I had an Aunt who was a soothsayer of sorts. She could predict things."

"We had an uncle like that," Adlai said softly, as an afterthought.

Frankie looked closely at the boy, but Walt and Dickie seemed not to hear or notice. Walt strayed away from the group, back to the bocce balls which he threw aimlessly, and Dickie kept his eye on the horizon, as if expecting a thrashing display of lightning.

They continued to drink and finished the game, as slowly, the sky took on an odd grey in its blue, like a blurred transition, not clouds, just a thin nearly translucent tone, then a dark rash, as the rumble edged closer.

At the first drop of rain, Frankie shook all of their hands and sent them away.

six

It rained steadily, though gently, as they drove back to the city. Pat asked them to meet him at O'Reilly's bar for a drink. They were in Dickie's car, the older brothers in front, Adlai in back.

Dickie drove recklessly and fast. "What's going on with Pop?"

Adlai leaned forward, and Walt turned. Their father was the one thing that unified them, that they agreed on and discussed, as if he were the errant child, they a triumvirate parent.

"Yeah, is he sick?" Walt said.

Adlai thought to speak of the document he'd read, but he did not. He felt that odd chill again, though this time it was pleasurable. He had a secret with his father, he realized. He had something they did not have and may never have.

"Is he drinking?" Dickie said.

"No. He's at the shop, whistling, talking to the customers. It's the opposite of when he drinks," Walt said.

Dickie sped up. There was a wild finger of lightning directly in front of them, a distant bellow of thunder, and the rain gushed. The windshield was overwhelmed, but Dickie did not slow.

"I need to ask you something." Walt glanced at Adlai, who had sat back in his seat again.

Without looking Dickie seemed to know Walt was considering their younger brother. "Go on, we're all working together now."

The rain was beating down in a steady, even rush.

"Adriana's father says he's going to take her away," Walt said. "I can't let that happen."

They were crossing into the city, and Dickie slowed.

"So what do you want?" Dickie said. Hands on the wheel, he turned and looked directly at Walt. "Tell me what you really want. I'm your brother."

Adlai watched the two, a frame of blurred water behind them on the windshield, as if that were the screen they were being projected onto. He thought again of the document, of that final night when Cahal talked with his brother Brandon. He suddenly felt haunted and frightened by what he'd read, as if it could harm him, as if the knowing of it could be a horrible thing.

"I want him to go away, to leave and go back to Argentina. I want to marry her and keep her here with me."

Dickie smiled. "Yeah, all right," he said.

The remainder of the ride was in silence, each brother drifting back into the familiar place of oneness. That slender connectedness of need concerning their father was obliterated by hidden desires, each one's ceaseless and solitary determination to remain hidden. Those desires that, in truth, were inescapably intertwined.

s.e.v.e.n

The three brothers sat together at a booth, forming a perfect triangle, looking at each other. The two older brothers, Walt and Dickie, had many times faced one another talking late into the night, bleary-eyed tales of girls and fights. But never had the three sat together in such a way. Adlai had always been away, sometimes near but never equal. Now he was one of them.

They were at O' Reilly's, a dark and empty Irish bar on the West side. Pat sat at the bar up front, talking evenly and slowly to the old barkeep, and left his boys alone in the booth in back.

"Why you look so fucking different?" Dickie said to Adlai.

Dickie was alone on one side of the booth. Walt and Adlai were across from him. He bought them all whiskey, the hard amber liquor in wide-lipped tumblers that were both elegant and dirty. Dickie was staring at Adlai, who colored but kept his eyes level.

Adlai sipped his drink. "I guess I'm getting older."

Dickie leaned across the table. "No. You look like the same Rat. But you move differently. You talk slower. If I didn't know better I'd swear you were getting fucked by some big tit broad. That would do it," Dickie said.

Adlai blushed deeper and looked away.

Dickie snickered and gulped his whiskey. "We are all gonna work for Corigliano. He didn't tell me what you two will do or when. Maybe nothing much at first. The point is he's thinking about all of us. Like a team. Even you, Rat."

Walt looked into his whiskey glass but did not drink. "You know what I need."

Adlai was the only one drinking.

"What's with that girl's old man anyway?" Dickie said.

Again Dickie looked at Adlai, as if the youngest brother's new inclusion was marked by a role of matriarch, the femininity in him so obvious so as not to be spoken of, this paired with an unmentioned assumption that the softer had instincts not known to the others. Adlai kept sipping his drink and shrugged. Dickie shifted his gaze to Walt. Walt downed his whiskey then began, wiping a yellowish dribble from under his lip.

"Adriana's father will force her to go back to Argentina with him," Walt said. "I need to get her away from him. We need to make him leave on his own. Go back to Argentina."

"Can't you just take her away?" Dickie said. "Fuck the old man."

Walt lifted the dirty tumbler, staring into its depths, as if some fortune teller's tea leaves would reveal a truth. "She refuses to run away. She says she can't do that to her father. She thinks we can convince him to see it our way in time, but I know that's impossible. He will trick her. He will get her away, and that will be the end," Walt said, this time more softly.

Dickie smiled. "Then we will make sure her father leaves this country alone." He took his glass and poured a small amount of liquor into each of his brother's now empty glasses. He made a toast. The chime of the tumbler's mingling was loud in the quiet joint

Pat rose and moved to them. He stood for a moment, then sat next to his oldest son, breaking the triangle.

"I'll figure it out, Walt," Dickie said.

"Figure what out?" Pat asked.

"Business stuff."

Pat leaned in eagerly, happily like a boy. "I'm glad to see my son's working together. That's as it should be."

He looked at Adlai, and the boy kept his eyes down and then quickly got up and went to fetch them all more whiskey, not knowing if Pat would share the secret, that tale he had read, that history. He was lately afraid of his father's stares. Adlai returned with more liquor. He sat, and then Pat began.

"I think I should tell you boys something," he said.

Adlai's shoulders fell, crestfallen, sure of what was coming, sure of what he would now lose. They would all know the story of Cahal, and it would no longer be special.

"Your mother. It's about your mother," Pat said.

Adlai sat up, listening.

"You cannot be made or broken by a woman. I think I always knew that. But I blamed her."

The three turned to him, listening intently, younger now, warmer with the latest whiskey, gentler somehow. There was the lightest toll of glass from the bar. The old barkeep was rinsing the dirty tumblers, aimlessly and with little focus, as the stains would never be removed.

"She left once you were all born, as if three boys were enough. Like something religious, like that would do me," Pat said. "She whored around. She was young and pretty and loose, and she whored about. I was young, and I worked the shop, and I turned a mean eye, I say mean because ignoring it was not what your mother wanted. Everyone knew what she was up to, and the more they knew the more I ignored it. I was never quite well after the war, and I felt less than a man, and she flounced around in summer dresses. There were always flowers on her dresses. I don't know why, but I recall that. She just did it like that, and I took it and was pitied, and then she left. One day she just left. I think she'd begun to pity me too, and that was too much for her to bear."

They all sat still. There was a calm in the silence, and they all felt it. They took it without grief or judgment, since they had never truly seen her or known her (though Dickie had scant memories), and she did not exist really, did not matter. It was as if she were that religious thing, that legend, something both revered and ridiculous, not believed yet feared, though now she was soiled and putrid. It was as if they had been born of something that never existed, as if she had not been part of it at all, rather that some long, dark, warm river had spat them up, she delivering them just so she could flee. Her sacrifice, of sorts.

The three brothers no longer looked at their father; they cast their eyes to the floorboards. Pat got up and went back to the bar. They listened to the sound of water rinsing over glasses, the muffled settling as the barkeep finished up. Pat ordered another whiskey.

"Let's do this right away," Dickie said, leaning across the table and grabbing the wrist of Walt, holding him like he wanted to yank him away. "Let's get this done for you brother. You understand? I will take care of this thing for you."

Walt did not move, nor did Adlai, nor, for a long while, did Dickie.

eight

Walt had a dream that he did not wish to share with Adriana. He was not like Dickie, not plagued by ceaseless night images that frightened him. He had never woken with the memory of nonsensical things like eels and bloody sawdust. He had always slept undisturbed and often thought that part of his older brother's problem was lack of pure sleep. That could be part of what kept Dickie mean.

But today, upon waking, the residue of a dream was bright and clear and it gave Walt pause. He shunned it, knowing he had to meet his girl. Walking to see her that late afternoon, though, he could not stop thinking of the dream. He was in a cotton field and it was extremely hot. The field was completely white since all of the bulbs had bloomed at the same moment. He was there, but he could not see himself. Then it rained soot, and the field turned black.

It meant nothing to him, but the fact that it was the first truly memorable dream that he could recall disturbed him, especially since it came after he made a deal with Dickie to fix things so he and Adriana could be together. He had not asked Dickie what his plan was. Whether he was going to strong-arm Adriana's father into leaving, or trick him somehow. Dickie was convinced it all had to be done quickly. If Adriana and her father suddenly left the country, all could be lost.

He paused at a street crossing. There was a frail tree, bleached in the heat, still and unmoving. He wondered how trees like that could survive the long, hot summer. He was meeting Adriana at a bar. As he continued, he realized he hoped a drink would calm him. If only she would elope with him, discard her father's demands. But she would not. She made that clear. He moved slowly down the street toward the small, nondescript bar he had chosen. It was a dive. Nearing the bar, he moved more and more slowly. He was uncertain and forgot why he had even asked her to meet. He couldn't tell her about the plan to get her father to leave. It came to him that if he got Adriana pregnant, she would have no choice but to marry him. But how could he assure that?

He stopped a block from the bar, near an alley littered with trash and a good number of liquor bottles. He realized he very much needed a drink. In the distance he saw a woman hurry into the bar, and thought it was Adriana and was afraid for her, being alone in that dirty place. But he could not move, because he needed to appear normal. He knew he was going to deceive her, to trick her, and he turned into the alley, into its dim shadowy stench and claustrophobic disgust. He bent over and wretched. Then he straightened himself, wiped his mouth and continued on, disregarding the lost and empty stillness in him that said turn back, the dim wretchedness that said, *This is not you.* He moved quickly to the bar, driven now by a new ugliness that he had not known existed in him.

nine

He bought Eva a dress. It was pure silk, deep, dark red, like blood mixed with hot tar, and it had these tiny bits on it that at first Dickie thought were butterflies, but upon closer inspection, he saw were nothing but flecks. When she entered the room, her with that shape, those breasts so full and flush against silk, the flecks swirled and blew like creatures flying. He decided to bring her with him, her in that dress, to his meeting with Frankie Corigliano.

It wasn't until he saw her and saw Frankie seeing her, until he felt the tension and the quiet fall over the room just because of her, it wasn't until that moment that he realized how proud he was to have her, and that he wanted to keep her around for good. He wanted to own her.

Frankie had an office downtown in the city. On the door it said Giuseppe's Cakes, which was a bakery Dickie had heard about. The office was in a small nondescript building, but once inside, it was all swank and glamour. Frankie had done it up with wood panels, leather sofas, a mahogany desk and a full stocked bar. It was like some hot-shot lawyer's office in a movie, Dickie thought.

"Can I get you a drink?" Frankie said to Eva directly.

He stood up, keeping his eye on the girl. Dickie felt Frankie's desire for Eva and was glad for it. He wanted Frankie to want something of his. He wanted the Wop to dream about getting under that dress, to ache for something that he'd never get.

"Have we met?" Frankie said.

"I was at your party," Eva said. She blew smoke to the ceiling. "I'll have whiskey."

Frankie went around to the bar. He was wearing one of his fancy suits, all buttoned up, shined-up shoes and slicked down hair. Dickie wondered how many guys he'd have to knock off before he'd be able to wear suits like that every day.

"Where'd you get that suit?" Dickie said.

Frankie faced the bar that lined one side of one wall, lots of fancy glasses and decanters. There was a big mirror that covered the back part of the bar. Dickie could see Frankie's face in the mirror. "A tailor in Little Italy," Frankie said.

"I'll have whiskey too," Dickie said.

He was watching Frankie's back, but also studying his face in the bar mirror. Frankie was staring at him, as if deciding whether he'd give him a drink or not. Dickie smiled, and Frankie smiled back, all through that glass reflection, and that seemed to break a mounting tension that neither of them fully understood. Frankie came around and delivered their drinks, then sat at his desk, giving his attention to Dickie.

"So you wanted to ask me something?" Frankie said.

The only sound in the room was the slow, light touch of ice on glass. Eva was swirling the liquor around. Dickie noticed the lights were not on in the room. He was in a chair facing the big desk where Frankie sat a few feet away. He wanted to move closer, but he didn't know how to accomplish that without seeming too eager.

"I know I just started with you, and this might not sit quite right but I need a favor," Dickie said.

Frankie sat back in his chair. From Eva came the gentle sound of ice on glass.

"Can I get you another?" Frankie said to Eva.

"She's fine," Dickie said sharply.

"All right."

Dickie stood up and moved to the bar to fill his own drink. Moving helped him think. He felt a familiar tension, a tightening across his back that steeled him in a fight. He took a deep breath. He liked taking things by force, not having to ask for them. But Frankie was different.

"There's someone I need to get rid of. It's personal. A family thing. But I need it to be real quiet," Dickie said.

"Of course," Frankie said.

"He's a doctor. My brother wants to marry his daughter, but he won't let it happen. I want to make it look like he left the country. I can do the job easy, but it's all the details where I need your help," Dickie said, facing Frankie now.

Frankie leaned forward in his chair, which made seeing his facial expressions easier.

"This is for your brother, Walt?"

Dickie nodded. He felt his shoulders rising, that faint call to battle he always felt when people mentioned his brothers. Frankie stood up and walked over to a window, looking out at the street, giving them his back.

"There is nothing more precious than family, am I right?" Frankie said. He turned from the window and walked toward Dickie. "You and your family will be part of my family. Which means you owe your allegiance to me. You get that?"

"My brothers too?" Dickie said.

Frankie reached the bar and refilled his drink. Then he filled Dickie's drink, then crossed the room and filled Eva's. He positioned himself in the center of the room, Dickie and Eva at equal distance from him now.

"I can use them at some point, leave it to me." Frankie said. "There are many ways to work with reliable men."

"Adlai. I don't know about him. He's not like us," Dickie said. "He won't be any use to you."

Frankie smiled. "He may surprise you," he said, lifting his glass. "To family."

Dickie, and Eva who was lost a bit in shadow, raised their glasses, and they all drank.

"You need to do it just like I tell you. Walt drives. Adlai keeps an eye out. You go in and do the job, then you call me," Frankie said. "Understand?"

Dickie felt a fierce shot of fire up his back. It was as if his skin were being ripped off, and some strange all but forgot fidelity, like a pact between he and his brothers, a pact too old to put into words but brilliantly alive in his gut, was being threatened. It was, he knew, some ancient call to battle. He also knew that at this moment, he was not the one in control.

"I can do it alone, like the guy with the boat," Dickie said. "My brothers don't know what I'm planning. They'll complicate things."

Frankie was still.

"You do it exactly as I just told you. That's how it works," Frankie said. "There is no discussion."

Dickie thought of his brothers, they each distant from him and not at all like him. There was a long dull moment where he tried to pull up in his mind's eye his dream, that ceaseless haunting thing that connected him to his brothers, because they were the two who would listen, who would ask him to tell it. The room which had been dim, grey and autumnal, like a dying winter day, slowly began to brighten, as if by some other-worldly force, as if a flaming eye were casting down on him, light and showing him this was the time to flee. Or the time for redemption. Unobtrusively, a woman in black had moved about the room bringing up lamp lights. She stood at the door waiting for some word from Frankie.

"You can see them out, Magdalena," Frankie said. "I'll get things set up so this can all go very smoothly for you Dickie."

Eva went to Dickie's side, and she took his hand, but he did not move. Frankie turned to the window, and Dickie stared at the man's strong back, the slithering pin lines that ran through his expensive suit. Eva tugged him a little, and because he could think of nothing to say, knew he had no power in this moment, Dickie allowed her to guide him out, like a beast secretly wounded, but afraid to let on even the slightest scent of blood.

ten

It was early morning, not long after dawn, which is how Frankie had laid it out. He was very particular about exactly how the job had to be done. Dickie had shut off the car not far from the Doctor's apartment building. He had a knife from the shop, sharpened and in a sheath. It was the type of knife used to bleed a pig. The blade would pierce the skin if barely touched.

Do it in the bathroom, Frankie said. Knock the old man out. Put him in the tub. Cut his throat. Do it fast and get out. Frankie's men would take care of the rest. No guns. He wanted a clean slice and dice. Best way to make a man disappear was in pieces.

Dickie wondered if Frankie was being a smart ass, making fun of his work at the butcher shop. But he went along with it. He just wanted this thing done. He thought of bringing a gun anyway, but at the last minute left it behind. There was something about the way Frankie emphasized every last detail. Like this was a test to see if Dickie would obey. He'd show that fucking Frankie. He'd do this job perfectly, then he'd start getting his power back. And then he'd buy Eva a mink.

Dickie did not tell his brothers the details of what would happen. Walt still thought his brother had come up with some way to convince the man, to scare him and make him see reason and agree to leave town. Adlai never said anything.

Dickie glanced in the rearview mirror. His brothers sat still, hands in lap, groggy and half awake, looking no more like brothers than some giant and a peasant boy. He hated that they were here. He didn't like involving his brothers in the dirty work. But Frankie insisted. Fucking Frankie.

From the back seat Adlai looked up, and their eyes met in the rear view mirror, and for a moment, there was something hot and urgent in that boy's gaze and harder then Dickie had seen ever before. It was as if he knew what was going to happen. Dickie looked away. He cleared his throat.

"I won't be long. You both get in front. Walt, you drive," he said.

"We're not going in?" Walt said.

"No. I'll take care of this. It will be easier this way."

In the stillness, they could hear their own breathing. Dickie realized he was sighing. He needed to get this done.

"It seems like it will take time. To make sure he understands," Walt said. "What are you going to say to convince him to leave town?"

"Just get in front. Have the car running. I'll take care of this alone."

"Then why are we here?" Adlai said.

Dickie looked again in the rearview and there were those hot eyes, too much to look at, like he was some damn fortune teller. Something was wrong with that kid.

"I'm going now," Dickie said, turning around to look at them. "Just trust me."

Then he was out of the car.

Walt watched his brother hurry up the sidewalk, and he thought 'I need to get out, I need to stop him. This isn't right.'

"So I guess we get up front," Adlai said. He got out of the car, then he sat up front. Walt did not move.

"I think I should go after him," Walt said.

"That would likely wreck it. I'm sure he has a plan. You know Dickie."

Things had not gone well with Adriana when Walt met her for a drink. She did not believe in this, that her father could change his mind. She said it was useless, which terrified Walt. Panic had overwhelmed him in that dark little bar, and he drank too much, and he began to think she was slipping out of his grasp. He didn't like turning things over to Dickie without knowing the plan, but he felt increasingly desperate. He knew Adriana's father could take her away at any time. He was a very smart man.

But this didn't seem right either, and he had a strong, urgent sense of foreboding.

"Well you best get up here," Adlai said.

Walt saw his younger brother's neck, the nape of it barely above the seat. He still had the look of a child. But he had changed. For so long, he was a shadow, an after thought, that other piece that had little to do with anything. Yet since his party, his turning 16, he had begun to speak up, and more than that, when he looked at you, his gaze was steady and strange and fearless. Walt didn't understand it at all. It was the look of a man who had been to war, or who had seen death.

He went out and sat in the driver's seat. Adlai turned and smiled at him. Walt wondered why they boy was so calm. It wasn't right.

"What is he going to do in there?" Walt said.

Adlai glanced out the window. Then he reached in his pocket, took out a cigarette and lit it.

"What are you doing?" Walt said.

"I'm smoking a cigarette."

There was a strange evenness to Adlai's voice. It was uncanny, Walt thought. He was beginning to sweat, though not from the heat, since it had broken and at this early hour it was very pleasant. There was a scent of jasmine. He tried to look in the driver's side rearview mirror, but it was cracked down the center, and everything was skewed.

"How long has it been since he went in?" Walt said.

"A few minutes." Adlai

Walt looked in the cracked mirror again to see if anyone was nearby, and he wondered if he could run to the building and stop this. Sweat built up on his face and was dripping down onto the seat. He did not know why he was so hot.

His younger brother was staring at him. "Are you sick? You're shaking, Walt."

Walt lifted his hands to the steering wheel, and they trembled then began to shake. He couldn't stop them from shaking. "You don't understand." His hands shook, and he put them on the steering wheel to try to stop them, but it didn't help. He still smelled jasmine, and he decided he needed to go in there after Dickie.

"You're in love. We do crazy things for that. I understand," Adlai said.

There was that low, steady evenness to the boy's voice that did not make sense, but there was a calming motion to it. It gave Walt the courage to go after Dickie.

"We need to go in there now. All right? We have to."

Adlai smiled. "Okay."

Walt got out of the car, as did his brother, and they walked to the building. Walt's legs were trembling too now, and he laced his fingers together to stop his hands from shaking. His body was in motion but not in his control. He had never fainted before, but he thought he could now. For a moment he stopped and leaned on Adlai. The boy was shorter and frail, but he held him up.

"You all right? It may be already over. It may be all right," Adlai said.

Walt took a breath and continued, at a swifter pace. They entered the building and went fast to the elevator and rode up, he was wet now with sweat, and in this wretched state of panic, but now more determined and hopeful because he was near.

Then they heard the gun shot.

The elevator doors opened on the Doctor's floor, and they both went quickly to the apartment, past an elderly woman in a robe with a ravaged and startled face who was peering out her door. They went into the Doctor's apartment.

Dickie was on the floor, gripping his own bloody leg. The Doctor, in a strange and almost lacy looking black robe, stood near the window, his face ancient in a hard morning light that was now rising, his hair wild, and his robe open, revealing glimpses of withering nakedness. He was smiling, and he had the look of a vile unbalanced beast.

Adlai went to help Dickie up. Walt was facing the Doctor.

"You think you can come in here with your cheap butcher's knife," the Doctor said, stopping to cough, and lean on a chair. "You don't think I know how you stupid animals think?"

The Doctor held a gun limply, and continued to cough, his robe folding open to reveal his limp, lifeless form and skin that had a slightly violet tinge to it. "I am of a line of Argentinean men who are not to be fucked with. You are ridiculous." His voice rose to a shrill note as he moved toward Walt, who stood in the center of the room. Walt's face was wet, was crimson, as if underneath his skin the flesh was on fire. The Doctor began to swing the pistol as if it were an appendage, not a weapon.

"You are a disgusting and stupid man--you are going to be put away in some place for men like you, a prison all of you. Your life is over," he said. "And my daughter never loved you. What a fool you are. She told me she had to get away from you, that you were a beast. We are leaving today."

The Doctor lifted the pistol over his head, as if he were going to shoot it in the air. The surge in Walt, which had begun not even that day, but rather the day before at the dark little bar when Adriana had begun to pull away, that surge of vile, black need, of heart-torn desperation, had come fully to the surface now. Walt saw not a man before him, more a soulless, evil and disgusting thing, like any bled and gutted carcass that had rotted and needed to be cast aside.

Walt moved forward only a few steps to the frail and half naked Doctor. He gripped the man by the neck, and with great force and that surging and now-clear blood-lust, he snapped his head to the left. As he held the man aloft, dead now, he felt finally calm, only distracted by his brother Adlai yelling that they had to go, and the hard, ragged and constant scream of Adriana, who had crept out of the bedroom and fallen to the floor.

eleven

A surge. A wailing from the insects in the country, deep country, black night, loose, slow airless country. The brute heat forgotten due to the scream of unseen and miniscule things, they overwhelming everything with their unifying power, their music.

The window was open, and there was no screen. Anything could crawl in. The black at the window was pure and silky, but the long, constant song of the bugs made it clear things were out there in the night. The kitchen was worn but not decayed, despite the fact that it had not been set foot in for years. There was no running water, but a creek out back and a well in use. An out house. There was a rustic table made of walnut. The smoothness of its edges gave the impression that someone had put much care into the making of it.

Dickie ran his hand along the edge of the table, fascinated by the craftsmanship. He figured his kin made the table.

He had surrendered to the constant noise, the crickets, tree frogs, cicadas, because after a time, the timeless and constant crescendos became like a wind in winter you could not bother paying attention to. It simply was.

"It was that robe. That flouncy robe the Doc was wearing," Dickie said. "It made me stop for just that second, so he could run like a woman into the bedroom. I talked low and slow just saying come out. Let's talk this out and get things straight. I had the knife ready, which is how Frankie said I had to do it. No guns, only a knife. I still don't get why Frankie made me do it that way."

Dickie put his hand on his leg at the spot where the bullet had been removed.

That scar ached something terrible.

"I should have just gone right in after him. But there was that girly robe and he looked half-dead already. And I had to get him into the bathroom like Frankie said. That made sense since I had to cut him. Then the Doc runs out, wild and shrill, like a crazy old woman, and shoots me."

It was as if the insects, the thousands out there in the blackness, were giving Dickie's hapless tale an orchestration, a weight that it didn't deserve. The outcome, where he and his brothers had landed, was increasingly desperate and dark, but the actuality of the episode, being outsmarted by an old man, was pathetic. Dickie knew it.

There was a window near the kitchen sink, and despite the chaos of night noise, Walt's voice swept in. He was cussing aimlessly. It sounded as if he had fallen in the back yard. Eva, in a loose robe, holding a grey and chipped dinner dish at the sink, looked out the window toward the sound of Walt's rant, which shifted from an angry growl to a softer cry not far from longing. She glanced at Dickie, then went back to washing things with the water she'd hauled in from the creek.

"He's got to stop drinking so much," Dickie said.

"He lost everything," she said.

Eva finished the dishes but remained at the sink, looking out into the night. Dickie studied her, the shape of her, and he wanted to have her there, in the kitchen. He was glad she had come along, though he both loved and hated his constant desire for her. He was shirtless, in loose boxer underwear, his hair greasy and unwashed, his face unshaven. He couldn't help but feel like a bandit, something he liked, but he knew that what he had done had put his brothers and even his father in danger.

Strangely, their father, Pat, provided the answer to their plight. The night after the murder, the three of them, crazed and clinging at one another like boys, ran to their father. He sat them down and told them what to do. There was this house, this run down place in the country a few hours out of the city. It had belonged to Pat's Uncle Brandon, who had willed it to Pat. Pat had left the house to rot, as if the memory of the giving was too much to bear, as if the past for him was an illusion he wished to never engage. The boys knew nothing of it.

He sent them here, and Dickie had insisted on Eva coming; a woman to help would be good. Walt and Adlai, though both now deeply against this, at the time were too distraught to question it. Adlai had muttered that night, over and over to them all and to Pat, about bringing Big Ed, that he would protect them, but Adlai was easily shut up. Pat told Adlai he would bring Ed with him when he followed later that week.

The house, despite being cast aside years ago, had survived, like an ancient heirloom lost in an attic corner. There were two bedrooms, a small living room and kitchen and a few sticks of furniture that had been left. The place had life about it, as if it had been lived in all along, or as if some ghost had lingered, thrown open the windows to keep air moving, shifted the few chairs and tables and lain in the beds. There was a layer of dust covering everything, nearly like a protective skin to keep the place from crumbling.

The first night they'd stepped in, Dickie felt, though his mind was ravaged and torn to pieces, as if he had been there, as if he belonged. There was a phantom-like other-worldliness to the place which struck him as odd and beautiful. He had not lingered on it though because he was so tired. He simply felt it in his bones. He thought it odd that the house did not smell like some discarded and ugly thing. It did not stink of rotting things or have shit from animals who'd crept in to take hold of it. It smelled sort of sweet perhaps due to the pungent perfume from flowering trees nearby. It was a home, he thought. He realized he never thought of the place he shared with his brothers, the apartment above the butcher shop, as a home.

Now, in the kitchen, he listened to Walt's lingering cry far out in the yard. Dickie wondered if his brothers thought the house odd.

"Adlai, you out there?" Dickie called into the living room.

There was a rustling from the other room, a soft and coy shifting as if a small animal had crept in to sniff about. Things were silent, then Adlai came into the kitchen. Eva turned and smiled, but Adlai stayed at the doorway.

"Come in and sit down," Dickie said.

Adlai did not move. The kid had changed, Dickie knew. Seeing a murder would do it. Plus, since his party, that cock fight and all that, he seemed to have grown up. He didn't jump when Dickie spoke; he didn't cower so much.

Adlai did come in, but he stood at the table. He too was wearing nothing but white boxer underwear. It was so hot, and there were no fans, only the water from the creek. They all had taken to wearing very little, and moving sluggishly about. Waiting on something horrible to happen, really, though none knew exactly what.

"So?" Adlai said.

"Sit down, I want to talk to you," Dickie said.

Eva remained at the sink, looking almost a little afraid. She said little to anyone other than Dickie. Adlai stuck a cigarette into his mouth, which he had been cradling in his palm. He struck a match on the table and lit it. Dickie looked at the kid.

"You think this place is funny?" Dickie said.

Adlai dragged on the cigarette, then blew a small ring and looked at Eva.

"Not funny like a joke, more like it was lived in, like somebody was here,"

Dickie said.

Eva smiled absently at Adlai.

"I don't know," Adlai said. "I guess I thought it would be more dirty. Animals nesting."

"Yeah," Dickie said.

Dickie turned to Eva and thought it would be nice to get her back in the bedroom. He'd take her there now. That would shoo away this creepy feeling he had.

"Is Pop coming? He said he was coming. We don't know what's going on in the city," Adlai said. "Yeah, he said that. He'll be here soon."

Dickie got up and motioned to Eva. She smiled again at Adlai, then followed her lover into their room. Adlai drew on his cigarette, then he stubbed it out and laid his head down on the table and shut his eyes.

twelve

Adlai woke from one dream, stepping hard into another, one set of screams turning over and over, as if being thrown around in distant air. Lifting his cheek from the kitchen table, he heard the screams and saw nothing. He sat in darkness, which furthered the sense of being submerged in a nocturnal netherworld.

His new dream, that dream he'd found after his birthday party, that dream of water and blue, had gone ugly lavender, rather, had gotten mixed up with blood and the floating carcasses of gutted sheep, floating aimlessly, and somehow, screaming.

Looking around the kitchen, seeing nothing but a wash of black, he heard the screaming still, strong and full of living things. It was a high-pitched cry, a screech. It was, of course, the damned cicadas, and he was alone in the kitchen of a strange and new house. Being only half awake made it all seem mad and magical, and he immediately yearned for Ed. It was a physical yearning. His body hurt, as if a rash of soars had blown onto him in the night, as if bones had cracked, and he were misshapen and old and bruised. He spoke aloud.

"Ed?"

Only cicadas returned his call, with their frantic cry. He did not hear even the drunken moan of his broken brother, Walt, or the furtive, half-muffled yelps of Dickie and that whore Eva fucking. Silence, save for the night things out in the yard. That strange, unnerving song. He hated it. The house, these insects. They'd only been at this hiding place a few days, and he felt as if he could not stand it another second. He needed Ed.

He thought again of the dream, as he knew it would dissolve, as dreams do. It would be completely gone if he stood and lit a candle and got a glass of water. He wanted to remember the details of those ugly gutted sheep, because he believed dreams meant something, but already, it was being stripped away from his mind, and the dryness of his mouth bothered him. Looking down, he realized he was only in his underdrawers and that he was aching, and he suddenly knew that he loved Ed. He also knew they would be together always. This was clear to him, though the timing of it, not in the man's arms, nowhere near him, but in a strange kitchen in the middle of the night, the timing of it was strange. But he accepted it as fact. It did not matter that he had not thought of it so fully until now. Plus, things often felt clearest to Adlai right after he woke. As time wore on, he doubted.

He stood up, still aroused, embarrassed despite the fact that nobody was around. That stupid woman Eva could creep in. He did not like her, did not trust her. He knew his dislike was due to his jealousy over the fact that she was here, and Ed was not. That Dickie, despite his botching the job and wrecking everything, still controlled their situation.

He pressed at his crotch to tame it, though that did not work, only made it worse, and he went to the sink for a drink, then recalled there was no running water. He'd have to go out to the creek. There was a side door to the house that led from the kitchen into the back yard and further to the woods and the creek. He stepped out, and there was a bright moon. He stretched, still thinking of Ed. Ahead, the moon was wild and full, the kind that seemed too large, and out of proportion to the sky. He could see the yard clearly with that bright moon, his feet cool on the downy grass despite the night's heat. The yard stretched out toward a wide field and an orchard of some kind after that. Off to the right of the field was a mild ravine that shot down to a creek.

He moved slowly, still a bit groggy, and came across dry scratchy patches of grass. He bent and touched the grass with his palm. There were a few dandelions on the lawn, and bending further, then crawling along the yard he plucked several, holding them together in a make-shift bouquet. He thought again of his lover, Ed, and he gave up trying to curb his lust. He continued to crawl, clutching the wild yellow weeds, until his knees hurt. He stood as he came to the edge of the small ravine that led to the creek.

His mouth was terribly dry. He took one of the dandelions and placed it on his tongue.

He'd read somewhere that flowers and plants held moisture. It was bitter, dry, and he spit it out. Beyond the constant cry of the insects, he heard the mild rustling of the creek. He was moved, alone here, under that unusually large moon with the handful of flowers, hearing the sweet call of the creek. He shuddered.

As he entered the ravine area, which was shrouded by willowy summer trees that blotted out the moon and offered therefore a darker, dreamier landscape, he noticed clumps of flowering bushes at the perimeter, almost like a gateway. He could make out small white flowers, and he touched them, then snapped a few off. That breaking sent out a rush of scent. As he fondled the tiny white bulbs, their fragrance came stronger, and he rubbed the flowers over his cheeks, then onto his chest. He would take Ed here, he thought, he would rub the flowers on Ed.

Adlai continued, feeling odd and giddy, into the shrouded ravine area, which sloped down to the creek. The ground was stickier, and there were needles of some sort pricking his feet. He moved more deftly, quickly across the area, the piney things digging at him and cutting into him. He ran a few feet, through darkness again, as if back into a dream. At the water's edge though, there was light. Above the creek he saw sky and the moon lashing its glow into the streaming water. He stepped in. The water was cool and soothed his cut-up feet. It barely came up to his knees. It was a shallow waterway, rushing down further into the ravine area, where to he was not sure. Standing on one leg, balancing himself, he removed his underdrawers, and cast them toward the shore, but his throw was short and they flew back into the creek, swallowed by the mild current, snaking downstream.

He stood naked for a moment, then gently, lowered himself down to a lying position in the creek, so the water was forced to rush around him, as if he were a torn branch fallen from storm. The cooling water swarmed around his head, swirling out and into and through him. He was mostly submerged, though not fully. He felt the water like gentle hands, like a rushing dream come back. With one hand, he tried to cup water to bring it to his parched lips, but it kept spilling out, so he flipped over and let water gush into his mouth, rushing forcefully, as if molesting and bruising his lips, choking him. So thirsty, he gulped, then flipped over again, letting the coolness take him.

He wondered if Ed could fit next to him, the bulk of that man in the narrow creek. Looking up, he again spied the moon, and for the first time that night, that week really, the insect's music, which was awash with the gentle cry of the creek, comforted him. It was as if they were now singing for him, as if it were a love song, a lullaby.

thirteen

It was dawn, and Pat was over an old wood burning stove shaking a skillet. He was the only one fully dressed, though the air was sweet, and the sun had yet to throw itself into the kitchen making things hot. There was merely a wash of soft light. The insects were silent, just a few distant birds calling to one another.

Dickie and Walt were at the table watching their father. Together the brothers had found an old ax in a shed out back and gone to chopping at things. Dickie was a bit melancholy, imagining an ax may have played a role in that life of violence and power he'd surely wrecked. Pat, who knew something of the crudeness of the house, their hide-away, had arrived late during the night with Ed, bringing abundant supplies.

He was frying bacon at the stove. Eva, just woken, stood at the kitchen doorway. She found a chair in a corner, away from the table and sat, covering herself as best as the scant silk robe would allow. She threw a scent about the room which they all vaguely noticed, despite the searing odor of the meat. They'd none of them spoken yet.

"Well it's done." Pat wiped greasy hands at his pants, looking about for something to serve the bacon on.

Eva went to the cabinet above the sink and pulled down the chipped china that had been left there. She held it near Pat.

"Come close," he said.

She did, and he deposited the fried strips.

"Thank you dear," he said.

She smiled and set the plate on the table, where the brothers went at it with bare hands, slightly ravenous, since they'd only had things in cans until then. Eva retreated to her corner chair.

"I have good news," Pat said.

There was a mild shuffling sound coming from outside. The kitchen door that led to the yard began to open, and Dickie stood up quickly. He moved to the sink, grabbing the rusted ax. He went to the door and raised it like some mad warrior. The door swung open, but no one was there.

"Who's in there," Adlai called from outside, hidden.

"What?" Dickie said.

"I fell asleep," Adlai called again.

Dickie, still holding the ax, went to the door and peered out. "Where's your clothes, Rat?" Dickie shook his head and moved back inside to the table to eat. "You best get back in the room for a bit Eva, he's naked as a jay bird."

Walt sat still, as if half-asleep, and Eva left the room. Pat went to the doorway and looked.

"You all right, son?" Pat said. "Wait out there until we get you something to put on."

There was a quiet, soft and lilting laugh from Adlai.

"Get your brother some drawers Dickie, so he can come in the house," Pat said.

Ed, who had been asleep on the floor in the other room, was in the kitchen now, holding underdrawers. He went to the door and stepped outside. There was an audible gasp from Adlai, then a rush of whispering.

"Eva, come on back," Dickie yelled.

They continued to eat the bacon. Ed came in from outside first, followed by Adlai wearing white underdrawers, many sizes too big. Adlai held them together at the waist, then quickly sat down in a chair at the table. He was flushed and smiling, his eyes darting to Ed, then back to Dickie who handed him a strip of bacon.

"You want to tell us why you're running around naked?" Dickie said. "Not that I give two fucks."

Eva crept back into her corner chair. Ed stayed near the kitchen door.

"So like I said, I have good news," Pat said. "It made the papers."

Dickie stopped eating. "Yeah, they talk about me?"

Pat took the black and greasy skillet to the sink. "She saved you, Walt."

Walt, who had moved little other than to eat—who in fact had moved ever so slightly since that awful night save to drink—looked up now from the table where he sat. "What?" he murmured.

"Adriana, she said it was three men, three black men who robbed them and killed him, she said she watched it all," Pat said. "There was an article in the paper."

Eva, off in the corner, made no sound save for the tiniest of sighs.

"What else?" Dickie said.

"There was an old woman. In the hall," Walt said.

Pat went back to the wood stove to check the fire. He put in a log from the floor. He had his back to them. "She was found dead. The old woman. She too had been robbed. A few furs and some jewelry," Pat said. "It was all in the paper."

Walt stood up. He was a big man, well built, though near Ed, he did not appear so large. He put his hand to his forehead, then he shut his eyes. Then he began to cry. They all sat quietly, awkwardly, and he fled through the kitchen door out to the yard.

"Must've been Frankie; he did his part. He made it look like that," Dickie said. "Maybe we're not lost after all."

Pat went and sat on the vacant chair. "You're brother is lost." He took Dickie's chin in his hand, and he looked closely into his eyes. "This is a chance son, this is a chance for you."

Dickie yanked his face away and stood so fast his chair toppled. Eva came to pick it up, but he pushed her away. Dickie looked at his father, this new man, this reborn species that seemed to think that, like some resurrected savior, he was their wise and ancient prophet.

"Don't ever touch me like that again old man," Dickie said. He turned and left, and Eva followed. Ed lingered at the doorway, then sat near Adlai, glancing at him furtively and often. Pat was at the stove.

"Do you want bacon, Ed?" Pat said. "We will all need to stay here. To make sure nothing resurfaces. It's been an ugly business, all of this. I closed up the shop for a while."

Ed nodded, and as Pat turned to the stove to cook, he reached under the table and swatted at Adlai's hand. He did not grab it or hold it, he simply swiped at it. Adlai sighed brightly.

"You seem to be happy today, son," Pat said. "Your brothers are troubled."

Pat was cooking, humming lightly, facing away from them, and Adlai went for Ed's hand under the table, grabbed the beastly thing, tried to squeeze it, though he had little power. Ed yanked his hand back in his lap and Adlai saw, from the side there, that Ed was aroused. Adlai blushed a high color and focused on his father.

"I will," Adlai said softly. "I will be strong, Pop."

Pat, humming more loudly, continued to fry the bacon, and the distant birds, more raucous now, sang a song familiar but somehow new and also chaotic, one crying to another, as the morning sun crept around and filled the kitchen with light and heat.

fourteen

Adlai had chosen a patch far off from the house, though not at all hidden, which Ed first balked at, but finally resigned to. It was a wide sunny patch of field with grass dried to nothing, some spurts of green, but mostly bleached out crabgrass and lone spikes of wild-flower stems burnt to disastrous peaks. They lay in the field, these two, one so large with mounds of muscle and flesh, the other lithe, tiny really, rolling about in the grass like the child he so recently was.

Adlai rolled over and straddled Ed, both of them naked and already slightly pinkish from the fierce sun. He liked to sit atop Ed, after they'd made love, to command him, much like a captain would his troops. Ed lolled flat with arms spread out, clutching the dried grass aimlessly, nervously, the weight of Adlai barely noticeable on his belly, just below his wide, pale chest. Adlai took a finger and ran it over Ed's eyelids. Then he pushed his hand up into Ed's mess of hair and yanked at it. Like a bear, just awake, just noticing a needy cub, Ed rolled the boy over and straddled him. He sat atop, the shadow of him eclipsing Adlai. He pressed his hands on the boy's shoulders, pinning him. Adlai feigned struggle, but liked it, liked to have Ed's full attention and weight. He could smell him too, the heat stoking up a scent, as beads of sweat fell from Ed's face onto Adlai's.

"I love you," Adlai said.

He had planned to say it that day, after his realization the night before, when he'd lost himself in the creek. But he didn't know exactly how or when. So there it is, he thought. He sighed, glad to have it out, shutting his eyes, not keen to look at Ed's face, or expression. He feared he may not like it. Adlai stayed still, eyelids shut tight. He felt Ed shifting back and forth, the sun pressing in when Ed moved to one side. He kept his eyes shut, feeling that odd shift of shadow then light. Then he felt Ed's tongue on his cheek, then his eyes, then his ears and he laughed and looked up at him. Ed's face was on his, and his eyes were startling and bright. Adlai reached around and grabbed Ed, pressing his tiny hands into all that bulk and muscle, around his ass and legs.

"You and me, we're stuck with each other you know that. Stuck together now," Ed said.

There was a rustling in the distance, and they both looked up, but the field was empty. It was a still, windless day. There was a small patch of trees not far off where the field met a hill. One of the trees had apples on the branches. The stray rustling came again, from that area of trees. They heard a low soft meowing. Ed sat up, then Adlai.

"Come on," Adlai said.

He ran toward the trees and the sound, feeling foolish and daring. Since the creek, he had been overcome with a constant, rushing giddiness. Running naked he felt strange, free in a way he'd never felt before. He wondered what would happen if anyone from the house saw him. How his brothers would react.

At the tree, shrouded under its shade, Adlai looked back. Ed gathered their clothes and was moving his way. He too remained undressed, but clutched their clothing tight to his chest betraying a soft shyness. The apple tree was vibrant, standing out from the other two saplings which had withered in the heat. Its branches remained hearty, and small green apples with blemishes of red hung in plenty. At the base of the tree was a smallish, wild cat staring boldly at Adlai. It did not move when Adlai reached down to pet it. Instead, it came to his leg, rubbing closely and purring, then bending back a narrow soft-haired neck and peering up longingly at the boy. Adlai picked the cat up.

"What are you doing with that?" Ed said.

Adlai turned, his pinkish skin softer now in the shade of the tree. The thin, brown cat hung limply in his arms. The cat reached a paw up to its mouth to lick it.

"So," Adlai said. "Do you love me back?"

The cat stared at Ed, as if too awaiting an answer. It held one paw in its tiny mouth.

"Yes," Ed said.

The sound of a shot startled them, though it was from the distance. The cat flailed a bit but did not leap away. In his mind, Adlai compared the sound of the shot to the one he had heard in the hallway, on the way to the Doctor's apartment. This shot was heavier, as if some thunder from above had come down. Far off, where the field led toward the house, they saw a man. He had his back to them and was kneeling in the grass. Adlai set the cat down and took his clothes from Ed. They grabbed their clothes anxiously—the cat watched, still purring, still licking its paws, but keeping an eye on Adlai. They were dressed as the man stood up and turned their way.

It was Walt, with a rifle, still a distance away, but coming toward them. Adlai knew the walk of his middle brother, the slow lumbering amble. He often secretly thought of him as oafish, though he'd never say that aloud. Walt was wearing dungarees and a long sleeved shirt. It was the clothing he had on the night of the murder. There was a stain on one arm and Adlai wondered if it was blood. Adlai watched his brother approach, and he tried to think of what he might say. He wanted to be a good brother, to offer something. He thought of Cahal and Brandon, those brothers, how one had helped another. Walt stopped at the trees, the rifle hanging across his arm, his face flat and dull.

"I thought I might find a deer," Walt said.

The cat crept closer to Adlai, pressing against him. The animal seemed to be afraid of Walt. They stood silently, Ed absently reaching up to pluck and eat an apple, Adlai standing with the cat near him, trying to think of what to say, but ultimately staying still, as Walt nodded, then strode away, the gun on his arm, like a hunter seeking not food, Adlai thought, but a sacrifice.

fifteen

The day was waning. Walt walked a long way, the rifle in the crook of his arm heavy and burdened too with some haunted power. It had belonged to Pat, who had brought it from the city, but how it had been used and where he'd kept it was a mystery. Walt imagined it may have belonged to Pat's father.

He was hot, sweat gathering at his neck and keeping his cheeks dewy, as he recalled the day of the murder, how he'd sweated and shook so much. He was used to being trapped in that memory and the subsequent grief. He felt oppressed by Adriana, that love, and felt her with him always now, sometimes only bits of her, as if he'd cut her up into pieces, an eye, a smile, that tiny hand of hers. As if he'd already carved and packaged her into pieces of memories never to be put back together again. It was a brutal remembering.

He also smelled her and blamed that partially on the countryside. It was ripe with odors, some sweet, some rank. Now, approaching a wooded glen, he caught whiffs of lilac. He recalled her smelling sweet, but already the reality and the memory were falling apart. At times, cloaked in a grief so dark his head ached, he felt a desperate need to hear her voice, but all that came to him was that horrible scream, the ragged and constant cry, as she came into the room and saw her dead father.

He wondered how far from the house he had gone. It seemed that he'd walked miles, but he couldn't be sure. Stepping from a pasture into the glen, which had a wide path skitting through a path of trees on either side, he paused, wiping sweat from his face. The sound of a shot would reach no one. He could lean the rifle onto a tree and put the butt into his mouth. That would stop it all. He continued forward into the glen, away from the late day sun, into the shrouded area, moving slowly. Ahead, a runty raccoon sat up on its haunches and observed him. The thing looked hungry, and glancing about, Walt thought that despite the abundance of trees, the land look malnourished, hungry and lost.

The raccoon dropped and ran, as if sensing the gun could turn on it. Walt lifted the rifle, and cocked it. It was a bolt action Winchester, still in good condition. He had shells in his pocket. If he shot anything, he needed to reload after each pull.

The area was still. In the silence, he thought of the butcher shop, the hundreds of carcasses he'd handled, carved and wrapped. They never seemed like things that had life. Even when a bled carcass came in, to be hung, head and hooves, it seemed artificial and soulless. He held up the rifle and peered down to align his eye with the front sight. Far off, an eagle cried, then cried again, and that swiftly brought her cry, that man dead, her father. He heard, not the cry again of the eagle, but that horrible grating sound and too, the snap as the Doctor's head turned to the left and the thump of the body to the floor and Adlai hollering. What was it Adlai kept screaming?

He lowered the rifle. His hands were shaking. His strongest regret was that he did not go to her, did not kneel and beg her forgiveness. Or accost her. Lift and force her out, make her go with them. Keep her as a prisoner until he could convince her to forgive him.

He listened for the eagle, but it was gone, as he thought: *But then she saved me.*

He lifted the rifle again, and in the sight was a wolf some ten yards away, staring at him. Like the raccoon, it was a scrawny animal. Not really a wolf, more a coyote, hungry and gaunt, skittish looking. It lifted its head slightly, and Walt shot the gun. The bullet caught the animal in the side, and it flopped to the ground. It was only a wound, as the coyote struggled up, and then fell back again.

It began to wail, as if calling for a lover, a savior to come drag it off to safety. It wailed more loudly, beckoning, and Walt went to it. The scream of the animal was escalating and horrible and he ran, thinking to rescue it, but as he moved, that noise rose and her face, that scream and something else, a deep and driving anguish, overcame him. Standing over the thing, it bleeding and flopping fish-like, he began to scream too, to echo it. Walt raised the gun and wanted to taste it, but that would not do, because she had saved him, and he could not wreck that saving with more death.

He shot the coyote in the head.

sixteen

Dickie woke, naked and wet, and for a moment he thought he was back in the city, on Eva's floor after a bath. He kept his eyes shut and ran a finger across his belly, which was damp with sweat. There was a small patch of pale hair at his belly button and he yanked on it, a habit he'd had since he'd grown hair down there. He liked that light tug of pain.

He'd lost track of days, of time. The room was dim, which could mean night or could mean late afternoon or a coming storm darkening the dull horizon. Eva and he had a small one-windowed room to themselves. They'd thrown blankets on the floor to sleep on. He tried to recall his dream, that dream he'd had all his life, that dream which haunted him and secretly made him feel unworthy, but nothing came. He had not recalled this or any other dream since the night of the botched murder job.

He realized now, that it was not simply that he did not recall the dream. The dream itself was gone. He was relieved, unburdened, and in truth, after the initial shock of things going so off track at the Doctors, he felt calm. Out here in this spooked-up little house, some forgotten shack of some forgotten relative, he felt at peace. Plus Frankie was on his way. Big Ed had told him that. Frankie was coming the next morning, and they were going to clear things up. If the mess was really wrapped up, if some fools had been fingered and were getting sacked for it, he could get back in the game. He could win back Frankie's respect. He could get Eva that fucking mink.

Near the room's one small window, he saw the outline of a dark shape. It was Eva. She sat smoking. He was trying to focus, to see her more clearly. He would never tell her, but the only real fear in his life was that of losing her. He'd felt a gut terror since the night of the job. There was an urgency that night, a throbbing through his body that made him drive to her house, get her in the car, get her up here with them. He needed her. He needed this fucking woman.

"Come here."

She turned, and he saw she was nude. She stubbed out her cigarette on the window ledge, looking out once more then moving to him. The shape of her, still so dark in the dim room, had such a beauty and a stillness in its movement that he felt momentarily choked up. He blamed that on this place, this house that if he believed in stupid shit, he would call haunted. It spooked him. But he'd never say that aloud either.

She knelt, then put her lips on his belly, then chewed on that bit of hair at his navel that he liked to pull on. She gnawed on it, which made him smile and feel like a kid for some fucked-up reason, then she lay her head on his stomach.

"That dream is gone," he said. "The one I told you about."

She didn't say anything. He liked that. How he could say stuff, anything really, and she'd just kind of purr at him and then maybe go down and start to lick his balls or his cock, or maybe just get right up on him. Other times, she'd just lie there, still. She always seemed to know what to do. He liked that.

"You want to get out of here?" he said.

He could see the top of her head, the long darkish hair. While in the past he would just look, now he put his hand there and she sighed. He put his fingers in her hair, then stroked her head a little.

"Where we gonna go?" she said.

"Back to the city. I'll get back to working with Frankie. But maybe we can get a place. A nice place. Jersey or Queens or something."

She sighed, then sat up, and he pulled back his hand. She straddled his chest, her big ripe tits over him. She smelled so good. He pressed his mouth up onto her tits, then licked at her neck. She laughed, low and dark, almost like a soft wailing.

"I'd like that. I always wanted a house with a couple of rooms," she said.

He lay back down, and she did too, her face on his chest again. He knew it wouldn't be easy for them. What they were. People didn't take to couplings like that. They both held one another, both knowing the same thing. They could get thrown in jail, shot dead. They sure as hell couldn't waltz into the justice of the peace and get married. He pulled her up on top of him again and started to kiss her mouth, getting ready to fuck her.

"You know what I'm gonna get you," he said, his mouth on hers, their tongues colliding, then her pulling away from him.

"What?" she said.

He liked that she was greedy too, like him. She didn't play coy or act like anything other than what she was.

"A mink. You want a mink?" he said.

She straddled him again and got him going, and he was gasping a little and starting to grit his teeth the way he did.

"You're too good to me," she said in motion. "You're gonna ruin me."

They were good now, despite the hard floor and the sweat building up and the sudden noise of somebody in the other room, talking too loud. They were good.

After, she got up and went to the sill and relit the butt of her cigarette. He looked at her from behind, and that fear came back, that she might leave, and he thought, *I can't ever let that happen.*

"You better come here," she said. "It's your brother. He's got a dog or something."

Dickie got up and went and grabbed her from behind because he was still hungry. Through the window, over her shoulder into the coming evening, he saw Walt, moving across the back field, dragging something big. The closer he got, the more they heard a thumping noise, that thing he was dragging. He was close now, Walt.

"That ain't a dog," Dickie said. "Damn fool shot a coyote."

seventeen

Adlai looked at the fallen thing, the beast, bloody on the back lawn and he thought, *'It's going to stink. It's going to rot.'* He recalled torn bits of wounded flesh, ghastly hunks that hid themselves under things at the butcher shop, making themselves known by their stench. As a boy, he'd been tasked with following the scent, like a hound, ferreting out the discarded and rotten bits to rid the shop of the odor. Once he'd found and hidden a ripped bit of hoof under his pillow, like a perverse pet. Later, he'd gotten rid of it.

He'd never seen anything so newly dead. He knelt by it. The coyote's side was sticky and carnival red, like candy shattered. The coyote's head though, where the bullet pierced between the jaw and eye, was still oozing and open, and he had an urge to push his finger in there, as he would similarly want to put a finger in a fan or a socket, but would never follow through. He glanced around the back yard, toward the field and off to the ravine where he'd found the creek. He was beginning to like this place. . He'd never spent time out of the city, and there was something soothing about it all.

The animal's left eye was wedged open in fear, wild and horrible, and that made it seem closer to death for Adlai, like the overly-wide opening of that eye told the tale of how it felt when realizing it would die. He stood up, feeling the shadow of Big Ed on him. He could smell Ed when he was near.

"You think animals have souls?" Adlai said.

"You mean like do they go up to heaven?" Ed said.

At that, the coyote flopped violently, one hard leap skyward as if in final death cry.Adlai threw himself at Ed. "I read that animals do that sometimes," Ed said. "Even after they're dead."

They were in clear view from the house, and Adlai stepped away, realizing he'd moved too close against Ed's chest.

"What will they do with it?" Adlai said.

Ed sighed, and the side door leading to the kitchen swung open, and Dickie yelled. "Come on."

"They're making dinner for all of us. Like a party," Ed said.

"We could go to the creek," Adlai said.

There had been a shift for he and Ed. To Adlai, they now felt as one, and more than that, it was as if it were just a matter of time before they would flee, run someplace where they could live together. What that looked like Adlai did not know; it was more a sensation in his gut, a knowledge that they would fit together more and more closely. It made him bold.

"There's a creek, down there," he said, pointing to the ravine. "We could go there."

It was a hot, still night. The kitchen door had never swung shut.

Dickie yelled again.

"Coming," Ed called back.

Adlai looked down again at the coyote, wondering if it may indeed leap once more, or if it had flown to heaven. He did believe animals had souls. Ed did not reach for his hand, but he did not move away either. He waited for Adlai.

"All right," Adlai said.

Then they moved, walking side by side, toward the house.

eighteen

Pat had brought a cooked ham on the bone wrapped in wax paper and kept on ice. He also brought canned things and a layer cake and whiskey, all from the city. They'd first tried to find chairs from around the house to pull into the kitchen, but Dickie thought it would be better if they dragged the kitchen table into the living room, which was larger and mostly empty. They supplemented the chairs with a crate from the yard to sit on and large boxes they'd brought that had held the supplies. It wasn't initially planned like a party, but they had to eat, and they were all together, and as they got it going, it took on an air of something special. Pat mentioned that Walt's birthday was that month. The boys were all born in summertime.

Eva put a flower in her hair and several from the yard in a can on the table and all the men dressed, having foraged about for several days in their underdrawers, shirtless like convicts on the run. Pat had brought candles, and Adlai set up rows of them in the living room to keep things lit as evening crawled in, and they all sat around the table with the food laid out. There was only one plate which the ham was on, so they decided to grab things and eat as best as they could. They all had cups filled with whiskey and were drinking.

The three brothers sat in a line, on one side of the table, facing Pat, Eva and Ed. Ed sat on the lowest box, being the largest and most able to hulk up and over the edge of the table despite being lower to the ground. Adlai was in a wide and ratty armchair, damp and left to die years ago. Walt was slumped in a hard wood chair, drinking; Dickie sat next to him in a nearly identical chair, smoking.

There was a calm. It was the first time they'd all sat, quietly together, not afraid. All of the windows in the house were open to the darkening night, and a breeze occasionally swept through and brought a scent of lilac. The evening was sticky, and there was a strange escalation in heat that seemed out of place, since evening typically brought a cooling. In direct correlation, the chaos of the night creatures, the cicadas and tree frogs, was building to a strange and unprecedented crescendo.

Adlai was used to the insect noise, as he was used to traffic in the city and the hard droning of his brothers' snores late at night. But now the insects were changing. It was as if they were warring, feuding over something lately erupted. Or as if their numbers had tripled with a wild dusting of locusts that had swept in from the north. Listening, Adlai recalled a recording he'd once heard of music on a piano, a strange and dissonant number full of harsh edges and alternating rhythms. Though the music was famous, he had wondered why anyone would write something so full of rage.

He drank his whiskey slowly. No one had yet started to eat, nor had they spoken. They all sat quietly. Eva had her eyes shut and was fanning herself very slowly with a small paper fan which had tulips on its front. It was quite pretty and he wondered if he could touch it.

"Where did you get that?" Adlai asked.

At first she did not respond. He had not spoken to her directly the entire time they'd been there. He did not especially like her, though now that Ed had come, he disliked her less.

"The fan," Adlai said. "It's nice."

She opened her eyes and looked at him, and Adlai thought "*She's a dangerous woman.*" Her stare...was unwavering, unforgiving somehow, with a look he decided was pure menace. He had previously seen her as a ridiculous whore his brother had dragged along. Now, with that glare of hers, he thought differently.

"I have had it for a long time," she said.

Then she shut those eyes and went back to fanning. Ed glanced at him across the table and smiled. Adlai smiled back, and Pat, who sat next to Ed, also smiled, and for a moment that old fear, that he had been caught or had been seen, came rushing back to Adlai. But Pat's look stayed with him, and it had no hardness, and he recalled that Pat had already seen, already knew and nothing had changed.

Pat pulled the plate of ham forward, then set to carving. Once he had a chunk in front of him, he continued to carve slices, then pushed the plate to Eva, who took a piece and shoved the plate across the table to Dickie. When it came to Adlai, he did not take any meat, just pushed it across the table to Ed.

Eva stood up, holding a bottle of whiskey. The dress she wore was a bland, pale pinkish shade, as if it had been tossed into a hot tub and allowed to fade. She moved slowly, like a slovenly cat around the table, filing the men's glasses silently. As she passed Adlai he could smell her, a lilac scent and more than that, a warm female scent that made him think, oddly, of his mother, though he'd never really seen that woman. He was an infant when she'd left. He drank the cup Eva poured and saw her at Ed's side, that sway and sultry shift of her, and he wanted to push her away, but he again thought of his mother, that far away woman, and he suddenly recalled a day when she had wandered around a table.

He drank, and shut his eyes and dragged forth that memory, or daydream, since such an early memory could be half-dreamed. It was a bright day in their kitchen, and his mother, Angie, served food onto the boys' plates, and she was singing something. In this glimpse, this memory fast escaping, he saw she had bright red hair, short and curled, and she wore a hard, starched-white dress. He opened his eyes, Ed staring at him.

"You should eat," Ed said.

Ed tore a piece of ham in half and pushed it across to Adlai, who took it up and put it in his mouth, more because he thought the meat may smell of Ed's hand which had touched it. There was never a moment when Adlai did not desire Ed.

He looked around at his brothers, wondering if he should mention the memory of Angie. Walt, head down, was gnawing at the meat. Dickie was drinking. They both seemed further away then ever. He no longer felt he was different, or isolated while they were connected sharing secrets. Instead, they both seemed lost, adrift and caught in their own madness.

As evening passed and night came, the room took on a softer, dreamier tone, lit by the candles. More whiskey was poured, and two more bottles came out as the rapid urging of the night creatures became passionate and deafening, until finally Dickie spoke.

"Those things are going crazy tonight," he said. "Those fucking crickets."

They all sat silently listening to the din. The breeze had died down. Pat filled his glass again and passed the bottle. No one ate much.

"It's the end of summer mating call. The males crying for it," Eva said. "Heat riles them up. And rain."

"Really?" Ed said, drinking.

"Yeah. I spent time in St Louis. They get it real bad there. So loud you can't sleep nights."

Eva's voice was taking on a mild slang, a laziness from the liquor. Adlai kept drinking, though he know he should eat. He didn't want to eat. He wanted to drink and rest his eyes. It was as if that noise was lulling him, lulling them all. Then Pat stood up. He lifted his glass as if to toast, then he simply took a drink and began.

"This house was your Uncle Brandon's," Pat said, glancing around the room.

"It was given to me. I will give it to you three. Same as the butcher shop. That was your grandfather's given to me; I told you that right?"

He continued standing, though leaned slightly on his chair, swaying. If there was no sound, no insects, the scene may have been awkward, so many pauses. But there was never quiet, so they all felt comfortable. "I think about what happened, that poor dead doctor, all that," Pat said with a slight slur. Then he shut his eyes. "But we came together here. Like a family. We never could have planned this. You can never really...never make something happen."

Then his voice drifted, and he sat and poured a drink and began to hum. The sound, an Irish song Adlai knew, was barely audible.

Dickie got up. "Adlai," he said, motioning to the kitchen.

Adlai followed his brother into the kitchen.

Dickie was maneuvering a cake out of a box. "How'd the old man remember to bring this?" Dickie said. "He can't remember what day it is, but he brings a cake."

He was snickering, and tottering from side to side, struggling to release the cake from its box. Adlai went to him and held the box while Dickie pulled the cake out. Dickie held it, then looked at his younger brother. Adlai did not remember the last time he'd been so close to his brother, staring at him, alone like that. It felt odd, and Dickie's eyes were wide open, his cheeks flushed with the whiskey, and he was smiling. Then he whispered. "Go get one of them candles."

Adlai went out and grabbed a small candle, then took it to the kitchen.

"Stick it on here," Dickie said, stooping a bit.

He put a round, fat candle firmly on the top of the cake. The wax dripped on to the lard icing.

"Come on," Dickie said in a strange, thrilled whisper as he move back to the living room.

Adlai followed, also excited. Dickie stood in the room with the cake, and everyone stared. There was a lull. Only the insects sang. Then, forgot by all, the stray and hungry cat came out of the shadows, as if from hibernation, slinking toward Dickie. It sat near him, licking its paws, and staring at the cake, then at the table of food.

"Come on, blow it out, Walt, come on," Dickie said, his voice high and pleading.

Walt stood up, unsteady, then went to the cake. He took in a deep breath, blew out the candle, then went back and sat and drank. Dickie set down the cake, but no one cut into it.

nineteen

The evening had evolved into something too black, too loud, though Adlai knew it was only the liquor. They'd all drunk too much, eaten too little. The birthday cake, left to sour and melt untouched on the table in the heat, was a feast for the anguished cat that Adlai had yet to name. He pulled Ed through the back yard across that stubble hard grass, toward the ravine and the creek. Ed was undoing his sweaty shirt, stumbling, drunker than Adlai despite his size.

"Where are they?" Adlai said, pulling Ed along, searching the trees for the crying insects.

The night's increasing chaos was the fault of the bugs, their never-ending trill maddening. Adlai did not understand how anything so small could be so powerful. He sat down for a moment on the ground, taken suddenly by the moon, milky and harvest-full against the black backdrop of night. Ed had his shirt half off, and it hung limp from one arm. He battled with it, yanking, until it fell off.

Their dinner party had scattered. Eva and Dickie to their room, Pat passed out on the floor, Walt gone, just gone. It was very late now. Adlai and Ed holed up in the kitchen drinking alone, before going outside. Now faced with that albino moon, Adlai's head dark with whiskey, he knew he would never be without Ed. This place and that creek had gotten into him, made him whole somehow, and Ed needed to get in it, get soaked in all that.

"You ever been baptized?" Adlai said.

Ed was staring at the bold moon, transfixed. Adlai stood and took his hand again, guiding him to the corner of the ravine.

"You're gonna like this," Adlai said.

When they stepped into the shrouded cloister leading them down, the sudden darkness, that blanket of black that swept on as the white bulbous moon disappeared, that dark caught them off guard, and they both fell. It was as if they had entered a cavern, sounds echoing now, and they stood and together made their way through the dark,down to the sound of the rushing water.

"Wait," Ed said several times, lagging.

At the creek's edge, Adlai looked up to find that break in the trees he knew, and through that, the wide pale moon. He stepped into the creek, into that slant of light, so Ed could see him more fully. Then he undressed, the warmish water flowing through his ankles and around his skin and making him feel slightly mad. He took off his shirt, then Ed stepped out into the creek and into that hard line of moon, and he pulled Adlai close, lifting him up as he kissed him, so their chests met, and he lifted the boy higher, so Adlai's feet dripped and dangled. Despite the liquor, and with what seemed to Adlai an unreal and Herculean effort, Ed held him aloft in a one-armed grip, and with the other undid and pulled off the boy's pants, so Adlai was naked, white, too white under that bone-bleached moon, like some flailing, young thing in a beast's grip. He kissed Adlai again, then released him and set him down, so he could get at his own pants, get them off and let them sift down with the current.

Adlai knew that they both were too drunk, that the moon was too bright illuminating them. This was not safe. But Ed's big hands hoisted Adlai again, his hard and gritty mouth at him. Adlai gripped Ed's hair and straddled him around the waist then pressed his hands on Ed shoulders and pulled himself up, as if Ed were a cliff he could climb. He was rising over him then coming back down, settling at Ed's waist, his face on the man's cheek, his arms solid around Ed's neck and up above, through one eye, he again saw that hard, bold moon. Adlai held tight as Ed gripped the boy firmly around the waist, then Ed angled him down sliding inside him, both of them gasping loudly and in unison, as the trees rustled and seethed with the insane beauty of their obscene coupling there in the rushing creek bed.

The sound overwhelming them was that of the water rushing, those insects, so they did not hear from far off the hard, sad yowl of the cat up at the house, and they did not hear the rustle of the branches, the slow approaching footsteps, nor even the first wretched gasp of a voice at once weak and righteously horrified. If they had heard, Ed may have looked up and turned away to hide their love making, may have even cast Adlai aside and stepped out of the creek with speed and force and raised his fists to stop what was coming. But they did not hear, nor see, they being lost in an overwhelming rush of what to them was magnificent.

Dickie was nearly on them when they finally did turn; they merging as one in sudden and unquestionable reckoning. Dickie screamed as he ran down the slight hill to the mouth of the creek and yanked them apart striking first at Ed who toppled, dropping Adlai, then falling back and hitting his head on a rock. Ed lay still in the water, face up to the gentle wash of night.

Lying naked in the creek, Adlai did not have time to stand before Dickie grabbed and first gripped his neck, taking away some breath, lifting him in the air shaking him, then with a wail of threats and condemnations as constant and as thrilling as the ceaseless insects, he hoisted his frail brother over his head and carried him up the hill and out of the ravine, out across and into the field. Adlai did not try to tear out of Dickie's solid grip, knowing his brother's strength and rage and knowing to fight was useless. Dickie ranted as he got out of the shroud of the ravine and into the open field behind the house, cursing Adlai over and over. He threw him into the field grass, down for slaughter under the white burning moon, naked. Adlai shook, waiting, terrified as Dickie stared at him with black searing eyes, the devil's eyes he thought, the eyes of the assassin. He thought of the sheathed carcasses delivered to the butcher shop back home, those defenseless dead things, and he knew how Dickie laid them out, hacked them and purified them, turned them into something clean.

Adlai's breath was short, and he touched his bruised throat wanting air as Dickie looked down at him then lifted his hands over his head, tearing at his own hair then screaming into the night sky quivering with some new level of rage and overwhelming grief. There was a moment of calm, then looking down at the naked boy, Dickie first knelt then set upon his brother, again starting up that animal wailing. Adlai felt Dickie's fists, saw the rush of trees and that moon. Then on the ground, he saw Dickie's black eyes again, and he shut his own eyes as he felt a smashing slice of pain in his cheek, then another, and he felt a tooth cave inward to his tongue and his face snapped to one side, and he tasted grass and blood. He felt some of his teeth set wrong in his mouth. Then the hands took to his belly and chest, a relentless pummeling, as the waves of pain rode into him, and he heard nothing really, just felt a now rhythmic battering until something inside his frail chest snapped, and he tasted the saltiness of blood and then again, hands on his face, and at once the voice came back wailing, and it was Dickie, yes it was Dickie. and Adlai looked up to try to see him, to try to see his brother's eyes, but instead he saw a wild halo of white, and he waited for it to end.

Walt woke to the sound of what he thought to be a storm. He dragged himself off the floor where he had passed out, and he rustled his father awake, then he realized it was his brother, Dickie, screaming in the field out back. Pat struggled to get up, and Walt moved quickly because he knew that rant, that rage, and he ran out to see what had happened. He thought at first they were wrestling, but Adlai was on the lawn, and he was not moving, and Dickie was lifting his arm slowly and with what seemed like great effort and even in the dark, even like that, Walt could see the long gashing stains of blood across Adlai's body.

Dickie raised and pounded again, until Walt ran to them and threw himself there, yanking at his older brother and screaming for him to stop, that he would kill him, that he had to stop and everywhere on that lawn was blood and stray bits of torn and pounded flesh, and the boy was mangled, as if he'd been bled and cut down, and Walt finally got Dickie away. But Dickie's madness was too deep, and he set on Walt, got into him and the two brothers met with fierce anguish.

Pat saw his boys, as he emerged from the house.

The three of them, Adlai motionless, Walt and Dickie so close, shaking and struggling, fighting each other as if in slow motion, as if two lovers set at one another with equal parts love and hate. The two were rolling closer to the youngest, their warring frames butting up against the youngest, all three tangled. Three bodies mingling in this ballet of violence, as if submerged, all three drowning, trying to flee from one another, but blind and stupid and caught in some horrible idiom of hopelessness that wound through them all their lives.

His sons, tortured under that now blood-red moon, those night sounds a dreadful symphony of grief, and those three boys, his three boys, his burden to love, his great failure, lost, he thought lost, lost, lost.

So he raised the rifle, and he fired three times. Finally, things stilled.

twenty

They laid Adlai out on the kitchen table, as they had so much meat in times past.

Ed hastily shoved off the gnawed-at, pinkish ham bone and the wrecked and soggy birthday cake, nearly demolished by the cat. It was dawn, and Adlai was bone pale, ghostly, though brought to colorful life with mad streaks of purple, fast-bruising on his belly, chest and legs, and a garish blanket of blood covering his chewed-up face. Walt was threading a needle, hunched over Adlai like a back-room surgeon, boorish and sweaty. The boy's breathing was ragged.

"Is he going to be all right?" Ed said.

Ed stood naked on the other side of the table, his head striped with threads of dried blood from where he'd smacked it on a creek rock. His eyes were wide, crazy, and he kept leaning down toward Adlai as if he were sniffing at him.

"Put some clothes on Ed," Walt said, holding up and examining the needle. "And stand back, you're stealing my light."

"Shit," Ed said.

"It looks worse than it is," Walt said. "It's a lot of blood, but he's going to be okay."

After Pat shot the rifle, aiming it to heaven and disrupting nothing save for a few stray birds; they all went still with the gun's sudden threat of death. The three brothers laid in the yard, not moving. Walt rose first from the bloody swamp of their falling out, standing and calling for Eva to help. He was not badly hurt, though his bloodied nose made a mess. Together, he and Eva hoisted Adlai up and took him into the house, then to the table in the living room. Ed emerged from the ravine, dazed, following after them. Dickie rose last, his fists bloody from the pounding he gave, his mind bruised and shattered, the residue of what he'd witnessed still on him. He refused to acknowledge Pat calling him into the house.

As Walt contemplated what to do with his battered younger brother, there came the sound of a car approaching. It was rambling at speed up the gravel drive to the house, a slick red roadster. Walt looked out, and there was Frankie Corigliano, who was expected later that day. Walt turned back to the twisted form of young Adlai, who lie naked and harmed on the table.

"I want to help," Ed said. He'd put on a pair of pants and had a wet rag.

"All right," Walt said softly.

Ed dabbed the worst areas of the boy's face with the rag, clearing it for Walt to try to make sense of the jagged cuts and slashes. Walt held the needle near Adlai's soft upper cheek. Ed squeezed Adlai's hand, which lay limp at his side. Frankie came in and sat nearby with Pat, who had quietly explained to him the drunken brawl.

"You came for Dickie?" Pat said.

"Yes, but that one is the best of them, looks like to me." Frankie pointed at Walt, who was slumped as he stitched. "Just had to wait for him to come around to my side," he said. "Maybe now's his time."

Pat sighed. "I see. Now I have lost him."

"The kid, oh he'll make it okay," Frankie said.

"No, Dickie, my oldest, the weakest really," Pat said.

They continued at the table, Walt working meticulously as morning came on bright and cheerful, unknowing, uncaring. Ed felt a squeeze from Adlai's hand, and the cat, oblivious and greedy, ran its ratty cheek along Ed's hairy leg. There was no sign of Eva or Dickie, and in the commotion, no one noticed the light purr of the engine when Dickie started his car and drove off.

twenty-one

Adlai looked out the window of the butcher shop at the falling snowflakes, so heavy and burdened he thought, sifting recklessly onto the city street, those pregnant wafers of snow. The Avenue had a landscape of country to it, as if a field lay before him, as if it could lead off to a ravine and a frozen creek.

Because of the blizzard, there were no cars, though a few boys were sliding aimlessly across the Avenue. One boy dragged a toboggan and another dragged an even smaller boy, who kept falling because of his too-large boots and too-padded coat. He fell, the smaller boy, and lay there content, fanning his arms out. Their laughter seemed abandoned to the storm.

Adlai turned away. He stood at the cutting table in the shop's window. He looked down at his work: the knives had been cleaned and scalded; the hog had been butchered, bled, cleaned, and chilled, ready to portion.

People were still out shopping for food, and he expected business. Their shop had become known for butchering in the window, offering passers-by a bit of a show that slowed them down, made them stare. Dickie had started that all back in the summer, back when people were afraid the heat would ruin the meat. Ed was at the counter, smoking, and Pat was reading a paper. Adlai was diggging his knife into pig skin when the door rang open, the mailman stopping by.

"Still out?" Pat said.

"Sure," said the mailman, handing Pat a sheath of letters.

Adlai scored into the pig, moving gently, wanting to go at it on a good angle. He made a long incision then paused. He had to take his time. He neither possessed Ed's strength, nor Walt's—who had moved into his own place and was around less and less, now that he was working for Frankie. Adlai pushed the knife slowly foreward into the pig. Pat was at his shoulder.

"There's no return address," Pat said.

He handed Adlai a postcard. The scrawl was nervous, childish and read:

I know he came out all right. I know that. I ain't sorry. But I'm glad he came out all right. And the dream is back at me. Every night. I guess some things ain't meant to change.

At the bottom, in hard angled letters as if stabbed onto the page, was the signature, *Dickie.*

Adlai stared at the postcard a long time, once Pat had walked away and gone upstairs. He studied each word, the tilt and slant of what each letter may mean, and he thought of his oldest brother, that one lost, at least for now, and he tried to imagine him writing this somewhere maybe where it was hot, maybe in a jungle. And he thought of his own nightly dream, that curse the brothers shared, and how he was grateful to have it, to tie him to the other two, even when it was brutal or dark. There was nothing else on the postcard, no dirt or stain of liquor or blood, only those letters, only the precise angle and jagged look to them for Adlai to decipher.

As he lifted his head he saw the boys bundled and ape-like in the window, staring at him, waiting to view the butchering but staring too at him, Adlai, who was not so much larger then they, this butcher-kid in a crisp white apron and now, wiping his face of fallen tears.

Adlai looked at the boys, as he felt a shadow on him, looming, and he saw the boy's eyes' rise, open wider, not quite afraid, but awed by the bulk of what approached, by the huge shadow it cast. Ed put a big hand on Adlai's scant shoulder, smiling gently at the boys in the window who were still waiting for the show. They smiled back, and Adlai sighed, happy to feel Ed's hands. He set down the postcard, and then he set back to cutting the beast.

CPSIA information can be obtained at www.ICGtesting.com
Printed in the USA
LVOW11s1108220415

435569LV00040B/318/P